REQUIEM FOR A SPY

A NOVEL OF NUCLEAR ESPIONAGE

RICHARD MILES
& JILL ROSE

Black Rose Writing | Texas

ISBN: 978-1-68433-785-9
PUBLISHED BY BLACK ROSE WRITING
www.blackrosewriting.com

Printed in the United States of America
Suggested Retail Price (SRP) $18.95

Requiem for a Spy is printed in Sabon

*As a planet-friendly publisher, Black Rose Writing does its best to eliminate unnecessary waste to reduce paper usage and energy costs, while never compromising the reading experience. As a result, the final word count vs. page count may not meet common expectations.

Cover design by Trevor Scobie

For my family

REQUIEM FOR A SPY

A NOVEL OF
NUCLEAR ESPIONAGE

PRELUDE
by Jill Rose

My uncle Richard Miles was born in October 1917, the youngest child of the Reverend Edwin 'Ted' Miles of Glamorgan and his wife Annie, née Jones, of Bala in North Wales. My father Roger was two years older, and they had two sisters: Marion (1909) and Margaret (1911). Edwin was a Presbyterian minister; Annie had been one of the first women to graduate from Aberystwyth College, University of Wales, and had taught French before her marriage. Although he spent his formative years in England, Richard was raised with a deep pride in his Welsh ancestry, as well as close family ties, a strong sense of duty and service, and the moral rectitude of his parents' faith.

Richard took his degree in PPE (Politics, Philosophy and Economics) from Exeter College Oxford in 1939, and almost immediately enlisted in the Royal Navy. He served with the Arctic convoys before being promoted to Lieutenant, at which point they discovered he had a hearing defect due to a congenital deformity of his right ear that, to Richard's dismay, precluded further active service, and he was sent to a shore establishment.

In the summer of 1942 Richard was selected as the Royal Navy's representative to the International Youth Assembly in Washington DC, along with representatives from the Royal Air Force and the Army. At the end of August, he and his companions arrived in the US capital, where he met the President's wife Mrs Eleanor Roosevelt, a sponsor of the meeting. Richard was subsequently posted to the British Embassy in Washington, where he would remain for the rest of the war, with responsibilities for White House Liaison with the Naval Attaché's

Office. Mrs Roosevelt took a liking to the young naval officer, and this was the start of a warm friendship between them that would last for the next twenty years until her death in 1962.

Richard later worked for the embassy's Economic Advisor Dr Redvers Opie, and in July 1944 was an adviser to the British Delegation at the Bretton Woods Conference, which established the economic order of the post-war world. He returned to England for a few months immediately after the war, working for the Treasury Department, and he was a member of the British team at the July 1945 Potsdam Conference, which formalized the division of Europe and inadvertently set the stage for the Cold War. By 1946 he was back in the States as adviser to the British Delegation to the United Nations and adviser to the UN Atomic Energy Commission, working with Sir Alexander Cadogan, who was the UK's first Permanent Representative to the United Nations, towards controlling nuclear weapons.

By March 1948 the talks were at a stalemate in the face of Russian intransigence. Soviet Deputy Foreign Minister Andrei Gromyko insisted that all existing bombs (i.e. American) must be destroyed before discussions could begin on international controls. Richard pointed out that this would leave the Soviet Union with a free hand to develop its own weapons; 'Miles Tells UN Reds Want US Weapons Destroyed So They Can Make Own', announced the *New York Herald Tribune* on 19 March. The meeting ended with a public spat between Richard and Gromyko as, led by Great Britain, the UN Atomic Energy Commission voted to drop consideration of the Russian proposal.

Richard's determination in not acquiescing to the Russian plan was more consequential than appeared at the time. In May 1944 a high flyer from the Foreign Office in London was seconded to the British Embassy in Washington. He was just four years older than Richard, and their paths would have crossed both socially and professionally. He became First Secretary, and from early in 1947 until the middle of 1948 he was Secretary of the Anglo-American-Canadian Policy Committee on atomic energy matters. His name was Donald Maclean, and in 1951 he was revealed as a Soviet spy who had for many years been passing top secret information to the KGB. Maclean defected to Moscow along with fellow-traveller Guy Burgess, the first two of the infamous Cambridge

Five to be exposed. It is certain, therefore, that in March 1948 Andrei Gromyko had far more knowledge of the American nuclear programme than Richard and his colleagues could have suspected. In his biography *A Spy Named Orphan,* author Roland Philipps points out that thanks to Maclean, the Russians were able accurately to assess the strength of the American stockpile of bombs. We can only speculate as to what might have happened had the Soviets succeeded in their aim to eliminate the American nuclear arsenal.

I remember Richard telling me, many years later, that he had known Donald Maclean, and that he had even written a roman à clef inspired by him. At that time I knew hardly anything about the infamous Cambridge spy ring . . . I was only four years old when the Burgess and Maclean scandal first broke in 1951.

Looking back on what I've just written about his early career and the exhilarating years he spent in America, it strikes me that my uncle was something of a Forrest Gump-like character, a participant in and an astute observer of some of the key events and most notable people of the time: Eleanor and Franklin Roosevelt, Winston Churchill, Roald Dahl (with whom he shared a house in Washington), Sir Alexander Cadogan, Kay Halle, Drew Pearson, Andrei Gromyko and, of course, Donald Maclean. Richard did sometimes talk to me about it, but to my everlasting regret, I never asked him to elaborate, to tell me more, and much of what he told me has slipped out of my memory banks.

One of my uncle's stories, however, has long been part of our family lore. Richard was a strong believer in the 'special relationship' between the United Kingdom and the United States. So when Churchill, on one of his wartime visits to the US, asked what Britain could do to cement the bond and show the country's appreciation for the help of the American people, Richard suggested that this would be an ideal time for the UK to switch to driving on the right as a gesture of solidarity. Churchill immediately shot down the idea, arguing that it was essential that the driver be on the left so that his sword arm was free in the event of an attacker approaching on the opposite side of the road! And so today the UK still stubbornly drives on the left.

I don't know exactly where or when this encounter took place, but I know it's a true story. It's been corroborated by Richard's friend, the journalist and socialite Kay Halle, a confidante of Winston's son Randolph.

I emigrated in 1970, and it was not until the early 1980s that I got to know Richard better. In 1982 my husband Allen and I were living in Rockville, Maryland, just outside Washington. Richard still had friends in the capital, and on one of his visits he took us to lunch with one of these friends – Richard Helms, who had been head of the CIA for seven years in the Johnson and Nixon administrations. Helms was tall and gentlemanly; he recounted that on one occasion, as he entered the Concorde in France, he had been frisked by French security and only later realized that one of the guards had relieved him of his wallet! We were amused by the chutzpah of the guy who pick-pocketed the head of the American Intelligence service!

I later learnt that Mrs Cynthia Helms was a long-standing friend of Richard's. As a young WREN she had worked for my uncle in 1942, and they had remained close. (In 2017, as I was writing my book *Nursing Churchill: Wartime Life from the Private Letters of Winston Churchill's Nurse* (Foreword by Emma Soames; Amberley, June 2018), I contacted Cynthia, who was then in her nineties and still living in Washington, and we talked about Richard. In February 2019 I went to Washington to give a talk about my book, and arranged to visit Cynthia at home. Alas, the city was engulfed by an ill-timed blizzard and I was forced to cancel our meeting. I had another opportunity later in the year, but after I received no reply to my emails I discovered, to my dismay, that she had died in the spring. Richard had been very fond of Cynthia and I'm sure she could have answered some of my questions about him, so I was deeply disappointed that I was unable to ask her.)

Richard and his wife Caroline had separated by this time (although they remained on amicable terms for the rest of their lives) and he was living on his own in a riverside flat in Kingston. On my annual visits to the UK, Richard would pick me up in his car after my flight landed at Heathrow Airport in the morning and take me back to his flat for coffee and a short rest, before driving me to my Mum and Dad's house in Chichester. I remember the glass French doors affording a view across to the Thames. The flat was filled with books and magazines, and I can still picture Richard relaxing in his armchair doing the *Times* crossword, with a glass of whisky on the table in front of him and his pipe in the ashtray at his elbow.

Richard worked for the government until he retired, although he never reached the most senior ranks of the Civil Service as he might have expected. He once remarked to me, rather ruefully, that "I peaked early". He believed that in those earlier days he had offended some of the higher-ups, and that had held him back, though I never learned more about who or why. He was moderate in his politics, a lifelong member of the Liberal Party and of the Reform Club. He was an enthusiastic mariner, a member and sometime Commodore of the Tamesis Sailing Club, and he kept an ancient motor launch in which he would sometimes take friends and family for excursions on the river – until the day the engine blew up with my sister and two of her children on board! (Fortunately, though somewhat shaken, no one was hurt, but that was the end of the fluvial outings).

He was warm, funny and smart, and though he had no children of his own, he was very fond of his siblings' children, his seven nieces and nephews. He and Roger had a close fraternal relationship. Richard was best man at my parents' wedding in 1942, and was godfather to my sister Lesley. When Dad died in 1990, Richard was with us, and together he and I went to the Registrar's office for the depressing task of completing the official paperwork, followed by a companionable drink in a nearby pub to try to cheer ourselves up.

In 1994 Richard moved from Kingston into Tan-y-Craig, the little house in rural Wales that had once been the family's vacation cottage, and where his sister Margaret had been living before her death. It was not an easy place for me to get to on my annual visits to Mum in Chichester, so I saw too little of him in the last few years of his life. I wish now that I had made more of an effort.

Richard died in 1997, and left Tan-y-Craig, with all his stuff still in it, to his sister Marion's daughter, my cousin Elaine. Fortunately Elaine, like me, doesn't throw much away, and she stuffed all his old papers away in the attic, where they remained for the next twenty years. In 2017, as I was going through my mother's documents for my book *Nursing Churchill*, I found four letters that Richard had written to his brother Roger from Washington during the war, full of delightful insights about his time there. I asked Elaine if she would dig around and see if she could unearth any more. She sent me a bundle of papers that had been living for all those years in a Tesco bag at the back of a wardrobe. It was mostly correspondence between our grandparents, Annie and Ted Miles, when Ted was serving at the front in World War One (fascinating stuff in itself!), but there was a handful of letters that Richard had written to his parents and sister, as well as some from my Dad, and some from Eleanor Roosevelt. Elaine also sent me the typed draft manuscript of the legendary roman à clef.

To my delight, the novel was complete; indeed, more than complete, as there were two drafts of much of the book, and even three of parts of it, as well as many hand-written notes and addenda. It was not always easy to figure out which was the older and which was the newer material. My challenge was to sort out the differing versions, to reconcile the inconsistencies, to fix the errors and make some judicious revisions and rewrites, and meld it all into one coherent final version that remained faithful to my uncle's original work.

The novel is set in the US and UK in the immediate aftermath of World War Two. Although ostensibly wartime allies, the relationship between the Soviet Union and America and her allies had already chilled into what would become known as the Cold War. The protagonist is an idealistic young British naval officer named Tom Davis, working for the British Embassy in Washington, who is drawn into the murky and dangerous world of spies and counter-spies, making him question all that he has ever believed.

I hope that my brief exposition of the backstory, and what insights I can offer into my uncle's character and career, enhance your enjoyment of *Requiem for a Spy*.

O, what a tangled web we weave
When first we practice to deceive!

–Walter Scott

CHAPTER ONE

Curiously, I had never seen a dead body up close before, despite having served in a naval cruiser on the Arctic convoys in the early years of the war. At sea, we believed we depth-charged a U-boat. We saw still-smouldering hulks of merchant ships in convoys we had sought to protect. Aeroplanes crashed before our eyes. Never did we see the victims. In Portsmouth a raid had buried us in the vaulted cellars of our barrack block. We were dug out. We never knew or saw the many corpses about us. The dead face of Patrick Marsden was the first show of death to have confronted me.

So I entered the room trying my best to look nonchalant, to give the impression to these hard-boiled cops that this was not the first time, even though I was sick inside with trepidation.

I managed to withhold any sense of shock at what I saw. Marsden had been seated at a desk in the window of the quite spacious bed-sitter. I observed the bed, nearer to us at the door, roughly made and apparently unslept in. I paused in the doorway, deliberately casting over the rest of the scene. I focussed on the bookshelf, recognising the distinctive bindings of Gollancz Left Book Club titles.

I moved forward. The body, in shirt and shorts, was slumped forward to the desk, where the head rested in a pool of blood. There was a blueish wound on the right, up-facing temple; the real mess seemed to be on the other side of the dreadful face. A rather pink and unhairy face, as I remembered, which now had the texture of a Stilton cheese. The lips, rather full and feminine, were drawn back in hideous tension over clenched teeth. His right hand was curled around a small handgun; I noticed that the nails were bitten down to the quick.

"So the doctor is satisfied that it's suicide?"

"Doctor ain't been yet, sir."

"What?" I exploded.

"He'll be here directly. But we seen a lot of these, sir. There ain't no doubt."

I'd woken early that morning in the comfortable little town-house I shared with the Assistant Air Attaché in Georgetown, a district I regarded as the most desirable in Washington DC. It was Sunday, late August 1945. Just a few days ago Japan had surrendered; the war was finally over. It was a little over a week since I'd returned from London, and the contrast between the two cities could not have been greater. I was looking forward to a leisurely day. I'd soon take a glass of orange juice from the refrigerator, have a tub, don slacks, a shirt and tennis shoes and join the softball game against the State Department on our own corner lot at 11:30. The Arthur Plimptons had asked us for drinks after. One did not bother to think where that would end. How to explain this world to the folks at home?

It was only seven-thirty. I lay in bed, enjoying being back. No round of family visits. No church parade this morning! But as I snuggled back, pulling the single sheet over me, the telephone rang. It was Boots, the embassy Security Officer.

"Tom. Put on your uniform. Try to look like an officer. Go to 4820 Connecticut, pronto. I'll put you in the picture."

Young Patrick Marsden, special assistant to our Counsellor (Information), had been found dead in his apartment. Shot through the temple. There was a revolver beside him.

"The cops are there now. Clear case of suicide. They, and we, don't want any fuss . . . What are you supposed to do? Why, look as though you know about this sort of thing. Agree with whatever they say, and sign the papers they will have ready. It's a diplomatic case, you see. As long as the embassy is happy, they will just record the death. No inquest or any of that stuff. Embassy will inform the relatives: all very sad . . .

"What? No, we have the disposal arrangements in hand . . . Yes! Think about a memorial service or whatever it is. Hey, how well did you know him?"

Not well. Not well, really, I thought as I headed the old Pontiac down into Rock Creek Park, to surface again near the Zoo to join up with Connecticut Avenue. Not at all, in fact! We'd exchanged pleasantries when we passed each other in the corridor or the canteen, but that was the extent of our acquaintance. I had travelled enough through the huge continent to begin to understand how important to the war effort our information service was, and how it had attracted fine brains from the press, radio and the universities, but also how pathetic it was in relation to the task. This was not merely boosting Britain but getting all those only somewhat united states to understand what the war was about; the war in Europe in particular and, most difficult, the sort of world we wanted after the war. Patrick Marsden had not been one of the front runners in this enterprise. He did not travel; never left his desk. He was not to be seen lunching with the press corps or at the salons where the Washington gossip circulated. He wrote reports, surrounded by press cuttings and copies of the Congressional Record.

He had lived alone in this apartment block where I now pulled up. It was an uncompromising rectangular six-floor block screened by a few conifers and neglected evergreen shrubs. There was no off-street parking, but I felt it was safe to draw in behind a couple of DC police cars waiting there. The janitor took me in the lift to the third floor. A large black policeman learned my business and led me to the boy's apartment.

As we approached down the bleak but well-polished corridor, a figure hurried out. It was Sylvan Ross, our Acting Head of Chancery, unshaven and tousled, a raincoat wrapped and belted round his spare figure.

"Tom! Glad you made it! Suicide! Terrible thing! You are in charge for us, now. Just get it all sorted out quickly, will you? Do what they say, if you think it all OK. Report when it's finished at the Annexe – security room." And he was gone.

I moved into the lobby of the apartment. Two policemen and a plain-clothes man filled the little space. There were no introductions.

"Good morning, Lieutenant," said the senior police officer, "we were expecting you." He pronounced it the American way, 'Loo-tenant', rather than the British 'Lef-tenant'. "Perhaps you could sign these documents." He indicated where they lay on the small hall stand.

I was being used and did not like it. The only possible reaction was to act as if I were in charge. "I'd better see what happened first," I said, and made to enter the living room.

"Not necessary, unless you really want to, Lieutenant; t'aint pretty."

I was not going to be accused of ghoulish morbidity, but, perceiving dimly that I had a duty to do, led the way in.

Now, distracting my gaze from that mutilated head, I asked, "That was Sylvan Ross here just now. Why . . . er, what did he say?"

"He agreed, sir, but said he was not here officially and that someone would be along. That'll be you, Lieutenant, I guess."

I was thinking how I'd have this out with Sylvan shortly, when the police captain went on, "Yeah, crazy business. Your gentleman says the stiff called him in the night. Says he can't go on. Your feller says he couldn't sleep so he comes on over. But he's too late and finds – this. He called Captain O'Malley here – he's the Diplomatic desk – he came right over."

"Yeah," said O'Malley. "Don't do any good to have publicity with the press nosing round when we get these diplomatic cases. State is notified, of course, and the FBI. But the embassies don't want no scandal and we go along with that."

"Of course," I said, "that's the usual form."

I had to collect my thoughts. Forcing myself back to the body, I tried to memorise details. I now noted the open book on the desk: it was a proof copy of the *Manhattan Project*. An introduction to the theory behind the atomic bomb. The embassy had been given advance copies.

It still rankled with me that I was being used, taken for a ride; not perhaps by the police but by our own people.

"I want nothing touched in here," I said. "I will be back later. I'd like to see the doctor when he's done – and then we will deal with the papers. But thank you, gentlemen, I'm sure you have it well in hand. The, er, Embassy will be most grateful."

As I moved to the door, the plain-clothes man, who had not yet said anything, moved ahead of me, and speaking over my head, as though I had not existed, said to the police captain, "Give me a call at the Bureau, Captain, when these guys are done."

The captain, an older man with bright blue eyes in a heavily lined face, offered me a cigarette as we waited for the lift.

"Don't fret about it, Lieutenant. It'll be as I say. But if you want to know something, have a word with the janitor!"

It was the janitor's wife who brought up the car. "Oh my, that poor young feller. Too much on his own he was. What they want, I always say, is a woman. It ain't healthy without a woman."

"That's all you need to know," said Captain O'Malley as we parted. "The janitor feller, nor I, couldn't have put it neater."

CHAPTER TWO

I drove back through Rock Creek, too early yet for traffic. It was still, and going to be warm. I pulled up by one of those picnic sites, to think for a minute about what I had seen, to calm down, to decide on what I was to say when I reported.

The sight of death still had me in shock. All the novels, films and radio plays about violence and killing seem to leave the surviving characters unshaken as they move to the next episode; a kiss and a clinch or a cuppa tea or the plotting of bloody revenge, or, as in the English whodunnit tradition, a quick bath and change before attending, with the other house-guests, an entertaining quiz game in the billiard room, when the super-detective explains everything and names the winner – the murderer. Here was I in the King's uniform, at the end of a ghastly war, and a single death could shake me? Yes, it could.

It was only a few minutes to the embassy on Massachusetts Avenue. I ran the car over the crunching dried evergreen leaves to the Annexe, a temporary three-floor box-like structure hardly visible from the road, but far more roomy than the Chancery itself, built to house extensions to diplomacy unknown before the war, which would grow, not diminish, as the emergency faded. Trade, shipping, aviation, education, science, food supply and financial policy were among the branches of the London bureaucracy whose agents had their names on the many doors of this pigeon loft and who now enjoyed the perks of being in the Diplomatic List.

The meeting in the Security Office was already in progress when I got there. The Security Officer "Shiny-Boots" was seated at the head of the table (heavy footed and toothbrush-moustached, he must have had a given name, but he was known universally as Boots). There was Sylvan Ross, still much as I had seen him as he left Marsden's apartment, and the Minister, Sir John Portent: quiet, pipe-smoking, content to let the Head of Chancery do most of the work, but, we believed, the hand on the wheel, involved in arcane issues of state we knew not of, and certainly the Ambassador's right hand – even his mentor. The Military Attaché, Colonel Hampshire, was there; and most surprising, Lord Zender. Seldom seen by the staff, Lord Zender slipped in and out; he was not formally attached but had a room in the Residence which was also his office when in Washington. Zender had been the Prime Minister's scientific adviser. He was a Nobel Prize winner for his work on particle physics. At his side sat Lady Marcia McKenna, known to one and all as Marcie, and listed in the personnel directory as the Social Secretary. I had no time to wonder why she was there.

Clearly the meeting had not been waiting for my contribution. Some paper was being drafted, and, indeed, the efficient Miss Sloman, Sir John's Private Secretary, came in as I did, bearing the transcript of the latest dictation. Even so, Sir John looked at his watch as I entered and observed that I had taken my time.

What had been happening? I made my report. "You went rather beyond your brief, didn't you?" said Sylvan.

Shiny-Boots frowned. "I told him just to sign the papers and get back here as soon as he'd done so."

Flushed and angry as well as still upset, I retorted, "I went on duty as a Naval Officer. I did not like what I saw or the rush with which it was being handled. I think I'm owed – you owe – I am entitled to an explanation." I sat down in a vacant chair, aghast at my boldness.

Zender spoke first.

"The Officer is quite right, of course. And it may be no bad thing to have shown the FBI that we are not merely stooges." Turning to me, he added, "It must have been a most unpleasant duty, young man. Death can be a messy business.'

Sir John said, "Very well, but we are five hours behind London. We must get this off straight away. Tom, I want you to read this page – just this bit which concerns Marsden's death. I will explain more later, but it is a matter of highest security and urgency. Please read it and give your assent."

I glanced over the few lines. Marsden's suicide was recorded with a confirmation from the local police authorities. Nothing else. Not a word about Sylvan or his near witness to the act.

"Agreed?"

I mumbled agreement. I was lost.

"Now, be a good chap, will you? See their doctor fellow and do what has to be done down there. Come up for a drink after."

Back at 4241 Connecticut Avenue, there were a few more cars and an unmarked black van. Police saluted respectfully. In the room nothing had been moved, except poor Marsden's body, which the doctor had examined; and, I noted, the *Manhattan Project* book – the bound manuscript that had lain open on the desk was now nowhere to be seen.

The doctor, his jacket slung over one shoulder, was only awaiting my return. "Well, that's it, Lieutenant. Poor young feller." He explained to me what had happened, and how it could not have happened otherwise. "Suicide, without a doubt."

My permission was sought to get on with the clearing up. White-coated men stepped forward. The body was straightened, the wounded head wrapped expertly and with care. No orders were given. Each man knew his job. In a silence almost reverent, the body was taken up, transferred to a grey bag, zipped up and borne from the room.

"Will that be all, Lieutenant? We have a cleaning-up squad waiting below. They will make it all hunky-dory as ever it was."

I signed certain papers, said my good-byes, and left with the doctor. "Nasty business," he said as we parted. "I should be at the golf club by now. Always on Sundays, it seems to me, these things. Nice meeting you. So long."

Sir John Portent, his wife, widowed sister and a teen-age daughter lived nearby in a largish 1920's house with Tudor-style front, furnished inside wholly by the British Ministry of Works to a standard thought suited to ministerial rank, comfortable but impersonal. A white-jacketed manservant showed me into a sunny chintz and flower-filled sitting room. After introductions the ladies left. Sir John poured drinks.

"This first! You probably need it. Chins up!"

It was a short dollop of Hollands gin. It dried the cold chill that had lain inside me since the morning's events. A longer glass was put in my hand. "Now, I have to tell you what you must know, and if you have ever read the Official Secrets Act, now is the time to remember it! Marsden died because he was a traitor."

"Good Lord!" I exclaimed. "A German agent?"

"No, no. You forget. That war's over. But an enemy agent nonetheless."

"Are we talking about our victorious allies, the Russians?"

"Yes, I'm afraid so."

"Atomic stuff? That would explain the Manhattan Report, which has disappeared, incidentally," I added.

"Fiddlesticks!" Sir John retorted. "I don't think he knew as much about it as I do, certainly not as much as you probably do. But yes, he was transcribing hush-hush documents and formulae on to micro film. Just a clerking job. Not a principal, just a cog in the machine."

"What about the Manhattan paper?"

"Forget it. He was probably trying to understand what it was all about. And that thing tells an awful lot, I believe. But it is going to be a published book, man! The Americans astound me. They are so hot on security but they publish this thing! I bet my bottom dollar that HMG would never have allowed it – never – till it was thirty years out of date!"

"Are they so hot on security?" I said. "Their Secret Operations lot seem mainly to provide plots for all these war movies they are churning out."

Sir John rose, then quickly drawing his chair closer said, "They are bloody good. Too bloody good. Their people picked up the trail that led to Marsden. Now they want more, please! Who is behind Marsden? Might it be the Ambassador perhaps? Or you? Or me? If Marsden had been picked up by the FBI, which might have happened today, God knows what would have come out! Frankly, the scandal is the side I'm paid to worry about; bother the secrets per se! So far we are the barely-trusted partner is this atomic thing. Already there are lobbyists in Washington for a 'go-it-alone' policy. A leak like this and we are out! Get it? Can't you just see the headlines? 'Britain leaks secrets to Reds'.

And we've sunk all we have to contribute, atomicwise, over here, in the American programme."

"So Marsden had to die."

"Marsden? Oh, yes, Marsden." Sir John got up, suggesting the session was over. "That was suicide, you remember? You are our principal evidence for that. You signed the papers – and you signed the Official Secrets thing, I hope. Stay for lunch if you like."

A note from Sir John was on my desk in the morning. Would I be good enough to arrange the funeral. Cremation perhaps? Or could I fix it with some local church? The staff would like that, he thought.

Why me? I thought again, or tried to; I knew not what to think. Only this, perhaps: that last instruction put the seal on my part of the conspiracy; it was a way of saying, "You're in it, up to the neck, until the grave." In my mind, I heard the prison doors clang and the key turn in the lock.

CHAPTER THREE

I've started this narrative with the death of young Marsden – his murder, as we came to know – because it was then that I became irretrievably caught up in the tangled web of deceit. That was just after the end of the war, in 1945. But to make sense of what followed you need to know the background and get some sort of picture of Sylvan Ross – my friend, mentor, and still an enigma after all these years – whose story this is.

The backdrop is Washington DC, during the eighteen months before the end of the war. I saw a lot of this man during that last phase of the war. It was through him that I became involved – after Marsden's death – in the later part of his story. I don't claim to have understood him though, but I think that, for starters, it is worth – as best I can remember after almost fifty years – recalling encounters and conversations that might throw some light on his character. And on mine too, I fear, but my excuse is that I was young at the time.

Then I will tell you what really happened to Sylvan, whose disappearance has remained an unsolved mystery of the Cold War, even to the present day.

I didn't really understand why Sylvan chose to take me under his wing, for I came to Washington as a complete outsider, knowing nothing of diplomacy or the whirl of diplomatic life that was to engulf me. At home in England I had never been inside a Whitehall department; I knew nothing of administrative procedure. Three years of war-time service in the Royal Navy had been my only training after leaving university. Ear trouble had cut short my sea service and, of all the shore duties to which one might have been assigned, being posted to the

Washington Embassy was a plum. I was to work for the Naval Attaché, Archie Struthers.

Sylvan Ross, seeing that I was a bit lost, a fish out of water, took me in hand, piloted me around, saw that I met people, and was the first to invite me to his home. He was about ten years my senior, I being then twenty-four, and I responded with a dog-like devotion. Not that Sylvan needed friends: everyone in the embassy and throughout diplomatic Washington admired him. In this new world of clever and important-sounding people, Sylvan seemed effortlessly to dominate. He was clever by any standard, full of wit but also of grace, of solid middle-class background with a tradition of public service. He had, after graduation from Cambridge, passed easily into the foreign service and was soon earmarked as a potential high flyer. When I joined the embassy staff he was a First Secretary and (as the post was temporarily vacant) Acting Head of Chancery.

This made him and his office the Clapham Junction of the communications network: downwards, transmitting the instructions of HE, His Excellency the Ambassador Sir Geoffrey Leeds, and the ceaseless flow of telegraphic messages from London; upwards, co-ordinating desk views on all subjects into briefs for HE, aides-memoire for the State Department or a counter-blast of telegrams to London.

Individual jealousies and tiffs were soothed and smoothed by Sylvan's calm judgements; who else would have dared to correct, as though it were a schoolboy's essay, the great Sir Robert Swaffam's memorandum on Nazi infiltration into the culture of the Amerindians of Guatemala?

"Thanks, Sylvan." Sir Robert had actually thanked him. "You have clarified my basic concept very nicely: good piece of work that. We can send it to London now. Well done!"

Sylvan's office ran smoothly, yet, however busy he was, the door was always open. He had been generous in the attention he had given to me, yet he seemed to find time for everyone. Never fussed, he could still be sharp with any foolishness.

Sylvan's In-tray was never as cluttered as mine soon came to be. "How do you manage to keep your desk so clear?" I once asked him.

"I throw away anything that has been there for a week. Whatever it was, it can't have been important!" He leant back, crossing his long legs on his desk, calm, but curiously alone in that buzzing, busy world.

In fact, as we all knew, he worked harder than anyone – often late into the night – alone in his office; but doubtless his adoring personal assistant was a factor ensuring good order in this, the hub of the embassy. How important it was I learned soon enough as I read through the piles of memoranda and telegrams copied 'for information' to the Naval Attaché's office. America, once the sleeping giant, stung into action by the Japanese attack on Pearl Harbour some two years after our war against Hitler had started, had, by now, emerged as the mainspring and architect of the coming victory. No ally was more dependent than Britain on American supplies. No other ally was there, after all, that had fought throughout, never been over-run and to have been hailed in the darkest days as the sole upholder of freedom in Europe. If only for this last reason, Great Britain was still accepted – just – as an equal partner.

So it was that, besides the embassy, we maintained in down-town Washington Naval, Army and Air Force missions and an army of civilians purchasing supplies of every sort to sustain a nation at war; buying or chartering shipping to convey these supplies home or to whatever front in the remotest parts of the world. A continuing task of the 'embassy stockade', as friendly Americans playfully called it, was to conduct this orchestra. The Ambassador and his team were primarily a pipeline for policy discussions between the two governments. Our political masters at home set a stiff agenda. They were desperate to maintain Britain as a full partner, but also, believing they knew best how to handle foreigners, friends or foes, they sought to exert a restraining hand on what they feared was American exuberance over the terms to be offered the enemy, plans to unite the nations of the world and for those parts of it (still marked red on the map) claimed by the British Empire, over the dissolution of which our Prime Minister had famously declared he did not intend to preside. Another issue, to become the dominant post-war problem, was still secret – the atomic bomb.

As Acting Head of Chancery, Sylvan had a finger in all these pies, yet he still found time to work on me. That is the appropriate phrase. It was more than friendly chats; he cultivated me in a literal sense, meaning that he forced me to think about things, to question my aims in life, to formulate ideas about the world after the war. He never lectured: it was always questions, questions, questions. I came to know myself; he remained hidden.

I recall our first meeting. Still new to the job, I was taking a snack lunch in the embassy canteen, sitting alone. I had not seen him come in but suddenly there he was.

"May I join you? My name is Ross – Sylvan Ross. You, I think, are the Naval Attaché's new assistant?"

"Tom Davis," I replied. "It's a pleasure to meet you, Mr Ross."

"Sylvan, please." He set down his tray on the table and shook my outstretched hand. "Poor old Archie. Natters on about too much paper work – but some people wonder what he has to do all day, what with all the admirals we seem to maintain in Washington nowadays."

I knew that Ross was a big shot in the chancery, which was over the way in the main embassy, the grand Lutyens building. I had not yet penetrated there; our office was in the Annexe, where also was this canteen, but I felt I had to stand up for my superior officer. "I've hardly settled in," I said. "But there seems to be loads of things to be done, and all this secret stuff – I'm rather overawed."

"Secret stuff? This atomic business, eh?"

"Well, if you say so. My chief goes on at me about not talking about it to anyone."

"Quite right, too, laddie; forget we ever mentioned it. Archie, though, your boss, is deeply involved. His pals in the US Navy Department are squaring up for the big fight with the other services for the prize of the first big bang development – for when, that is, the boffins report that a big bang will really work."

I knew nothing about all this at that stage and was relieved when Ross switched the line of conversation. On reflection I realised that I did most of the talking, in response to his prompting questions. At the end of it, I had given a complete profile of my life and background, and even of my rather woolly middle-of-the-road politics and philosophy.

I found myself recalling something my dad had said as the Spanish civil war was forcing public attention on the ideological struggle between the Communists and the Fascists, with their Nazi backers. "Ideology," he had said, "is not the same as Idealism. Ideology is the assertion of a doctrine that has to be served at whatever cost to one's self or to others. Idealism is the search – never ending – for the Ideal – the right, the true and the good."

"So you would say you are an idealist, eh?" asked Sylvan. "Open minded, eh? An open mind is at least a shield against the devouring dragons of ideology, whether religious, political or just faddist that beset us."

"If the mind is strong – very strong – as well as open, then you might get by, but many of us are not so strong-minded and are swayed by either side."

"So it is the strong-minded who settle for compromise? What do you say to that?"

This was logic chopping. I was too young to admit to compromise.

"Can't be right," I said. "Compromise, that's like appeasement before the war when we nearly sold out to Hitler. There has to be one – and one only – right course to take."

Sylvan shifted back to a more personal probing of the issue. "You can become confused about long-accepted loyalties. What you would once have died for can become an abomination. Any of us may, by luck or virtue, be given exciting jobs, but we can get out of our depth, cannot make the best of them. We cannot make the key decisions – except . . ." He had suddenly become remote and his eyes gazed without focus at the ceiling.

"Except?"

"Except when we have an ideological commitment."

I remember looking at him sharply, but at the time I did not really take in what he was saying. He rose then, and as he picked up his tray resumed brightly, "I hope you are bidden to the Ambassador's party tonight?"

I confessed to knowing nothing about it. He said, "Disgraceful! I'll see about that! Marcie will give you a call to say you are 'on'. Probably be pretty boring – a lot of southern congressmen and their, er . . . ladies: all madly pro-British but slave owners in all but name. They abolished slavery, as you may have read, but it goes on just the same! Anyway, you must start meeting people – lots of southern belles who will just 'lurv' your uniform. See you then!"

The sun shone on Sylvan in those days and I was stimulated and not a little puffed up because he kept up his interest in me. We met, not so much in office hours, occasionally in the canteen, but more and more frequently in the evenings, often late into the night. After all that followed and half a century later, it is hard to recall just how he looked, although the warm impact of his personality is still vivid. Later, press articles and then a book were written about him, and in them were pictures, mostly snapshots, of family, of university reading-parties, of punting on the Backs in Cambridge. In these, the man I came to know is recognisable and helps my 'identikit' reconstruction.

He was tallish, slim rather than thin. He moved easily but not as an athlete. The Ambassador had us all play tennis with him from time to time: Sylvan was remarkably inept – I was a much better player. He liked bridge and poker, but I was never bidden to these sessions. His hair was lanker and cut longer than was then usual, though clean at the neck. A long neck with an obtrusive Adam's apple. Above it the face was sharply chiselled with high cheek bones, a Scottish sort of face that Raeburn might have painted, and there was a trace of Scots in his accent. He seldom raised his voice, but always there was that musical quality, always suffused with good humour as was his mouth, always ready to smile – for all that a smile revealed his terrible teeth, stained by endless chain-smoking. This, and a habit of tapping his teeth with a pencil and abruptly chewing the end off any pencil that was to hand, were the only signs of any tension he may have suffered.

Now I can see him better. I see him in those hot and humid Washington summers. He used to wear a blue and white seersucker suit and a blue, polka-dot bow tie. As the ancient air conditioner thumped and dribbled away in the window space beside him, he would work away at his desk with his coat off, in his shirt sleeves, and, as he collected his thoughts, tap away at his teeth with that confounded pencil.

CHAPTER FOUR

The Naval Attaché, Archie Struther, and the Assistant Naval Attaché, a captain (engineer), were away much of the time, and though outgunned by the big naval mission and the operational teams down at Norfolk, Virginia, they were in cahoots with American opposites over some very hush-hush developments, notably on submarines. Sylvan said one night, "It sounds out of this world, but someone was telling me yesterday that they are working on submarine-based missiles. Instead of firing torpedoes they will fire rockets – missiles like those disgusting German things – up into the air!"

"What?" I exclaimed, "from under water?"

"I wouldn't know about that, but I'd rather supposed that you would know all about these things."

As he spoke I remembered seeing rough pen-and-ink sketches among the NA's papers; they had meant nothing to me then, but now I guessed what they were all about.

"Now you mention it," I said, "yes, I have seen something about this! I can't remember much about it, but I will look into it." (I said this, anxious perhaps to keep my end up. It was silly really, since at that time I was no more than a paper-keeper for my seniors.)

In the absence of both senior officers, I secured the drawings, no more than sketches torn from a foolscap writing pad. I brought them round to Sylvan's house the next evening. They meant no more to him than to me, but he turned them this way and that.

"Another swig, I think," he said, "I'll get another bottle." He was out of the room for a few minutes. "Couldn't find the damn corkscrew," he apologised. "But, hey, you'd better take these papers."

He handed them back to me.

"It looks to me as though Archie has been doodling. He is an old submariner, isn't he? Twenty thousand leagues under the sea and all that. Still, Verne was writing all that in the 1860's as I recall; I don't suppose there were any real submarines, were there, before the turn of the century?"

He was refilling our glasses as he spoke; his hand was shaking slightly. I sensed that he was more interested in these scribbles than he was letting on.

I returned the papers to the NA's safe, exactly where I had found them. Neither of us referred to the incident again. I felt it was trivial enough, but it had been wrong to take papers out of the office – any papers – let alone someone else's. And such a pathetic motive – to show off before Sylvan. And Sylvan had known this.

There was an occasion when he pulled me up for talking, at some reception, about the important people we had to deal with. At that stage of the war the Prime Minister, heads of the services and the like flew in for consultations. Only top people flew those days, in unpressurised bombers or flying boats: "Bomber Harris flew in last night" or "Did you know the Foreign Secretary was here yesterday?" – such was the gossip in the canteen. They came with no red carpets or bands, but briefly and silently. Any of us might be called on to serve as temporary assistants, if only to carry their papers or find them their favourite cigarettes. I was talking airily about such contacts to a complete stranger when Sylvan appeared from nowhere and took me off.

"You're an absolute bloody fool," he hissed. "That girl is the daughter of the Secretary of State for Air. I don't think she was impressed. She's very smart."

I murmured apologies for a breach of security.

"To hell with that. Of course you don't talk about these things. But that's not the point. You were trying to show how important you are – showing off. And," he added, "not for the first time either."

Receptions at Embassies, parties with Georgetown Hostesses, filled our diaries in those days; there was precious little wartime austerity here. Once I'd settled in, the work proved to be easy and largely routine, and 'showing the flag' at these and more public occasions was all part of the job. Juniors, like myself, gave their own parties, exhausting our allowances of duty free Scotch or gin, stabilised only by packets of nuts and crisps. The morning after one such party I was to attend some committee and met Sylvan on the way in.

"God! You look disgusting! Where were you last night?"

"I'm not sure," I said. "I think it was in Georgetown. This morning someone gave me a shot from a jug left over from last night. Gin and It – five to one – and the melted ice, of course, but it was covered with flies and things; the screens were pretty ropey, wherever it was. Ouch! Oh, for a cup of coffee."

This time Sylvan was quite gentle with me.

"We all get blotto at times, but watch it, Tom, or you will start rotting away. You're under-employed, that's your trouble. We'll have to do something about it; you have quite a good brain actually."

A transfer of duties did follow, but it is worth recalling one incident before that because of its bearing on a much later twist in this story.

Unless down-town on official business, most people ate in the embassy canteen, manned by voluntary rotas of embassy wives and families. While there were always some 'safe' dishes for British tastes – cottage or shepherd's pie, a nice distinction – the American style was taking over; lots of salads (for many it was a first encounter with coleslaw), Maryland chicken or the ubiquitous 'Chicken a la king'. There was cheese and fresh fruit to follow, and ice-cream, but also, to make us happy, a choice of recognisably British puddings. All together it was good, and cheap. Sometimes, on fine days, the younger people would take cold food from the canteen up the little path through the wood behind the embassy to picnic on the grassy slope that led up to Wisconsin Avenue. There Sally or Hermione, queens from the cypher room, would lead the way. Both had had some ballet training in the course of their upbringing and would dance on the green in the shade of the trees, enticing their swains to join in, which they did, until everyone collapsed in a heap, rousing passions quenched by laughter. After lunch, all would be back to their jobs on time.

But one grey and humid day, while I was eating in the canteen, Sylvan came up behind me and leaning over said, "See you for a minute please, when you are through: my room in, say, ten minutes?"

The Chancery had emptied for lunch but when I came in, Sylvan shut the outer door to his office, then the inner door.

"Thomas, you went to the Soviet Embassy yesterday at 11 a.m. You stayed there till 12:30. Was there any good reason for this?"

"I . . . I, er, yes," I stammered. "The Assistant Naval Attaché, Lieutenant, er, whatsit – no, Captain Sodkin – asked me to look in."

"Why?"

I explained how the Russian Assistant NA had approached me in the Navy Department car-park where I had just come away from a routine visit. The Russian, trembling with anger, had complained that he had been insulted by the Marine guard at the entrance we had both used. He had noted that I had been waved through with a casual salute and a "nice day, Loo-tenant!" while he had been diverted into the guardroom and had to wait for an escort. He had been treated like a prisoner, he said, before being ushered into his appointment. How did I explain this? Could we talk some time? The invitation to the Russian Embassy had followed. It had taken the form of a call from the Naval Attaché himself, Captain Sodkin.

"What passed?"

"Nothing much really. We sat before a low table. There was vodka and caviar set out. The Captain showed me how to take my vodka. It was the very best, he said."

"And?"

"And then he called in the lieutenant. The incident at the Navy Department was gone over. If you really want to know, I think they were trying to suggest that at this stage of the war, the Americans were becoming a bit careless about their allies; that they treated us as tiresome relatives, not partners in the coming victory."

"Did you agree?"

I flushed a little before answering.

"Of course not. I didn't have to respond. They did not make the point directly. The NA then went into a lengthy spiel about what a fine job the Royal Navy had been doing, especially on the convoys. He really seemed to know what we had been through, and talked about the Murmansk run. He said it was his dearest hope that our two navies would work together always, as good friends and allies."

Sylvan remained silent, tapping his teeth with a pencil.

I added, "But Sylvan, we do, don't we? We do get a bit fed up when the Yanks, the army people especially, seem to think that they and they alone are fighting this damn war. The French hardly make a secret of how they feel about it, and look how our information people have to nudge the press to remind them that we are still in there. Pentagon briefings would have the press report nothing but the heroics of GI Joe. Now the Russians –"

Sylvan cut me off with a gesture.

"Don't go there again, Tom. Don't get mixed up with them. If they ask you round say you are busy. You <u>are</u> a busy man, aren't you? – or you should be."

All this was said with unfamiliar vehemence, almost between clenched teeth and without looking at me at all. But then Sylvan looked up at me – I had stood throughout the interview – and said in a more relaxed tone, "Anyway, you won't be tempted. I've arranged your transfer, at least in principle. Archie – the NA – will be sorry to lose you and won't let you go until he is promised a new slave. He will fill you in."

It was an odd arrangement. Archie Struther showed me the last Admiralty signal on the matter: "Officer to retain use of his rank," it concluded.

"Meaning?" I asked.

"I dunno. What it says, I suppose. You can still wear your uniform with the wavy stripes when it suits, and I guess you are still subject to naval discipline – Kings Regulations and Admiralty Instructions and all that. Now, this is the job. You are to go over to the Chancery to help Hopkins, the Economics Minister . . . used to be an Oxford Don, now a Treasury wallah. I expect you've met him. London say they have no one to spare at the moment. Poor chap, he has all these post-war plans on his plate, including the solvency of our own dear country. He tells me, by the way, that we are already broke three times over. But there's more to it. As you know, a lot of us are involved in this atomic project. I've kept you out of it so far, but Hopkins is in charge of negotiations over long-term development; so as well as learning something about the science you will be deep into the politics of the bloody thing."

And I did and I was. I sweated to master the new agenda. My degree in economics may have helped, but now we were grappling with facts and theories way beyond the old text books, even beyond those of John Maynard Keynes, who was even then at the Treasury master-minding us from the London end. But this atomic business! We learned about the fission process and then about the Bomb. Even as we were still battling Nazi Germany together, the Washington stage had been darkened by shadows of mistrust. Britain had impressive scientific capability, but was seen by some as a loose card in the inevitable struggle for nuclear supremacy.

The UK had pooled all its resources with those of the US and Canada, and our own boffins were out there in the secret places of the Western deserts developing this monstrous thing. There was a long way to go but one saw figures – estimates of its destructive potential. Hopkins, and in due course I myself, had to have some knowledge of the technical developments in order to carry out the central task, which was political: to see that the UK kept a finger on the trigger of any weapon that might emerge, and, looking cannily ahead, on the future control of nuclear power, mindful always that it was not to become an American monopoly.

In a high-level committee, UK met with US and Canadian opposites to ease problems and review progress. And who was the British Secretary to this very secret gathering? Of course, it had to be Sylvan Ross. This was one of a range of administrative duties he took over at that time; the regular incumbent had returned from sick leave, so he had relinquished the Head of Chancery job that he had held temporarily.

After first attending one of these meetings, Hopkins being away, I told Sylvan how relieved I was to find him there. "Not really surprised, of course. I know you have a hand in just about everything round here."

"Nonsense, laddie. A good secretary does not need to know about the subject in hand. The art, for which Whitehall is famous, is pen-pushing and using the King's English proper-like! All I have to do is to write up the minutes – the sort of minutes that make Permanent Secretaries purr! But why the relief?"

I explained the loneliness of the job. "It's not just loneliness, it's all this secrecy! I have to lock up everything I learn. I do, and throw away the key. But sometimes I feel I want to burst – at any rate, talk to someone."

"Well," said Sylvan, "I really am an ignoramus in these matters but since we are on the same team, I guess you can let your hair down with me from time to time."

And we resumed our old camaraderie. It was good to be able to talk and to clear my own mind by outlining the new problems as I saw them.

CHAPTER FIVE

D-Day came as a complete surprise. The first person up at the digs I still shared with the Assistant Air Attaché at 3412, O Street, had the job of putting on the coffee and turning on the radio. Our first reaction to the news was to challenge each other to admit to being in the know. Unsuccessfully. But we had learned that whatever secrets each had to nurse, the security system was pretty good. There must have been people in the embassy who had been working night and day on the Washington end of the operation, but there'd been no leaks.

Most of our Service people had been on active service earlier in the war. We pictured to ourselves the approach to those beaches, the dread of air attack on cargoes of khaki-clad soldiers, the barrage of fire as they waded ashore. One could only imagine the days of build-up, the troop and truck movements through the wooded lanes of Hampshire and Sussex. Some wished they could have been there. Others thanked God it was not for them.

Throughout that day every news-flash was seized on. Later in the afternoon word was passed that we were all to go into the Residence. A staff officer 'put us in the picture' to the point of assuring us that everything had gone remarkably well so far. The Ambassador said a few words and all were invited to partake of Sir Geoffrey's usual offering, a glass of sherry – or tomato juice. As we came away, Sylvan said, "Thank Heavens it did!"

"Did what?"

"Go remarkably well."

Hoping to get a clue as to his involvement, I asked, "Did you think it might not?"

"No, you ass. I just can't help thinking what it would have meant for us if it hadn't."

"Utter disaster! I can't imagine we could ever mount the same effort again."

"I've no idea of the military implications. I just mean, think of the fuss if the Germans had been tipped off! Think of the witch-hunts! Every Department of State, every embassy would have been ransacked for the – er – traitor! It was that sort of little administrative problem I had in mind. You service chappies have not a clue to the problems we administrators face!"

I recalled the dressing down Sylvan had given me following my call at the Soviet Embassy. Security was obviously a worry for anyone in charge of such a load of secret and confidential papers – and of idiosyncratic people such as an embassy contained, especially this one. There were, of course, German agents in Washington. There were embassies of countries not involved in this war at all, whose diplomats were nearer to the fascist and Nazi way than to the way of the democracies. Our staff had been put on their guard against 'maggots at the core of the Corps Diplomatique' as our Security Officer Boots had put it.

But what about the Russians? They were our allies. And though they were now on top in the East and the race to Berlin was on, they had suffered losses and hardship without compare. They played hard to get in Washington. They kept very much to themselves. Indeed I had thought it rather good to have been invited to call.

In so thinking, there was an element of defiance, a backwash of disgust, at the crude 'anti-Red' skirmishing, not only on the Hill in Washington, where Congressman Martin Dies and his fellows were seeking glory by 'exposing' 'lefties', 'Reds' and 'Commies' in public life, in the Unions and the Government service, but also in much of the press and, from what one read, throughout the heartlands of America. Anyone who had held a job under Roosevelt's 'New Deal' was liable to be pilloried and slandered.

Sylvan was still grumbling as we walked back to the office together. "You'd think, from that briefing, that Britain again stands alone, this time on the edge of victory. But it's an American show, of course: they are in the saddle now."

I retorted, "You'd think from the news flashes we've had all day on the radio that the Yanks are in there all on their own! I'm glad and relieved to know just what we've done. And, I've said it before, we've got to keep our end up. We all love the Americans of course, but really, sometimes –"

Sylvan cut me off. "Come round to supper tonight, we can talk some more."

After supper we sat on in his 'yard', as the Americans often style their gardens. His was the sort of yard common to many of the houses below the unfinished cathedral where the streets traversed little ravines running down to Rock Creek Park. The garden area is left pretty much to nature, but a firm, wooden terrace is built out over it from the house – big enough to give a party on. In this case furnished with a rocker, cane chairs and a dinner table where we had just sat. Mauve sunset light filtered through the dark, looming trees; fireflies danced and crickets kept up their endless, busy noise.

"Now, what you were saying about the Americans – no, half a mo', let's go indoors." He closed the screen doors behind us and led the way to the kitchen, freshly cleaned up by his wife Bella, who had gone to bed, but redolent still of the casserole she had given us for dinner.

Sylvan poured another round.

"Tom, it's not just us that the Yanks will trample on, it is the whole world! With their trusts, combines and 'international companies', now backed by unmatched military power, they can take over everything! Let me tell you, I fear the Americans more than I fear the Russians! I hate America! Not all Americans, mind you, but America, the symbol of greed – capitalism!"

"You mean we have to stand up against the Americans?"

"No. Ass! We are nothing. On my reading, the USA will come out of this war unchallengeable, wealthier than when it came in, able to buy up the world, and if anyone doesn't like it, there is the Bomb. Only one country can stand up to America – the Soviet Union. And only one philosophy can stand up to unbridled capitalism – communism!"

"A tenable theory, but odd, coming from a top Foreign Office man, and in practice it would mean that Uncle Joe Stalin would have to match the US nuclear arsenal – bomb for bomb. Now that would be a terrifying prospect."

"Not really. All the options are pretty grim, but the best hope may be a balance of power – of terror, if you like, so that neither side dare use the bloody thing!"

That this picture of the post-war world would be spot-on accurate was unthinkable at the time. Sylvan, it seemed to me, had had too much to drink, and I told him so, adding, "How can you ignore this United Nations thing we are going to launch? And I know that the President – President Roosevelt has authorised a plan to hand the whole works over to an international agency. You've got to hand it to the Americans; there's real imagination for you! And it makes a lot more sense than your gruesome scenario."

"Oh, yeah, sense to the Americans, yes: for who but the Americans will have the plant, the technology and the boffins to run this control agency? In one move they get to control the world!"

"Steady on," I said. "That depends on the structure of the Agency; as you know we are working on it right now. We, the French, and in due course the Russians – and just about everybody – will be protected by built-in safeguards."

"You make me laugh. If the Russians join this United Nations thing at all, they will fight the atomic agency plan to the death! They want their own thermonuclear industry and they want the bomb. They are well on their way, and a front – a flimsy front – of international bureaucrats won't stop them!"

"What about us? The UK? You realise that Hopkins has left me to make much of the running in the present round of discussions. It's incredible really – and a bit awesome. Are you telling me that it's a waste of time?"

"Come off it, Tom! You should know – this man you are working for, Hopkins. What's his job? It's this: to make damn sure we get our bomb! When it comes to 'international control' we will be in the same boat with the Russians, determined to do our own developments, determined to prevent an American monopoly."

Yes, I had known this, but there had been no grand policy statement by the government, and there were powerful voices at home and round the world calling for international control of this new and unpredictable force, so there was hope that sense would prevail.

But Sylvan was right about Hopkins' immediate orders. "So," I said, "you are telling me that the Foreign Office at least is determined we keep our own bombs?"

"Fortunately, British foreign policy is constant in one respect: it requires that you never mean what you say. We will say – Ministers will say – 'Hurrah for international control' – while quietly working to undermine it. So much smoother than the poor old Russians, who can only say 'Nyet!'"

In the pause that followed I reviewed the discussions I had had recently, with the Americans, yes, but also the French, the Dutch and other 'exiled' Europeans with missions in Washington, and with the Chinese – Chang Kai Shek's people as they were at that stage. I reported regularly to London but got very little response. I had been a bit concerned about this and had consulted Hopkins, who had told me, don't worry, just keep things ticking along. "Keep them happy," he had said, "You're doing fine."

"You mean I'm just a part of this front?" I asked Sylvan. "A fall-guy?"

"You said it. I didn't."

As the war drew to its close, I didn't want to believe that the post-war pattern would indeed develop as Sylvan had foreseen. A brave new world would be born: this time we just <u>had</u> to get it right. For all the mud that Sylvan had slung at America, I had seen and touched, even been fired up by, American liberalism embodied in the Roosevelts. I would stand by them. Yet Sylvan had preferred that the awful Russian monolith should be built up to a point when it could challenge this healthy vision.

"Old chappie, there would be real changes if the Russians were boss. Life in the British Isles would really change. They'd let us form the Government, but it would be pledged to cutting out all the deadwood, the Clivedens, the big money men and their international deals, and the working class would come to its fulfilment."

"Come off it, Sylvan. Beddy times! You've had too much to drink! And where, pray, would you and I for that matter end up, with our well-known 'solid working class' backgrounds?"

"Probably in front of a firing squad. Goosh night, ol' chappie. See you in the morning."

After the lunch break the next day, strolling back from the canteen, I asked Sylvan if he enjoyed his work.

"Enjoy? Enjoy? It's not British to admit to enjoying work. But yes, if you must know, I love it. I live for it! The FO is super, really. You may start as a Third Secretary, but you get responsibility from the start. Before you've had time to unpack you may have a coup on your hands, or perhaps just a demarche from the President of Zenda. It's up to you, and no one else, to assess and advise action. Then there are only a few rungs on the ladder till you are at the centre – or feel you are – at the centre of everything – at the centre of power. Ministers depend on you for advice, so you mould the instructions you then put into effect. D'you know, one of my first bosses in the FO, just before the war, joined Midas Oil, or some such. Now he is stinking rich, top of the heap! Rolls, chauffeur and a mistress. But he is bored stiff with the job."

"Which is?"

"Oh, sorting petrol coupons, or arranging nationwide allocations of heating oil to one-armed, bed-ridden pensioners – or summat like that. He was over here on some mission recently. 'Sylvan,' he said to me, 'you may still be as poor as pisswater, and I'm stinking rich, as you may have read in the gossip columns, but I will swap jobs with you this moment, if it suits.'"

I was relieved, and said as much.

"Forget last night!" He laughed. "I can't recollect it myself. Ah, yes. Forget it – beyond the following brief resume which I will dictate as follows. Mr Ross observed that keeping the ship afloat, however rotten it might be, was the prior requirement for all, but for some was the additional responsibility for designing a safer ship and a sure haven for it. There were difficulties here; for, as Mr T.S. Eliot had noted in another context, 'Between the idea and the reality, Between the motion and the act, Falls the Shadow.'"

He glanced at his watch. "Tom, it's late! Back to your desks, slaves!"

The jocularity, the jokiness, betrayed rather than concealed a certain tension. He had spelt it out this time. Was it not the huge looming shadow of The Waste Land, of The Hollow Men? Did it not fall upon all of us, if we allowed, even for a moment, thoughts about the appalling devastation of the war, our piddling individual efforts to win it? And what was to follow, for us, for the world? For what would follow? Crushing retribution, economic bankruptcy, unemployment for the returning heroes – all as "last time"? Why should we think otherwise? What was new? Well, the atomic bomb, of course. But Sylvan was, I felt intuitively, speaking of another shadow.

In the months that followed I stuck to my work, facing down the suspected truths that that evening with Sylvan had exposed. The tempo of the office had speeded up after D-Day, and Hopkins had me dogs-bodying on a host of the problems in his charge. In April I mourned the death of President Roosevelt as much as any US citizen. But then in May came V-E Day, Victory in Europe, and finally the end of this long war seemed to be in sight.

At the beginning of August, and with no prior notice, Hopkins was called to go to London for consultations. I went with him. We landed not in London, but at an airfield in Oxfordshire whence we were whisked to a secret destination, a manor house somewhere in the Cotswolds. Never mind what else passed, but we knew that day that Japan was about to receive the first blasts from an atomic bomb.

I was given leave to go home while Hopkins went to London on further business. I dreaded facing family and friends with their questions about my work or, indeed, Washington life; if the one was covered by the Official Secrets Act, the other was so alien to the ancestral suburbs to which I had returned that it was better left unreported.

The visit was so sudden and so short that there was little time for intimacies. Even my family were treating the home-comer as a visitor from another planet. There was a church supper they had to attend and I went along, as also to church on Sunday. After the strain of the polite and inconsequential small-talk, it was a relief when Hopkins came in the

Foreign Office car that would take us to Poole, where we boarded the flying boat for the flight to Baltimore.

Just before we took off word came through that the first bomb had been dropped on Hiroshima.

CHAPTER SIX

Now to arrange poor Marsden's funeral. I gained admission once more to his bed-sitter, to glance over the shelves, perhaps to find a clue to the dead man's religious affiliations, if any. There were the Left Book Club titles I had first noticed: they covered pacifism, imperialism, and the prescriptions for social reform to be found in so many households in pre-war Britain; ideas that the war had quickened and might yet help re-shape the battered but purged country. I found a Bible, lightly thumbed, with a plate pasted in the frontispiece indicating Patrick Marsden as the recipient – 'for diligent study', from the undersigned, the superintendent of his Wesleyan-Methodist Sunday school.

There was a Methodist Church up Connecticut Avenue in a new development near the Maryland border. The minister was most helpful; he proposed the service should be at the crematorium rather than at the church, and offered to take it. No hymns, I had thought, but the dear man said that his organist, a volunteer, was always glad to play, and that some of his choir ladies could be on hand. He would find a Wesleyan hymn we would all know.

Pumping my hand warmly he declared that America could never do enough for 'England'. Not only had 'England' given John Wesley to the world, she had upheld the torch of freedom throughout this terrible war. What sweetness after the cynical sophistries of Washington dinner parties! Must get out of town more often, was my mental note. Meet the real people.

The service was on the following Wednesday. Quite a sprinkling of staff attended. There was old Missy Rankin, who had lived in the States since the First World War. She was the doyenne of the clerical staff.

There was Cheevers, who ran the typing pool and kept the stationery, and many others, known and unknown, for the news of the suicide was now public so there was curiosity as well as sorrow in the eyes turning towards the black casket as it was carried in. Of the senior Chancery staff there was no one but Marcie, the Social Secretary, and then, almost at the last minute, Sir John slipped in and sat at the back.

When everyone had gone, and a few words were had with the pastor and his kind friends, someone took my arm. It was Marcie. "Drinks, please," she said.

Marcie directed me to the Chevy Chase Club, only a mile or two back along the road. I followed her Packard convertible, fazed at this sudden turn of scene and company. Everyone adored Marcie. While she seemed to permit no intimacies, she was a ready friend and guide to all who came to her. I had had no good reason to do so. Now she had summoned me. She was an 'Hon.' if ever there was one. She was said to be the daughter of a Duke and her mother came from the Irish peerage. God knows how she had come to this job, but all knew that Lady Gertrude Leeds, the Ambassador's wife, quite depended on her. But so did everyone else.

"You did that very nicely, Tom," she said, as a waiter took her coat and another hurried up to take our order. "How about a horse's neck? Yes? Two, please, Charles, and very strong but lots of ice!" She excused herself for a moment, "to tart myself up," she said, improbably.

I lay back in the deep armchair before the low table at which we had been seated. Through the open windows came sounds of tennis and bathing. An elderly foursome went out to ready themselves for golf. The club was not busy on a mid-week morning. It was restful, delicious. It was a top peoples' club then, quietly but elegantly furnished.

Marcie returned. Her customary silk blouse was pale grey today, and her only jewellery was a single string of pearls and a pearl in each ear. If she wore make-up, you had to be expert to notice.

Had she been a member of this club for long? Surprise must be allowed that the impoverished British had feeding rights at all in such a place. I had been there before, but only with the richest and nicest Americans I knew. Some such I said as I toasted her with a brimming, ice-cool glass. "And thank you for this. I've hardly earned it."

"You have, you know, arranging the cremation and all that, and writing to the poor boy's family. I told John he'd have to find someone else besides me; I just could not have coped! You know we shipped their Excellencies off to Montana last night. That will be the forty-third state; the Ambassador is determined to visit them all before he retires. Yes. That kept me busy – telephones from the Governor, train schedules altered, and what shall poor Gertie wear? Can't you just see it! So yes, Tom, I am grateful for your help this week."

Hugely content with the moment, the setting, the company, but not believing that the momentary high could be sustained, and tied to the convention that office hours had to be kept (this was, after all, a Wednesday, not some dreamy week-end), I said I'd better be going, but that it had been a wonderful break in such a godawful day.

"Nonsense! You have to take me to lunch. But first – Charles! Same again, please! Just the same! Last lot was perfect! Now, let's see what they've got today."

Marcie led the way out to the awning-draped verandah where a buffet was being laid out and two chefs busied themselves with carving, fixing a variety of salads and dressings and preparing avocados, removing the great stones, arranging them on ice-packed bowls for serving. Into, onto and over them piles of shrimp or crabmeat or a mixture of both were arranged. I still marvelled at the abundance of such exotic treats in this country.

"I think a couple of those, Tom, don't you? They are ready, and, as you were saying, we haven't got for ever."

"But I was to take you out, I thought?"

"As you like, dear boy. I just thought, as we were here, we might as well get on with it."

There was no point in disturbing a dream that seemed not to have run its course. As we ate, and over coffee, she told me a bit more about herself. "You didn't know Daddy was Minister here, just after the last war? Everyone here loved him very much. That, if you must know, is why I can still come to the Club; he was made an Honorary Member, and all the family too! But it was a bit too much for him, poor man; he became a dipso."

"Your father, the Duke? You surprise me."

"Oh, no! He died when I was very small. Don't really remember him. But Mother married again, much later on, and the Daddy I knew was this Foreign Office chappie. He and John were at Eton together."

"You refer, I presume, to the good Sir John Portent, our present Minister here?"

"Yes, of course! Who else? Incidentally, he'd be quite glad if you dropped the 'sir' business. Just say, 'Hi, John!' when next you meet."

Marcie was telling me that to be one of 'Us' you only had to behave like one of 'Us'. My levelling, Presbyterian instinct could not buy this. I said, "And if the good Sir John was so addressed by the messengers, the security guard, or his personal private secretary, would that go down well? Would that be OK by you, Marcie?"

Some last shot in my locker of leveller's ammunition had found some sort of target. I persisted, risking this unexpected new friendship:

"Marcie, I'm thinking about this new world we are to have now that the war is over. Is it 'Sir' John's victory, or John's? I have to stand with the Johns, Marcie, even if it means being shot with the rest in Burford Churchyard."

"Oh, for Heaven's sake, Tom! You sound just like Sylvan when he is a bit blotto."

"Really? Go on."

"I suppose you know I adore Sylvan?"

"Splendid chap, yes. What's so hot about him?"

"Tom, you ought to know. What is great about Sylvan is that he believes in something! Even if we all end swinging on the lamp posts, Sylvan believes a new and better world's being born – or could be."

This was indeed the Sylvan I knew, but I wanted her to go on. "Odd. Unusual in the Foreign Office?"

"Yes. Unique. Bound to lead to trouble, of course, but most refreshing, don't you think?"

I was more interested at this point in Marcie. With, as far as I knew, no qualifications except her breeding, she was clearly on the inside of the whatever-it-was, the plot, the conspiracy, the secret design which I felt sure, after the last few days, was afoot. Had she dropped in by accident on Churchill's secret headquarters in the darkest days, a job would have quickly been devised for her. Had she boarded Lenin's armoured train, carrying the fuse to light the Bolshevik revolution, the comrades would soon have been confiding their secrets to her and seeking her advice. Something of the strength of her personality was getting through to me and it was more than her blue blood. I tapped tentatively on this well-armoured exterior with a question of my own.

"What do you believe in, Marcie? Do you believe in anything?"

"Me? Oh, I don't think I have to." She gave a short puzzled laugh. "I believed in this war. I hate the Nazis. My sister fell for some beastly Nazi Count. He was high up in the SS. God knows what happened. We think she shot herself in the end. Then, yes, I believe in people. I believe in people who know their own mind; who get an idea, and go after it, hard!"

"Like Sylvan?"

"Sylvan has great ideas, but he is in a muddle still. And I fear for him. He is impatient. He can't afford to be! He should just work to get to the top first. Top Foreign Office chap! He could be, soon enough, too. And then! Then he could act, speak out. Go into politics. That would be best, I think. Then, he could change the world – well, Britain, anyway, and that would be a good start."

The breastplate image. This was Athene! The goddess Odysseus knew, popping up, when needed, for advice, or when she thought advice necessary. Her clear, grey eyes were Athene's. Aware of the future, seeking to guide her protégé, acting not from her beliefs but acting out her role as goddess. Gods and goddesses did not have beliefs; they were believed in. But Athene and others less clearly remembered, however wise and well-informed, were not the ultimate in deities, I recalled. Others, higher on Olympus, had the fate of men and the universe in their hands. These, the likes of Athene, came among men to advise, warn, and if possible correct, to share their sorrows, to love them.

This reverie, induced no doubt by all the brandy, was broken by a sharp prod from Athene's spear.

"Wake up, Tom! I have a plan. Follow me down to my place. Park your car on that M street lot, the other side of Dupont Circle, then come on over. There's more to be done."

Protests that I should be getting back to the office were brushed aside.

"It's already three in the afternoon. You can write today off. You couldn't do any work, anyway, the state you're in!"

CHAPTER SEVEN

With the windows rolled wide open, fresh air did its healing work. I was roused, pleased at having penetrated the disguise of the goddess (they always come among men in disguise) and eager to do her bidding.

Marcie's front door was open. It gave directly onto a large square room lit by high windows. From a balcony at the far end, down a broad, uncarpeted stair of oak, came the goddess. She had now assumed the guise of a desirable woman, bare-footed, clad only in a kimono. No words were spoken. The goddess enfolded the mortal. The button marked 'desire' was pressed firmly. Dazed, the mortal was led back up the staircase. There, in a white room, white carpet, curtains, bed and bed drapes, he was undressed, piece by piece, each piece hung on a rack and put into a fitted cupboard that stretched down one side of the room.

Then he was propelled gently on to the white bed, and examined, piece by piece, inch by inch. Gently, gently, expert hands explored; soft caresses, strokings, followed, hands and then soft lips moving as gently, here and there like bees darting from flower to flower. The body stirred, responding in kind, taking a lead from the gentle pressures exerted by the goddess, this way and that, the guiding pressure a dance or skating instructor can apply to the eager learner. Limbs enfolded, intertwined. The mortal head sank between the god-like breasts. Bodies rose and fell, rhyming as one. The God Pan, seated in a corner, played louder – and faster – on his pipes. Hosts of maids, youths, fauns and satyrs ran madly through the room. We rose and wildly laughing, joined the dance; round and round over the bed, over a chair thrown in the way, until the mad pursuit was ended. Falling back to the bed, bodily law took over; ecstasy began.

The sun was low when I awoke, low enough for it to make dappled patterns on the upper walls and ceiling as it peered through the trees into the unfamiliar room where I lay. An alarm bell sounded in my head but its call was smothered in a huge sense of contentment.

I would have dozed off again, but there was the Goddess, kimono-clad but now with some sort of shift underneath, kneeling by the bedside table, pouring a cup of tea.

"One for you? Earl Grey. Hard to get now. Only for special occasions."

"Is this a special occasion? I had the impression you must do it quite often."

Marcie turned on me harshly. "God! You absolute swine! Get up, get out. Now!

So real was my own shock at the words that had slipped out, so abject my repentance and so genuine the assertion that I was just waking from the most wonderful dream I'd ever had, or ever could have again, that I was forgiven.

"But only because your horrid remark was true in a way."

I risked neither a comment nor the movement of an eyelid.

"It goes with the job – when things are very, very serious, that is. Then I'm ordered into action. It's me who found out that they were getting close to that poor Marsden boy."

Warmed by what we had done together and chastened by my too-quick remark, no distaste or even curiosity shaped my tongue or posture.

I just laid a hand on hers and said, "And Sylvan?"

"No! No, no. Sylvan I love. Yes, we come together. We love together. Not in love, you know, but we just love those moments of loving. Those were special occasions – my days off – and his."

"Those were? No more?"

Marcie had sunk to her knees beside the bed. Then in an urgent tone she said, "Sylvan is in danger, Tom, he might have to move at any time."

She rose, paced up and down the room, hugging herself. She continued, "He will need more help than I can give him. We need another hand. Sorry, Tom. But that's why I've asked you here."

I suppose I looked hurt, for she went on, "Sorry again. Let me put it this way. I asked you because I need you. I like you, Tom, because you have something of Sylvan about you. Just a little and, of course, you are not as clever as he is but you have the same sort of ideas. You want to change things some day, and in the right direction. Perhaps you will."

"I doubt it," I said, "But it is sweet of you to say all this and I think you are – you are the cat's whiskers!"

She laughed softly and pulled me down beside her on the edge of the bed.

"And you are a great lover. Can't think where you've been all this time!"

A light kiss on my brow, and I knew that I would do anything she asked and this I said to her.

"I knew you would not let me down," said Marcie, rising at the same time and resuming her pacing. Speaking fast in a matter-of-fact sort of way she said, "Yes, I love Sylvan. But listen. Sylvan, like me, does secret work for MI5 – you know, the anti-espionage people. But he is also in hock to the Russians. They have some dirt on him – have blackmailed him for years. I don't know the full story."

"So Sylvan is working for the Russians?"

Marcie looked at me mutely, then said, "Tom, I don't know, I really don't know. Given the hold they have on him it has to be possible."

"In his position it just can't be true!"

"And supposing the Americans find that it was true! 'Top British Diplomat exposed as Spy!'"

"And supposing, as you say, that the FBI or whoever had detected that Patrick Marsden was a spy too, are you telling me that Sylvan killed him – to cover his own tracks? Marcie, for heaven's sake! A traitor as well as a killer – and you want me to help him out?"

"I've not said this. These are your guesses. You may as well know this though: it was MI5 who snuffed Patrick."

This was little comfort. Who else of our small team of po-faced diplomats was our man from MI5, our own licensed killer? It could just as well be Sylvan again.

"Marcie, it just is not on. How can you live with it? If things are as bad as I suspect, then he might as well take his own life, follow Marsden."

"Oh, we thought of that, we've even talked of a suicide pact," she said in an even tone, "but it would be too melodramatic, and just think what the papers would make of that. Besides, it's not necessary."

I was shocked by what she said but tried to keep my expression neutral as I asked,"What have you got in mind then?"

"This is it, Tom. Sylvan needs to clear his name, get free from all this intrigue. Suppose he was able to bring off some tremendous coup . . ."

"For . . .?"

"For Britain! More particularly for the Foreign Office. It would be very hush-hush of course. No headlines; but if the Russians found out he had double-crossed them, they could denounce him as much as they liked and no one would listen – no one who matters, anyway. And if the Americans had suspected him they, too, would be flummoxed. Sylvan would have redeemed himself."

"And I am to help?"

"Yes, you have promised me! The plan is just starting to take shape. I am already working on the details. I'm not sure yet where you fit in, but it's a very small team. Sylvan wanted you on it, but I thought I'd make my own recce first. You'll do, Tom – no, more than that. I'll need you to see it through."

"I still don't know . . ."

"Yes, you do. You have promised me to help."

"Tell me a bit more, for God's sake."

"No. Enough for today. Sylvan will fill you in when necessary."

"But –"

"But me no buts." Another kiss and she melted into my arms again. "Just say once again you will help me."

I did so with as much conviction as I could muster.

CHAPTER EIGHT

I bedded myself that night in warm dreams of Marcie, but at dawn woke in a sweat over what she had been telling me about Sylvan: that this important chap in the foreign office also worked for our secret service, as she did too. But then, that he was in hock to the Russians! My friend Sylvan Ross? And then, she hadn't said it but I had: could Sylvan have killed Patrick Marsden? I would have bitten off my tongue before giving voice to the thought, but the thought was there as I woke.

Marsden had not taken his own life. There was now no doubt about this. Yet it was <u>my</u> signature that had certified his suicide at that strange, hurried inquest at the embassy – a cover-up if ever there was one. Cover-up for whom? I had seen from the inside something of Britain's fight to develop an independent nuclear deterrent. The stakes were high. We had need of ruthlessness too; so behind the bland front put up by the embassy staff there had to be some hard men. The meeting with Sir John Portent and Lord Zender had shown that these amiable establishment figures could be tough and swift to act when they had to be. Boots, the Security Officer, also – I knew that he was an ex-policeman. And Sylvan – was he ruthless too?

One did not have to accept that our people killed him. It must have been Russian or American agents: they did that sort of thing. Most likely the Russians: supposing that he was their agent and that American sleuths were on to him, they might well have decided to eliminate him. This seemed as good an explanation as any.

But what had Sylvan's business been that morning? I had not seen him since and now dreaded what I would hear when next we met; or, as bad, perhaps nothing would be said. I was already on notice that this conspiracy into which I had been drawn was a conspiracy of silence. It had been the same with the bomb, talking about it to no one but Sylvan. After the atomic bombs fell on Japan, when at last everybody was talking, the relief had been enormous. Now I was imprisoned again: I did not want to talk to Sylvan; was there no one in whom I could confide?

As I was leaving for the Office the phone rang.

"Is that you, Tom? Marcie McKenna here. I've got to go to a party this evening. Will you come as my escort? It's at Lewis Grearson's. What, you don't know him? Of course you do. . . That's right! The columnist man from the *Washington Mail*. Good on you. I'll pick you up."

Cool as a cucumber! Not a word about yesterday.

She came earlier than expected. In the working day she was always well turned-out, sober-suited and efficient. Now she looked stunning. A long-sleeved shift of loosely woven mohair, tawny coloured with glints of gold, fell loosely outside a black, divided skirt.

"This is from my 'relaxed intellectual' shelf of useful disguises!" she said gaily in response to my frank and happy stare. "Lewis likes what he calls intellectuals. Thank god we don't have them in England! All you have to have in America is a university degree – and they're two-a-penny here, same on the continent of course – and Lo! you're in! An intellectual! Never went to a university myself. You did. You'll go down big."

We got into her big green Packard drop-head. It was open to the still-warm September day.

"I came early, thought we could drive round for a bit, perhaps put you in the picture."

I spoke of my confusion following Marsden's death: was she going to explain?

With a mock frown, taking her eyes off the road for the moment, she said, "Hush, Tom! John Portent warned you, I think. Official Secrets Act and all that. Remember? Best forget it ever happened!"

"One thing I must know, please! What is Sylvan's part in all this?"

I saw her lips tighten but I persisted. "Sylvan is my friend and mentor. I feel sometimes he has taken me over. He got me this job I'm doing now. But he shaped my ideas too. I was always a liberal; just a family tradition, you know. Sylvan has made me think more clearly about all that, and I get a glimpse now of his really radical ideas for changing things – what you were saying last night – changing the world! Now he frightens me, or am I frightened for him?"

She didn't respond. I added irrelevantly, "I'd love to see him before this Un-American Affairs Committee in Congress. He'd give them hell!"

"I'm sure you'd do very well yourself," Marcie said evenly. "I know you are very well trained – even read your Marx. You've been vetted pretty thoroughly, you know."

As I had come to Washington by a chance war-time posting, had been before no board or filled up any questionnaire, I declared my disbelief.

"I assure you, we had you vetted. The usual British form is to say 'He's probably a good chap, or they wouldn't have sent him to us'. Now – and it's a bit late in the day with the war over – in M15 we are beginning to be a bit wary. So think of yourself as rather important! That's one of your weaknesses actually, thinking yourself important, but we decided to overlook it."

"Well, thanks a lot!" I retorted, then not wanting her to think I was peeved, added quickly, "Is that all part of your secret work – and Sylvan's?"

"My main work, as you know, is looking after the Ambassador's social calendar and the whims of Lady Gertrude. But, yes, you had to know sooner or later; and I <u>will</u> tell you more about Sylvan and, as I said yesterday, Sylvan will tell you what you have to do. We're nearly there. Still early. Let's stop for a moment and I'll tell you what I meant to say – put you in the picture about Lewis Grearson and his pals."

We stopped by a rough path a little above Grearson's house. We were on the same bluff as the house, overlooking the Potomac. Only a tram ride from the city centre, but another world. Below was a cataract where the river foamed over its rocky bed; the steep bank opposite, above the dark shadow of the gorge, was bright with autumn colours. We sat for a moment on the smooth rocks atop the bluff.

"You are about to enter the snake-pit," said Marcie. "If ever you can keep your thoughts to yourself, now's the time. Lew is a liberal. He hates these witch-hunters as much as you or I do. His column has been quite useful to us occasionally, but he is a witch-hunter himself. Can't help it – it's pathological – that's why his column is syndicated through every scandal sheet in the USA. And why he is so rich! And he is feared. If he fingers you, you've had it. Mainly, he is exposing the real baddies, but if he smells scandal anywhere, he and his sleuths are on to it. He keeps a stable of jackals and they don't all share Lew's nicer instincts. Let's go then, but watch your mouth."

We moved down to the house that Grearson had built for himself in this strange suburban wilderness.

Our host was on the porch with some of his guests. "Marcie!" he exclaimed, throwing an arm round her shoulder. "Good to see you! I was afraid you might not come after all this unpleasantness."

"Meaning?"

"This young fella of yours being killed."

Marcie blinked, as though not fully comprehending. "Oh! This suicide? It was rather awful. I never met the young man. I expect I will have to find out all about it."

"But was it suicide, Marcie? Was it?"

Marcie's response was to introduce me. Then she said, "You have a mind like a midden, Lew, digging for dirt as usual. I'm going in to find myself a drink. Tom here may put you straight. I believe he knew the man."

I explained that I had not known the man, but that it had been my job on behalf of the embassy to see the body, the police and the doctor; there had been no suggestion that this was other than a suicide.

Someone else was listening, a short, sharp-looking man – one of the jackals, perhaps. Lew Grearson turned to him.

"You heard all that, Carlo? Knocks your story out of the ballpark, eh? Tell it to this man. I'd better go inside to see that everybody's happy."

"So, Carlo, what's all this nonsense about?"

"I work for Lew – a stringer, know what I mean? Collect material for the column. But the FBI, too. They give me assignments. A buddy of mine there told me that J. Edgar Hoover himself is convinced that the Russians have a man in your embassy. "

"Is he mad?" I exclaimed.

"My reaction exactly, sir. But then this, er, suicide last weekend; the CIA are said to believe he was a Russian agent."

I had to find out more. I probed carefully. "So you think the Russians killed him, before he could be exposed?"

"Why!" exclaimed Carlo brightly, "that's a possibility! I was just following the lead in the CIA story."

"Which was?"

"That the Brits killed him, before he could be made to sing and expose the big shot behind him."

To give me time to think, I fished out a cigarette and lit it, coughing heavily to cover the palpitations that almost stopped me breathing.

"Carlo, you are clearly an old hand at this game, but there are two flaws here. First, on your own admission, all this is second-hand – hearsay. You've never met J. Edgar Hoover, have you? Or spoken to anyone in the CIA? No. So no wonder Lew was cool about the whole thing. The secret of his success is that no one can challenge the evidence set out in his columns. But second, think about this: the Brits, as you call them – the Embassy – could not have thought that this Marsden chap was working for the Russkis, or they would have been on to him soon enough." And I made to go inside.

"Point taken, sir. Anyway, Lew, you know, is real soft on you Limeys and I know when he does not want to follow up a story. But it will stay on file. We've lots of unfinished symphonies at the back of the store. You never know: years later, maybe they're dusted off and the coda can be written. Nice meeting with you." And he extended his hand in the American way.

Inside, Lewis Grearson was ushering a small group towards another room. "Come on, let's hear what Ezra is up to."

There was only one Ezra. It had to be our own Ezra Hamburger, professor, world renowned philosopher. In the midst of this spacious, calm room, lined to the ceiling with shelves of books, was Ezra, cross-legged in a deep leather armchair. Standing, seated or kneeling around him were half-a-dozen or so eager listeners. It might have been a seminar in his native Oxford.

"So, Ezra, to put it in a nutshell, you are saying that freedom is simple to measure – it lies in the absence of restraint; that there is no ideal government that will guarantee freedom?"

The speaker, bow-tied, with an oddly striking thick fringe of greying hair, moved to the fireplace to knock the ashes from his pipe.

"That's Jerry Khon," Marcie whispered, "from the Justice Department."

"So put, my dear Khon, it sounds a small shell and a very small nut. But let me sum up."

Putting his fingers together, the professor summarised the way mechanistic materialism had limited freedom. "If, as the scientific materialists argue, human-kind is – are, that is – just another lot of machinery, responsive only to the environment and external stimuli, what is left of choice? Judgement? Concepts of right and wrong? Dulled by the opiates of materialism we become fatalists, and worse, prey to the great manipulators, the ideologies of fascism and communism . . . strange sects and cults. 'Freedom for the Masses' we are conditioned to cry out, and suchlike slogans, but we've lost the hallmark of our humanity – freedom to choose and judge for ourselves. Happily for you in thrice-blessedAmerica –"

There was a disturbance behind us. It was Sylvan, evidently blind drunk. He stumbled as he missed the short steps down into this room from the main hallway and his glass fell to the floor. Everyone was looking at him. Marcie froze.

"Still churning out that crap, are you Ezra? You're right on one point though; what was it you were going to say about the great Manipulator? Blessed America! Bugger America! Freedom? Freedom to exploit the world!"

Marcie recovered, moved swiftly to turn him round and propel him back up into the hall. Lewis broke the stunned silence. "I never cease to wonder at the freedom of the British public servant to speak his own mind while unflagging in his duties. Refreshing, isn't it, after some of the zombies we meet in this swollen bureaucracy of ours. Now, everybody, an interval; there's food next door."

My apologies were accepted coolly and without protest. I hurried after Marcie and Sylvan.

"Here's Sylvan's keys, Tom. Take his car back to Tilden Street and tell Bella that he will be along later. I'll sober him up a bit."

"I must have a word –"

"Yes, OK. Call me later," she said over her shoulder, as she bundled him into her own car. "Oh Sylvan, you stupid . . ." I heard her grumble, between near sobs.

CHAPTER NINE

I did not see much of Sylvan in the weeks that followed. He was away for quite a time on some job and I did not deliberately avoid him, but, knowing how close he was to Marcie, I felt awkward about day-to-day contact while harbouring the secret of my own encounter with the Goddess. More inhibiting, though, were the fathomless questions about Sylvan raised by that encounter and his embarrassing exhibition at Lew's.

But one day Sylvan breezed in to my office. 'Breezed in' suggests a cheerful entry, and so it was.

"Tom! Happy coincidence: You are going to New York tomorrow and so am I. Let's go together."

"What, drive?"

"No, let's take the Pennsy Rail-Road. I'll have Susan get tickets and book us in at the Barbizon. And I've wangled an invitation to come to your show too!"

My 'show' was to attend a party on the British aircraft carrier *HMS Ferocious*, then in New York on a good-will mission. With some recollection of my having been in the Navy, 'they' had sent me to represent the Ambassador, who was away again, while other senior members of his staff appeared to be otherwise engaged.

We made our separate ways to the Union Station and found our seats in the club car. Sylvan, ebullient, ordered highballs for us both.

I was not responsive, having these inhibitions and at a loss after what Marcie had told me about Sylvan.

Sylvan chattered on for a bit, then fell silent, fishing a paperback out of his pocket. I stared moodily out of the window: through Baltimore, looking at the distant masts, funnels and cranes, and, adjoining the tracks, the busy scene at the Baldwins Locomotive works. Amid lines of dead-looking old locos were shining new ones. The flash from an opened firebox fanned the clouds of steam to puff-balls of orange. It was noisy in the old coach and silence was mutually acceptable, but as we slowed for the crossing of the Susquehanna River, Sylvan slid from his club chair to the seat beside me.

"Cheer up, old chappie. I think I know what ails thee. It's Marcie, isn't it?"

I wanted to back away but there was no room.

"Marcie has told me all about your little romp together. She said you were great. Bully for you, Tom. Great Lover, eh?"

I assembled my defences. Sylvan was a married man. He had no more claim on Marcie than I had, but I expected a warning to lay off. But no.

"She said in so many words that she felt she could rely on you and, incidentally, that she had the impression that you don't sleep around much. I'm glad if it's true."

It was, but there was no need to reply. I said, "What about you, Sylvan? Married man?"

"Tush, laddie. Yes, devoted husband and father. But as you will find, occasional moments alone in the arms of a Goddess are extra-phenomenal experiences, never to be missed. Odysseus positively depended on his encounters with Athene, although the whole thrust of the *Odyssey* is his struggle to get back home to Ithaca and his waiting Penelope. I struggle, Tom, I struggle to get back; I can't tell you . . . but I promise you Athene helps. Helps no end."

Amazing! Sylvan had already cast Marcie in the image I was forming of her. The shared vision restored some warmth to my feelings towards Sylvan.

"Yes! Goddess," I said. "That's how I see her. She doesn't really belong to this world."

"Yes, but we do Tom." His face clouded. "But, no. Truth is, Tom, I'm not sure if I do either."

I shushed him up, muttered something about working too hard, take a break and so on.

Sylvan remained a riddle, now a sinister one. I remained on my guard, but at least our feelings for Marcie no longer stood between us, rather it bound us closer.

We booked in at the Barbizon. Much used by the embassy people, it was not the smartest place on offer in New York, but with its view over Central Park it set the visitor on New York's wavelength, as did the balance of that evening with friends on Fifth Avenue with a penthouse also overlooking the Park. The party ended up in the early morning at the Blue Angel nightclub. Next day we went to our different contacts before meeting up for cocktails at the hotel and a cab down to the piers where *HMS Ferocious* was docked. At the pier head, her raking stem seemed to reach out over us and the steady trickle of fellow guests making for the gangway, yet the ship herself was dwarfed by the eighty thousand tons of the *Queen Mary* in the adjoining berth, her three enormous smoke-stacks gleaming in the late afternoon sunshine.

Handshakes with a reception committee of senior officers were followed by attachment to one of several parties being conducted round the ship. Food and drink were on offer and accepted at every turn. Apart from the Consul General and some other New York-based staff, we knew no one, so having done our duty and drunk more than enough, I suggested we should leave. Sylvan said, "Tom, I want to tell you something. Let's get out on top again."

From the cavernous hangar where we were, we found a lift which took us to the flight deck. We strolled aft along the length of it to the great White Ensign trailing lazily from its staff astern. The sun was almost set. The Hudson River ran before us in streaks of bronze. Across the river, lights were coming up like pinpricks in the black silhouette of the New Jersey shore, black against the red glow of the setting sun. The warmth of the day quickly gave way to the chill of approaching autumn.

"Was your ship as big as this, Tom?" asked Sylvan.

I explained, as I had certainly done before, that my sea service had been confined to convoy duties on a small and very elderly destroyer. People don't take in what you say about your world – they are fully occupied with their own – until or unless they find themselves transposed as Sylvan was at that moment. His eyes ranged over the carrier and the great liner nearby, now aglow with lights and with wisps of smoke rising from her funnels.

"I envy you all the same," said Sylvan, "and with your lovely ships here I am suffused with an intense glow of patriotism."

"I never doubted your patriotism, Sylvan – well, hardly ever, so spill the beans. What's this all about?"

"I'll tell you. I've been working up a scheme that has amused me, but I was in a bit of a limbo. There was no purpose to my plan. Now I know. It will be the great patriotic act of atonement."

Sylvan drew me down to the locker on which he was sitting. He spoke low and fast.

"Listen. You know about Los Alamos, the nuclear weapons centre in New Mexico? Well, quite a few of our best boffins are working there. One of them, a famous chap actually, is in touch with the Russians. They have some sort of a hold on him. I say one of ours, but Sergei Bronski comes from Eastern Europe – worked with Rutherford, became a refugee. Now he's a leading theorist in the thermonuclear field."

"So?"

"If the Americans get on his tail there will be all hell to pay. You know they are nervous as cats with all these foreigners working over here. They suspect everyone, not least the British. At the moment we are beggars at their table. If they come to distrust us, the present nuclear co-operation will end, but, probably worse, pop goes that 'special relationship' that keeps the pound sterling afloat – broke though we be – and the island economy just ticking over, given daily injections of dollars."

"So?"

"So, before the FBI or the CIA or whoever gets on to his tail we must get him away."

"Have him recalled?"

"No, if he is playing traitor the establishment can no more use him at home than could the Yanks. No. We've got to whisk him out. 'Lift' him, as they say. We have a little time. As of now no one knows he is playing footsie with the Russians –"

"Except you, it seems," I interjected. "Sylvan, how on earth do you know?"

Sylvan, for only a fraction of a moment, seemed taken aback. He said abruptly, "It's my business to know. And you may as well know this. He's not given the Russians much, but they are giving him a channel to exchange notes with an old contemporary of his – a Soviet scientist, a colleague from pre-war days. What they want is not secret drawings and plans; what they want is Bronski himself – and, if we don't lift him, they will!"

I quizzed Sylvan further: "But, why are you telling me all this? What can I – or any of us – do about it?"

Sylvan was tapping his teeth with a swizzle stick, pocketed after his last drink below.

"We are going to do it. I have a team, but I will need you too, old laddie. Being on this ship has given me the idea. We can get our man to the seaboard, but how get him to England? Why, obviously on one of these splendid ships! There are lots of our Navy ships repairing in these US Navy Yards. You know all about ships. With all your Navy connections you could fix up that end of things. Think about it."

I was aghast, yet could only laugh out loud. "Sylvan, you're mad. Let's go."

It was on the late train back to Washington before Sylvan put me more in the picture.

"We can talk here. Even at the Barbizon it's not safe."

"They could bug us there?"

"Certainly. You know I do business with the CIA. They don't trust anyone they do business with . . ."

"Nor their own people, so I've heard."

"Quite so. So I expect to be bugged. In this game you've just got to watch your back all the time!"

"Well, Sylvan," I said, "the whole thing seems improbable to me, and now you add a persecution complex to complicate the issue!"

Sylvan stayed silent. Minutes passed before he spoke again.

"It's no good," he said. "But look here. I'm meeting with John Portent tomorrow – that's almost this morning – at 11 a.m. Please clear your decks and attend. An extra hand will be needed and I'd like you to take this on . . . a sort of fifth wheel, d'ye know?"

"But –"

"But me no buts now. Portent will agree to your coming in with me. He knows we'll have to act before long. And when you have the whole story you will not, I think, want to back out either."

I knew things were moving, though there was no specific part assigned to me in the development of the plan. I was a bit miffed at being left out, but Sylvan promised me that I would have my orders in due course and anyway, wasn't I busy enough on my official work?

CHAPTER TEN

Indeed there was plenty to keep me occupied that winter, as the challenges of peace replaced the challenges of war. The relationships between erstwhile allies continued to cool. In March, former Prime Minister Winston Churchill, who had led Britain so heroically through five dark years of war but who had been turfed out of office within sight of the finish line by an electorate weary of blood, toil, tears and sweat, gave an electrifying speech in Fulton, Missouri. "From Stettin in the Baltic to Trieste in the Adriatic, an iron curtain has descended across the continent," he warned us. I remembered that when I was growing up, Churchill, then just a back-bencher, had been accused of overstating the threat posed by the Nazis. But of course he had been right then, and I wondered if he was being equally prescient now.

Sometimes I wondered if Sylvan's Bronski scheme had just been a figment of my over-active imagination. But during these months he was working determinedly to bring it to fruition.

I put together the following account, not only from the post-mortems held by the conspirators, but also from Sylvan's report and from memoranda notes by Sir John Portent, the Minister, as well as conversations much later on when he proved a true friend at a difficult moment – but that was much later in this story.

It had been some months earlier that Sylvan had reported to Sir John that the FBI suspected a leak of secret information from the Los Alamos Laboratories. It was arranged for Sylvan to visit Los Alamos as the escorting officer when a party of British VIPs were visiting. He had met and talked extensively to Bronski on that occasion; entirely openly and above-board while going round the plant, but also very privately, at what sounded like a sort of guest house outside the laboratory reservation that was one of the few off-limits resorts to which the senior staff could escape from the shop talk and sometimes oppressive tedium of their own close-knit company.

Returning to Washington, he told Sir John that Bronski was probably the trouble spot.

"God, man, I hope you can back your story. He's a top boffin, you know, and he is one of our chaps. Couldn't you have chosen one of those verdammt Germans disguised as Americans as your prime suspect? There are dozens of them to choose from wherever test tubes fizz and magic formulae are, er, formulated. What's your reason?"

"The man was frightened, I could tell."

"Hardly good enough reason to shoot him. Might not others as percipient as yourself – if such there be, dear boy, if such there be – might not others have detected the signs, the nervous twitch, the wetted pants?"

"It was this party that made him on edge, I think," Sylvan explained. "One of the visitors was an old acquaintance from Cambridge days. I dare say he keeps his feelings under wraps all right the rest of the time. Anyway, the Americans don't suspect him as yet."

"Come on now, Sylvan. You won't be wasting the time of this Holy Office with a cock-and-bull story. What do you really know about all this?"

"The Russians will lift Bronski out of Los Alamos the moment it becomes necessary."

This statement, delivered in a dead-pan voice, shook the Minister. As he told me later, it was less because of its dramatic content, but because Sylvan, not for the first time, seemed possessed of knowledge not given to ordinary mortals, not even diplomats. It wasn't supernatural, of course, rather it was underhand, underworld intelligence. Sir John thought he knew who were Sylvan's masters – those intelligence agencies in London, M-this and M-that, not accountable to Parliament. They were allegedly accountable to the Prime Minister alone, but from what he'd heard, even the PM was not aware of all their tricks. Sylvan was one of them, he was one of their instruments. Or was he? Did 'They' possess this affable and brilliant man?

Sir John went over to the window. Not looking at Sylvan, he said, "I know, of course, that you have connections outside the Office that we agree not to speak of. But you've brought this one to me. I have no basis for doubting your story. What am I meant to do about it?"

"We pick him up first –"

"Sylvan, you exasperate me! Pick him up? Kidnap him? We – you and me? Preposterous. This cloak and dagger stuff is for your Secret Service chums –"

"Don't trust them. Ours, theirs, anyone's. They are all mixed up together – and they will fight like hyenas for the body."

"You would defy the Americans over this? You know very well that our mission is to preserve the sacred relationship at all costs."

"If Bronski is caught out, Anglo-American relationships go for a burton."

"Er, yes," Sir John agreed. "It would be a disaster, an unmitigated disaster. And we know he is working for the Russians?"

"Yes. He doesn't actually pass out blueprints of bombs, or anything like that. He is a particle physics man, whatever that is. And all he does is to exchange figures, formulae and particles of ideas in this arcane area with an old pal in Moscow who thinks on the same lines. Freedom of scientific exchange and all that sort of thing."

"But he is compromised, and the Russkis have a hold on him, right?"

"Right. He is in breach of their security laws and ours. In the present atmosphere there would be no mercy for him."

"Is he a . . . er, communist? Ideologically where do we place him?"

"I've no idea. I find all that sort of thing confusing, myself." Sir John looked sceptical, but allowed Sylvan to develop his plan.

They had further talks. Sir John was won over. At their final meeting, he said, "So the embassy will do this. No one else will be involved. The world will never know, but we will have saved this man from his, er, folly, saved our country's reputation, and, I hope, will retain the services of a top man we really need. I will fly to London. There is only one man you and I can trust and can give the word. Our

Permanent Secretary at the FO, of course, and it will be up to him to take it to the PM if he thinks that is the form.

"I will send you a signal. How about 'Bombs Away'! Were you at the Air Marshal's for the showing of that RAF propaganda film?"

"No. And no," answered Sylvan. "Could you try 'Perm/Sec grateful'?"

"Well, yes, if you like – it won't look as startling to the cypher room staff."

The signal to go ahead came soon after Sir John returned from London. Sylvan had had the assurance he had desperately wanted, that he was trusted – and trusted to carry out a scheme that he knew well would be utterly distasteful to the Foreign Office. There was also the implied assurance that a defection by Bronski would have been as damaging as he had guessed. He went to work.

Marcie, of course, was his first lieutenant. It did not appear that there was any other of the staff as involved as these two in under-cover operations – although they could never be one hundred percent sure of this as it was of the nature of such clandestine work that one agent might not be known to another. Boots, the Security man, would have a part in this: he knew all the dirty tricks, was tough and athletic, and had helped them in other deals.

One more hand was needed. Sylvan decided on Roger Ritchie, another colleague at the embassy. Roger's father was English, but his mother was American, and he had many friends and relatives in this country. Roger had got to know the American West well from childhood. He had actually worked as a cow-hand on a Texas ranch and was familiar with the country from Texas to Colorado. It was this knowledge of the region that Sylvan wanted now. Roger had an easy manner and an assured self confidence, which was surely the basis of his promise as a career diplomat, coupled to the fact that he was linked to one of England's oldest families and had a private fortune of his own. It went without saying that he was temperamentally suited, and would accept. 'Anything for a lark' would be his school-boyish response.

The plot was simple enough in concept. At the right moment the conspirators would spring their man, whose co-operation could be induced, supposing that by then he would be wise to the alternatives.

But a hue and cry would surely follow. The man had to be spirited away and eventually smuggled out of the country – to Britain. That would be where I came into the plot. Timing was critical to success. The conspirators had no option but to trust Sylvan on this. They never learned his sources. The American and British intelligence agencies were hand in glove on most matters of security. Strong bonds survived from joint operations in war time of fantastic complexity, ingenuity and daring, but it was not to be supposed official assistance would be available from the American agents in a plot to snatch their own quarry from under their noses. It might be supposed that there were agents in the American camp with whom Sylvan had contacts and who leaked to him. If so, they were traitors; and if he dealt with such, who else might he not be dealing with?

Not only Sir John came to regard the man as a bit sinister. Sylvan, however, cheerfully allowed to his team that he was not omniscient: they just had to trust him to know when to act. "If I don't get it right we are all for the dog house anyway. Back out now, if you must."

But no one did.

CHAPTER ELEVEN

What they needed was a base. Somewhere handy to the Los Alamos laboratories where they could lie up and wait for as long as might be necessary. It would harbour their transport, be a centre of communications and the command post for the operation. At once Roger offered a solution. An aunt of his, living in New York, also kept a home near Santa Fe. She intended to spend half each year there, thogh seldom succeeded. He would make enquiries.

"Many thanks, Roger. Your entrance fee will be refunded at the door," quipped Sylvan, for whom this was becoming a high experience.

"Now, transport. Another one for you, Rog. First, everyone must be independently mobile, and you must not be seen in company with each other going or coming. Boots can help there. He knows all the rail schedules – and air services, such as there are. But we will need cars, too. Cars all round! Then think about the return east. A wild-eyed professor in the back seat might attract attention. For once money is no object, I think we can say."

Roger was very happy with his assignment. He was a vintage car buff. He liked nothing better than to join the chauffeur under the bonnet of the Ambassadorial Rolls, which was just old enough to be interesting, to fiddle with it and tune it. His solution for the escape vehicle was to purchase a Canadian 'Camper', a motorised caravan in which a small family could live comfortably for a vacation trip. He could visualise a secret compartment somewhere, perhaps in the bulkhead behind the driving seat. A double bulkhead, wide enough, just, to take a man. Who could do that? Well there was a chap near Toronto who'd rebuilt the timber frame for a Bentley Weyman saloon – wonderful job, good as new.

"Do it," said Sylvan. "Canada too. Very good idea. If ever the cops have a call out for the van, people who may have worked on it and all that, it may be harder to trace."

One idea sparked another. "No, the van had better not come near the site; fast getaway in one of the cars, switch to van fifty miles away – hundred miles away. Think about it. Work out what the Army are now calling the 'logistics' of it. You have time. Probably a couple of months, maybe more, before a Red Alert is remotely likely."

When these arrangements were in hand and Roger had his Aunt Sissy's blessing to use Piñones, the Santa Fe home, he and Marcie made a preliminary reconnaissance. They travelled independently. Marcie went by the Super Chief train to Albuquerque with two nights on the way. Roger drove his convertible, taking seven days to study the route and alternatives for the eventual return – presumably to Washington. Aunt Sissy's man, Pedro, picked up Marcie in Albuquerque. Pedro and his amiable wife Concepcion lived on the property, kept it in condition to receive their mistress and guests at any time, maintained the grounds, cared for the horses, and lived themselves not uncomfortably in their own little house on the compound. Roger went straight there.

Long afterwards, I visited the area and stayed with Roger and his aunt at Piñones, so I can clearly picture the scene and the events that the participants described later.

Piñones is a rambling, adobe-style home. It lies like a lioness in the desert scrub. At one end of its tawny flanks is a squat tower, the lioness's head as it were; round it, like lion cubs, are the outbuildings – Pedro's home, stabling, and a large garage and workshop The far horizons are bounded on the east by the Sangre de Cristo mountains, and on the west by the James Sierras. Although there are peaks of 13,000 feet or more they seem only as thicker pencil lines framing the picture of the desert. Through the vast bowl of the desert the Rio Grande meanders. Distances are hard to judge for eyes unused to such space.

The afternoon sun caught and held some glinting silvery structure in the far distance across the wilderness of desert and scrubland.

"Los Alamos," said Roger. "Twenty miles away." There was not another building to be seen.

As darkness crept over the valley, the rays of the westering sun broke through to touch the pencil line of the Sangre de Cristos that formed the distant horizon, and the black line of the great mountain range was silhouetted against a sky of burnished red for a few minutes only; then darkness, alarming, black. Then the gentle blue gown of night, studded with stars, enfolded all.

The pair of them would sit on the broad terrace, long after Pedro and Concepcion had cleared away dinner. Across the deeper darkness of the valley a single light showed, a tiny, hard, unwinking pinpoint of light set on some tower or chimney in Los Alamos.

"You thinking what I'm thinking? I bet they are looking at us."

"Bet they are! Better put out that cigarette!"

They laughed together, but both had felt that they were on the edge of dark events.

They stayed long enough to get to know the area well. They explored Santa Fe, about six miles off, the main routes in and out, and the byways, some hardly more than trails, leading up to the mountains. They exercised the two quarter-horses, which were fat from lack of activity. Marcie and Roger were competent riders and used to western saddles. Far out on the plain, surrounded only by the small pine-like bushes that covered the ground for as far as the eye could see, Marcie again had a sensation of being watched.

This time a sharp, chilling presentiment. She shouted to Roger to come up and he was soon at her side.

"Sorry chum," she said after a moment.

"You mustn't let this thing get on top of you, old girl."

"It won't, I promise you. We are going to win this round. And I trust Sylvan entirely. No, Roger, it's what happens after – after that and after that. I thought when the war was nearly over that would be it. Now the war is over, but this, this, this, goes on. There has to be an end to it. There has to be . . . there has to be an end for me! What will it be, Roger?"

Marcie freely admitted to these fey moments, declaring that she was of Irish stock, but they did not inhibit incisive thinking. Between them they worked out alternative schemes for the actual kidnap. Together they studied every foot of the proposed kidnap area.

They left Santa Fe again by devious ways, Marcie back to Washington, while Roger drove up to Colorado. Other contacts of his had a ranch high on a great mesa on the western slopes of the Rockies. The lesser and nearer peaks were fantastic enough, changing colour and, it seemed, their very forms with the play of light and cloud. Far to the south-east Pikes Peak, much of its 14,000 feet hidden by range after range of foothills, still showed head and shoulders above the rest. Roger had arranged to leave his car at the ranch and return to Washington by rail via Chicago and New York. Now he studied the land: this might be the place for the camper to wait. He arranged for that too.

It was June before they were called to action stations.

CHAPTER TWELVE

As the weeks passed the conspirators came and went – Sylvan, Marcie, Roger and Boots; mostly they were away. Only John Portent and I were left, so to speak, at base. Occasionally I would see Sylvan briefly, in passing, but when I asked him about his progress he would merely say, "Best if you don't know at this stage, dear chappie; safer that way. Your turn will come in time." I pretended to a deal of frustration at being left out of this key part of the plot but it was a bit of an act, really. I did not see myself charging about New Mexico on horseback defying the FBI – or the Russians – with a gun in my hand, or facing the consequences if the whole thing was a flop. John Portent was nervous as a cat, but did not show it. I warmed to this hardened old diplomat. He did not have to remind me what the consequences for <u>him</u> would be if we failed, and he read my mind well.

"Just stick to your job, Tom. They also serve who only . . . well, you know the rest, and you know there's more to be done. How are you getting on with the shipping-out plans?"

I had just about completed a time-table of sailing dates for both naval and merchant shipping to British ports for the whole Atlantic seaboard. This covered three months, but it all seemed a bit futile without a firm date to work to. I said as much to John Portent.

"Sylvan thinks July at the earliest. The devil in him knows how he finds out about these things but he says the Russians won't move before then. It is only when we know they are going to snatch him that operation counter-snatch can be justified. Only then will Bronski come to us willingly, indeed, I would hope, with some show of gratitude."

"Sounds rum to me," I said, "and we just hope the Americans don't decide to close him down first?"

"Just a hope, dear boy, but Sylvan's antennae seem to extend into that quarter also, and he thinks we are safe."

"Minister," I said, "I have an invitation to spend a couple of weeks around the Fourth of July with friends up Cape Cod way, Martha's Vineyard actually. Should I cancel it?"

"No, no, we all need a bit of a recess. Kidnapping on a public holiday wouldn't be cricket, and Sylvan is a gentleman – or so I used to think! No, go ahead. Have a break."

June passed, hot and sticky in Washington, but the vacation season – the first full summer of the post-war era – had begun. Washington was going for a sleepy siesta; it was already strangely quiet. Not that there had been no time for vacations during the war years, but this year was different. No longer was Mom harassed, on her own with the kids, surviving each day on faith, determined to believe that Pop would return – and in one piece. Now it was Hubby at the wheel of the wagon as the family moved off to the chosen vacation land.

Then it was my turn to take off. John Portent had told me not to worry, he would telephone me if it became necessary for me to return to Washington. He gave me his home number and said I could call him if I needed to.

My host, Charles Weaver, had, over the past year, been one of my contacts in the US Navy Department. He was still there, but on the point of release, back to New York and a partnership in the staid and solid merchant bank that bore his family name. It had been a bit of a shock, really, to find that this American sailor, so easy, so helpful, so modest, was a big name in Wall Street. Now he and his family spent the summer at their place on Martha's Vineyard. Gracie, his wife, had driven there from their home on the New Jersey coast near Redbank to open up the house. Charlie, with his teen-age son and daughter already at college, took me up in his elderly but sea-worthy cruiser with its twin Packard engines. We stopped for an overnight stay at Fire Island Inlet, where the night was spent in tale-spinning and reminiscences with the head of one of the big oil families and his guests. This strange and lonely house on the seaboard marshes was but one of the family retreats. It's worth recording only because they knew Sylvan, loved to have him as a dinner guest: "He'd shock the daylights out of some of these tycoons when he put on his anti-American act. It was great fun!"

On, the next day, to Menenempsha, the fishing port on Martha's Vineyard. Gracie was there with her truck to greet us at the wharf. She drove us up in the evening light to their vacation home, the highest point on the Island – 'The Top of the Mark' it was called, a one-storey, shingle-covered edifice, weather-beaten, crouching at the hill top in a shallow nest of gorse and broom. The Fourth fell on a Thursday this year, so the three of us enjoyed a simple supper and watched the local fireworks. On Sunday friends and neighbours showed up for drinks and a barbecue to celebrate the country's Independence Day, elated that for the first time in five years we were not at war.

Everyone was assembled in the one great room, the floor covered with a scatter of fur rugs, cushions and bean bags to sit on, as well as some deep armchairs. In the fire-place a few logs smouldered. Although the day had been hot, the evening was cool.

"Fetch me another beer, will ya, Tom!" called out an elderly man whose name was Jay. I'd been told that he was a senator from Texas, and an oil man too, but tonight, in his faded jeans and casual shirt, he looked just like any other vacationer.

"Shush, everybody! Listen!" The news was coming over the radio. "Some big-shot scientist has disappeared, vanished, vamoosed."

The bulletin was short, with few details. More drinks were poured, then everyone burst out talking.

Although witch-hunts for 'Reds' had never let up, this was a time before spies, traitors and defectors had become the standard fare of news-hawks and novelists, so the disappearance of Bronski dominated the party chatter that evening. Bronski it had to be, of course. I was having palpitations. I kept out of the conversation as far as possible. But the guests were a well informed lot. "Yes," I heard someone say, "this Bronski was a top boffin at Los Alamos."

"With a name like that he sounds a Russian, but nowadays I suppose he may just as well be American."

"No, actually, he's British."

"You don't say!"

"Is this right, Tom?" asked Jay.

I had to speak up, and resolved to make that plug for Britain that our information staff were for ever urging us to make.

"Yes, whatever his origins, he is a Cambridge man. Worked with Rutherford at the Cavendish Laboratories on the historic first splitting of the atom. We lent him to you to work at Los Alamos. He is the tops. Three things I suggest of high significance we have contributed to the American technology of today and her war-winning potential – radar, the jet engine, and the brains of Sergei Bronski!"

Good natured cheers and grins greeted my high-falutin' effort.

Then someone said, "I seem to have heard that he was one of those against the bomb. Maybe he has killed himself rather than go through with it."

"Not bloody likely," said another, "betcha he's sold out to the Russkis," and another, well into his cups, "Don't trust these foreigners, least of all the Limeys. They'll have the skin off our back yet. How many billions have we lent them in this lousy war? – and they never paid their last war debts either."

So often had the dollar sign drifted back in as the measure of national sacrifice. It was not worth fighting the point. I melted out on to the porch.

Charlie followed me out. "A worry for you, Tom, eh? You are pretty deep into this atomic thing now, aren't you. Any ideas?" All Charlie knew was that I had been assisting, in some quite junior position, in the planning of an international control organisation. He had, of course, no inkling of my involvement with the Bronski affair, but he was not one of these people who distance themselves from those they take to be their inferiors but, rather, one to bolster them up, ignoring inferiority of status or rank. Another like him was an Air Force general who had taken me to lunch in his Officers' Mess. We were both in civvies. I was a lieutenant, as he well knew, but he introduced me to one and all as Commander – "Commander Tom, of the Royal British Navy."

So, when I said that I really needed to use his phone to call the office, Charlie did not bat an eyelid.

It took a few minutes to get through, but Sir John answered on the second ring.

"Tom! Yes, the – er – package was put in the post on Friday. The people out there managed to keep a lid on it for a couple of days, but the press were bound to get hold of the story sooner or later. Don't worry, the package can't possibly get here before the end of the week. You stay there and enjoy the rest of your holiday."

And I did enjoy relaxing in the sun, sand and sea of the Cape in the company of thoughtful, intelligent friends. There was no more real news: speculation about Bronski's fate was being kicked and re-kicked into life by rumour, only to fill the daily pages and radio news slots between the canned music and advertisements. By the end of the week I was anxious to get back to Washington. After a quiet word from Charlie, Jay – Senator Firbaker – kindly offered to take me with him when he flew back to town in his private plane, which was hangared in nearby Edgarton.

It was a Sunday. The Duty Officer I contacted at the embassy was as amazed by the story as any one else. I rang round. No sign of the conspirators, and John Portent was not at home that day.

On Monday I took a chance in contacting some of our intelligence people just to see how they were taking it. There were lots of them in Washington: naval, military and less identifiable civil agencies. In the Pentagon and in the Navy Department there were doors marked "British Intelligence Dept: Keep out" or "No unauthorised Persons beyond this point" – and to establish their bona fides the agents would wear conspicuous plastic labels with two photos and the relevant details. These they would 'forget' to remove when, late and careworn, and carrying bulging despatch cases full of secret intelligence, they arrived at cocktail or dinner parties, thereby establishing that they were something rather special.

But that afternoon Marcie called. She would pick me up. We were to drive down to join Sylvan and Roger Ritchie at a cottage Roger had rented on the edge of Chesapeake Bay.

Cherwell Cottage was a dreamy little place, with a small fenced paddock, with open grass-land rather than a garden running to the very edge of the water. That night the water was still as glass, the cooling on-shore breeze barely touching its surface. A great orange moon hung low above. A few distant lights showed along the bay shore, too far away for their dancing reflections to reach us, try as they would. It was a lonely place.

After supper, Sylvan said, "You will be amused to know that this is where we brought Bronski."

Their tale had begun.

CHAPTER THIRTEEN

Again, I piece the story together from what Sylvan, Marcie and Roger told me that strange night on the shore of Chesapeake Bay.

For much of the late spring and early summer they had been back at their routine duties, and it was not until the end of June that Sylvan gave the word to move. Yellow Alert only. Take up positions!

The camper had been checked out and pronounced ideal for the job. It was mounted on the chassis of a light Chevrolet truck that had plenty of power. A new engine had been installed. All its mechanics had been gone over meticulously. Inside, there was a nicely veneered cabin, with fitted berths, a sink, and a lavatory built in to one half of the front bulkhead. The other half was now a concealed compartment in which someone could sit quite comfortably cross-wise in a narrow but adjustable chair and foot-rest combination. The rear panel of the van was decorated with stickers indicating the many sights and places visited by the previous owner: the Athabasca Glacier, the Calgary Stampede, Yellowstone National Park, the Grand Canyon. "Let's leave them," said Boots. "All part of the disguise."

"Good thinking," responded Roger. "Wait. Half a mo. Not this one, or this." They carefully scraped away one proclaiming the charms of Santa Fe and another of Aspen, Colorado. "We've never been there, have we?"

Boots drove the camper to the Colorado rendezvous, again provided by Roger – another case where Roger's friends, the owners, were away; this time they lived in San Francisco. The people on the estate made Boots at home. He helped repair a truck and a harvester (Boots, too, liked and knew his mechanics) and learned to ride horseback. His host, the caretaker, was an old cowhand and had ridden in all the stampedes in the West.

Marcie and Roger made their way by separate routes to Piñones. Then the wait began. One of them had always to be on call, but more exploration was necessary. They had been alerted that Moose Lodge, a rather seedy saloon off the road up to Taos had previously been used as a dropping point and might well be the place where Bronski was to be lifted.

Mostly they stayed at the adobe; it had treasures enough to detain them. There were books galore: priceless first editions that the libraries of Oxford, Paris, or Padua would have cherished, signed copies of contemporary works, many of whose authors appeared to acknowledge some debt or other cause for warm devotion to members of Aunt Sissy's family. Paintings and sketches that crowded the walls were, many of them, significant for similar expressions of devotion scribbled on them by their creators; there was also a Matisse, two Braques and a beach scene by Sisley, small, but outshining all else. There was music – a magnificent gramophone and neatly-catalogued records for every mood and taste. There was a chess set, exquisitely carved with an inlaid table, incorporating the chessboard to match. They played chess; they played music. If they did not have to agree on what they liked, they had time to try everything.

Roger had no preferences in music (though an eye for the pictures). "Just makes a nice background – if it's not too tinny. Mustn't interrupt one's train of thought."

Marcie liked blues and mood. She was gently footing it round the room to the soft strains of a pre-war number, 'Why am I so Lonely', and humming the tune. She broke off, coming up behind the settee where Roger lolled comfortably with a section of last Sunday's *New York Times*, and said, "Roggie, dove. I'm glad you have a train of thought. Wish I had. The train I'm on just rattles and rattles. You haven't a time-table, have you? I might find where it is going."

At that moment the telephone rang.

"Red alert! You've no time to lose. Subject is due at Moose Lodge at 7:30. He will be in his own Hillman Minx. He won't be followed, but the FBI will be up there somewhere." Sylvan's voice faltered and broke.

"I'm sorry, chappies, I hope to join you, but go ahead. You know what to do!"

That gave them four hours. Boots, two hundred miles to the North as the crow flies, was alerted. They got out large scale sketches they had made of the drop area. The Moose Lodge, built for the tourist trade but sadly decrepit after the war years, stood on a small eminence to the side of the road that wound up to Taos. A bed could be had there if you asked, but the rusting Coca-Cola sign across the front porch and the rotting picnic tables in the front yard were uninviting. It had been used, before the war, by tourists on the way up to the Indian centre of Taos; now it was a resort for local farmers and their families, a meeting place for a drink, for a game of pool.

The road winds up and up, and under deciduous trees the country seems quite lush and intimate by contrast with the great plain below. The nearest roadside habitation was two miles back down the road from Santa Fe. Here a community of dropouts had taken over some old sheds to set up a weaving shop, where they also made jewellery and pinewood furniture. There were local folk in scattered homesteads through the steep woodland above and below the road, mostly Hispanics, and these people must have maintained the small church or shrine standing back from the road that Sylvan had told Marcie and Roger to make their base for today's action. Sylvan would join them there. The little building lay on the other side of a narrow stream that hurried and gurgled by, even now, in the dry season. Its tin roof and other cheap repairs could not disguise its probable ancient Hispano/Indian origins.

Inside, altar lamps hung in dull blood-red bowls and a few candles were usually lit, but you needed the help of the single light bulb to see its more garish detail. Decorations of bright paper tinsel and tin were all about; between them brightly painted Holy Families and many saints peered out. In deeper recesses were grotesque figurines in pottery, shelf upon shelf. Few could be called pretty; many designed to be hideous. "Spooky" and "Disgusting" were Roger's epithets. Marcie, who did not go for churches as a rule, loved it.

"These," she interpreted, "are the souls of the damned. But here, they are about to find peace with this charming family and these jolly looking old saints." She picked up and fondled a woolly lamb from a

Manger scene. "*Agnus dei, qui tollis peccata mundi*," she intoned, clearly and gravely,

Roger had again sensed this mood of foreboding upon her. He hurried her out into the sunlight.

That had been two days ago when they had met on their separate reconnoitres. Now they took Roger's car only. The 8-cylinder Oldsmobile, secreted in the Piñones stables, was now quickly loaded with two small bags of their personal things, two powerful electric lanterns, some rope, a rifle for each, and three hand guns.

Their plan was to go beyond Moose Lodge and return as if from Taos for a quick peek at the state of things at the place. They were both dressed in checked cowboy shirts and well-pressed jeans. Both had good quality western hats. They would appear to be well-heeled tourists. In one plan, they had fixed a spot some distance south where they could intercept their man as he came up from Los Alamos. Just how was as yet uncertain. As they drove, details took shape.

"That old church is our base, we can store our things there."

"*Agnus Dei –*"

"Stop it! Pay attention."

"OK, I'm with you. There's a steep bit on the bend just further up. We could push Bronski's car over the side there. It's a terrific drop."

"Good thinking, girlo."

"If they trace it they may expect to find Bronski inside – but he would have fallen out on the way down. All those eagles and things would see to the rest."

"Not a bad alternative solution, if the worst came to the worst."

"It won't," said the prophetess.

CHAPTER FOURTEEN

On the way up they checked the site of the hold-up. Looking back down the hill, they chose a position from which they could identify any car coming up. They would use the lamps, now covered with red paper, to suggest some sort of road block. And Marcie's ravine was there, on a right hand bend. If you failed to take the bend and went straight on, the drop below would be at least 300 feet, they thought. In the already fading light they could just be assured that there was nothing that could check the fall. There was nothing, except for a low bank along the curb, surmounted by a rickety row of posts carrying two rough lengths of unsawn larch. These could be moved in a trice when the time came.

Still no sign of Sylvan. Roger wasn't put out. "We'll manage," he said.

Marcie steeled herself to agree. "But he'll come," she insisted, under her breath.

Now it was time to push on toward Taos. They soon reached a pueblo where they bought a large and gaudy Indian bag with worked designs of beads and dye, and an armful of bright painted toys and geegaws to complete the illusion of tourism. They wondered whether a call on the Lodge was, after all, necessary. As they approached with half a mile to go, Marcie spotted a car, up a side trail, but facing the road though generally hidden from it.

"That was a police car – patrol car. My guess is that the lodge is invested – is that the word? Invested – surrounded by cops and G-men looking like stags and tree stumps."

"Right, of course. The American army will be outside and the Russkis inside. But if they are out for a red-handed catch, won't they want an inside team too? Well, that settles it. We'd better go and see. We've just got time."

Apart from two local farm trucks there were two automobiles in the yard which the sensitive antennae of our team registered as not belonging.

"Do you see," Marcie pointed out, "they've been turned around, like the police car. For a quick getaway, don't you think?"

Carrying their more conspicuous tourist shopping, they barged through the swing doors into a large bar room with bare wooden floors and a scatter of deal tables. At one of these three men were seated, strangers, like themselves, but inconspicuous. All wore sports jackets, flannels. By the bar there were three more men, in well worn jeans and scruffy Mexican riding boots. Propped easily against the bar, smoking and sipping their beers, they might easily pass as locals. A third group was there. Two half breed Indians and an old, bent, thin-faced man wearing a tattered deerskin jacket over a torn check shirt. He had a wispy beard and sucked, seemingly out of habit rather than smoking pleasure, on an ancient but empty corn cob. He looked like some trapper who might have come west with Davy Crockett.

All this two sharp pairs of eyes took in before the proprietor had time to come from behind a curtain at the back of the bar to offer his hospitality. The two 'tourists' looked quizzically at each other. Marcie broke the moment's silence. In a loud voice and in what was later declared to be a perfect plains accent, she proclaimed, "Honey. No! You kid me not! You take me right back to the hotel in Santa Fe!"

She turned and marched out, clutching her parcels. Roger wisely held his tongue but spread his hands towards the proprietor with a despairing but sympathetic look as much as to say, "You see how it is? We all have these little problems." The old man in the corner cackled, lent backwards on his rickety chair and went on tapping his teeth with his empty pipe.

"Brilliant!" muttered Roger as they got outside. "May I say that was brilliant? I'd no idea what we should do next."

"Thanks, pal, but we'd better think out our next move rather more carefully."

"If we are going to stop this Bronk, I guess we have twenty minutes at the most. Where the hell is Sylvan?" Roger grumbled. "What are we going to say to the man? Shall we pretend to be the Russians? How can he know we are his pals, his saviours?"

"*Salvator Mundi*. Why, that's Sylvan's JOB! That's why Sylvan has joined the party! He knows the man. Sylvan Salvator!"

"What? What are you muttering about? Is Sylvan already here?"

Marcie smiled knowingly. "Yes, Didn't you notice him in all that crowd? Stood out a mile. See how he tapped at his teeth with that silly old pipe just like he uses a pencil in the office?"

Roger had no time fully to digest this development before he slid the Oldsmobile into its prearranged hide, facing north this time. The plan was to drive back up to Taos, once the first hue and cry had passed, then over the mountain roads down to the Colorado plain, approaching from the west rather than along the main Denver highway from Santa Fe, which went under the eastern lee of the Rockies.

"Then perhaps he will join us."

"Hope so. How will he know where we are?"

"He told us he'd meet us by this church place," Roger reminded her.

The two were still crouching by the road when one of the farm trucks came down from the direction of the Lodge. It slowed as it came to the little shrine; a figure vaulted over the tailgate, steadied himself and looked about.

"Sylvan! Here we are!"

He scrambled down the bank to join them.

"Well done, kids – and Marcie, darling, that was quite brilliant."

"I know, Roger told me. But how, pray, do you know our plans?"

"I have my spies, you know. Captain Ross's Own. 'The Desert Scouts'. Those two villains I was with have kept an eye on your preparations here and heard much of your chat. I approve entirely. Bronski should show any minute, I'd say. Lucky he has that little Hillman car. To most people they are a heap of trouble. We had a clear entry to the US market after the war, this car was our spearhead. But as usual, there were no spares! No service! Another British last!"

"It is nice and small. Poor little Minxy! It's the big push for you."

"It's only quarter past seven, and I expect he will be late."

"No. Look! There's something coming now."

The lights of a car came and went as it followed the winding, tree-covered escarpment. It would be some minutes yet. Time for Sylvan to explain how he had shacked up at the weavers' place down the road. He had got close to them a year ago.

"Then you could have planned all this properly on the spot and not risked our amateur necks."

"Not so," said Sylvan, adding that he had arrived only two hours since. "These things have to be played by ear," he said, "*Solvitur ambulando*! Besides," he said handsomely, "I knew I had a first class team on the spot. Now, Roger, you stop the car with your old lamps. I don't think the rope is necessary. He will have to come to an almost complete stop anyway as he changes down for this bend."

It was the little Hillman all right. It was brought to a stop without difficulty. Sylvan did the talking, quickly and incisively. Bronski did as he was bid, though quite bewildered by this new turn of events; he had thought he was only leaving some papers for collection. He had had no idea that he was bound for Russia, still less that the indicator board had changed, and that he was now on his way to Britain. He was obliged to assist as his car was pushed to its doom, then to hurry back with his captors to the little church. As they crossed the stream, Roger pulled over the two planks that served as a bridge. "They've probably got dogs, if they start searching round here."

In the church they had stored a bag behind the altar, with a complete set of gear for Bronski, and some food and liquor of which each now took a swig. They had their guns. Sylvan accepted the spare hand-gun, while swearing he had no idea how to use it.

Marcie's and Roger's plan now was to wait in the hope that (a) without their expected caller, everyone at the Lodge would quickly disperse; (b) if the US agents moved on the Russians anyway, if there was any sort of fight, again they must hide till all was quiet. It was not thought that the US agents knew exactly where the usual letter drop was situated, only that it was 'near' or 'at' the Lodge. Hence the probability of many agents scattered through the woods (confirmed by Sylvan's scouts) and the likelihood that if they suspected that they were at first misled, they might spread the search as far even as the conspirators were holed up. They dared not move down the hill to Los Alamos and Santa Fe. That way the whole organisation would be lining up to trap the supposed Russians. The posse at the Lodge, small or large, would simply be driving them into the trap.

"You are too full of plans, my kiddos. Look, we are ahead of time. Don't wait. Go! Go now!"

And they did. Sylvan watched their tail light, then sauntered down the hill to his temporary base.

CHAPTER FIFTEEN

That was the gist of what they had to say – Marcie and Roger that is. Sylvan added little, just beamed as the story unfolded, stirred up the little pile of glowing embers in the grate, and poured us drinks.

They told me the rest of the adventure; how they had driven all night up the line of the Rockies to the Colorado hide-out; how in the fresh morning air they had rested, eaten an enormous breakfast of eggs, sausages, pancakes and coffee before Boots brought round the camper in which Marcie's and Bronski's belongings were installed. Bronski, dazed at first, had become wholly cooperative. He told them how he had been tipped off about the Americans being on to him, which was why he had brought with him all his major work. He had intended to pass it to the Russians. He was now kitted out in a flaming shirt and corduroys that had been found for him. The journey had been made with no haste. It was made to appear a vacation tour and that's what it was.

Sylvan had to leave, to get back to Washington. We stayed on, Marcie and Roger reliving their experiences for my benefit. Roger opened another bottle.

"Bronski <u>was</u> here, you say! Did you get him away? Is he in England?" I asked.

"No. Rottenest thing. He had become most cooperative and a good companion, but he wasn't well on the journey. We were just unloading when he had a stroke – a mild one, fortunately."

"So where is he now?"

"Boots and Marcie took him back to the city, he's in bed at the Residence," said Roger. "Marcie fixed it. You know that the

Ambassador is retiring? He and Lady Leeds have gone home and will only be back after Labour Day for the formal announcement, the farewell functions and all that. So we have what is effectively an empty nursing home at our disposal."

Marcie took up the story.

"He might have died, but fortunately, professional service is on tap at our nursing home. Said to be the best medic in town, at least the Ambassador thinks so. He's some sort of Arab, Egyptian I think. The Ambassador is Arab-mad, you know, like many of his lot at the FO, so this chap Masudi is his pet – anyway he has not killed our man. He should be ready to move quite soon."

I didn't have to ask Marcie how she was going to keep Bronski's presence a secret until we were able to get him out; I knew she could be trusted to do this. I asked what the next step was.

"That's where you come in, dear boy," answered Roger. "We hand you the baton, yield the torch, sink back exhausted! Just work out a little plan, will yah, and rid us of this unfortunate person."

Marcie went on: "John Portent and your boss Hopkins have agreed you shall be released from all other duties for the next few weeks." She sat on the edge of my chair, laying an arm round my shoulder. "Don't worry, they've done quite a lot already. John will fill you in and give you your sailing orders. Look, Tom, this is the score as of tonight. Sylvan has done what he set out to do. Bronski is now in our hands . . ."

"What? Yours and mine – and Roger's?"

"Well, yes, for the moment, But don't you see? It is now for HMG – His Majesty's Government – to do something about it! Now the might of Britain – what remains of it – is being marshalled to bring him home. Admiral Somerstown is in charge; I expect you know him."

I confessed I did not, but that I had met up with his charming WREN steward whose main duties seemed to be early morning tea and to prepare his little rowing boat for his daily pull on the Potomac before breakfast.

"Well, no matter, because his executive arm is no less than your former boss, our Naval Attaché."

I blew out a sigh of relief. "Jeepers! You frightened me, thought I actually had to do something!"

"But you do, dear Tom, you do. All they had to start on was your list of sailings to the UK. They've decided not to risk their necks by using a Navy ship so they have got a freighter lined up, and as admirals just can't go dashing about fixing these things I think the plan is for you to smuggle him out. Back to Washington for all of us first thing tomorrow! You'll get your orders then."

I slumped back, aghast at responsibilities looming but still shapeless, but in another part of me pleased that I was to be given the job. Lulled by the warmth of the room and several glasses of a rather fine Burgundy, I relaxed in the comfortable armchair and listened to the back and forth between my co-conspirators.

Marcie hadn't finished with her explanation. "It was the Prime Minister and his old pal Alfred Zender who latched on to Sylvan's scheme and authorised it – without a clue about what they would do with Bronski once he was in their hands. They can't display him publicly; the latest we hear is that Zender has a place outside Cambridge where he might install the Bron, give him all the test-tubes he needs. And there he will be immured, a prisoner for life!"

"I suppose we could have killed him," mused Roger. "We could have pushed him over the side, in his car. Why didn't we kill him, Marcie?"

"First, our orders were to bring him home because he was useful: second, because, because, because we don't work for the NKVD – although I wonder sometimes, whose war is this, anyway?"

"Light against darkness, dear girl, that's what it is; though whose light, and whose darkness? In the morning the light is in the East, in the evening, in the West."

"You cribbed that from Sylvan," she said.

"What if I did? Don't you ever crib? Toss off a line of Shakespeare or something from the Psalms? What's good bears repeating. Sylvan has a lot of truth."

"I don't mind his 'Light at eventide', which must refer, I suppose, to our glorious Western Civilizing Mission. But the light of dawn in the East – that's a bit rum. A bit radical, don't you know? Tends to suggest the Russians have something to offer."

"Can't see Uncle Joe Stalin as a great humanising influence," retorted Roger.

"He is just a historical accident. It is ideas that matter."

"Ah, yes. And such a pity that every time, ends and means get fouled up. The nicest ends become prey to the nastiest means. Why is that, I wonder? Some of these socialist ends are fearfully jolly. Chicken in every pot. Car in every garage. Just what we ought to have. If capitalists were smart, just such would be their proclaimed ends. They alone have the means – the capital – to get there These poor bloody Bolshies haven't got the means, so they try a short cut, with Uncle Joe!"

Marcie clapped her hands. "Well done, Roger. Didn't know you were a philosopher."

Roger poured us all some more wine, ignoring my rather feeble protest.

"I believe we had some sort of unwritten agreement not to discuss this," he said to Marcie, "so at first I just assumed that Sylvan, this key man in the Foreign Office – frightfully pukka and all that – had a special assignment to get close to the Russkis, as part of his official duties. But is this his duty, Marcie, his painful assignment? Or is it his sense of principle, something the poor man really believes in?"

Marcie had risen, and, in the way she had, was stepping round the room to a tune that none but she could hear.

"Marcie, you must have shared my astonishment. How did he know so much? The Russian Embassy may have extended him the courtesies due to a diplomatic colleague, but would they have told him about Bronski? Of American plans to expose him? Of their plans to lift him? It doesn't make sense! He could only have got all this gen if he was one of them – part of their team!"

Marcie hugged her arms around her chest in what looked like a defensive posture. "I don't know, I don't know, I don't . . ." she whispered.

My brain was not so befuddled that I couldn't take in the significance of what Roger was saying, that our leader was – as good as dammit – in touch with the Russians. But had we not suspected it all along? How else, over these past mad months, had he planned this escapade?

"Do I shock you, Marcie? Come to think of it, Sylvan always was a bit of a Red, going on quite openly how different things would have to be after the war. He was cock-a-hoop when Labour got in last year. He's a Bolshie. I'm more than worried about your Sylvan. When we get back to our desks in the Chancery, and we are only two doors apart – I just won't know what to say to him."

Marcie spun around to face him, on the attack now. "For heaven's sake, Roger! Haven't you and I just assisted him – held the basin at least while he kicked the teeth out of the Russians? Hasn't he fooled them at their own game? Yes, a mad scheme but an act of high patriotism! The sort of thing that wins the Victoria Cross for chaps – like single-handed capture of a machine-gun post, or driving your torpedo boat against all odds at the side of a Hun battleship!"

"I'm still not happy, Marcie. OK. A pay-off for past misdeeds. But has he settled the balance? Dammit, was he working for the Reds? And for how long? I've given my reasons for fearing this. I haven't used the word before, but is he not a traitor?"

For a moment I thought Marcie would strike him. She stood over his chair and fairly hissed into his face: "Keep your bloody thought to yourself! Forget it, Roger. Forget it! We are still in charge of Bronski. Don't bugger things up now!"

We'd all drunk a lot. We parted to our beds with no more being said. Roger had voiced my own fears exactly, but Marcie was right. The job was not finished.

CHAPTER SIXTEEN

So Archie Struther, the Naval Attaché, had been brought into the plot. Well, some one had to give orders; this mad scheme was now official business.

Bronski's disappearance was by this time world news. The US authorities had only said that he was missing. When speculation multiplied, when some columnists came near to the truth in saying that he was against the atomic bomb and some suggested that he had defected to the USSR, it was *Pravda*, with surprising promptness and with no circumlocution whatsoever, that declared this to be nonsense. The paper paid tribute to Bronski's great achievements, reported his known distaste for weapons development, and even volunteered the idea that on this account 'and in the name of the Peoples of the World' he had taken his own life rather than be further involved in the scheming of 'imperialist circles' to develop the bomb. And this was the dominant theme thereafter in the world's press.

The wrecked Hillman had been found, of course, but now, a new discovery. Some miles down the fast-flowing creek at the foot of the drop, just before it joined the Pecos River, Bronski's jacket was found. Inside, his wallet: intact with money and his identification papers. On this, Marcie tackled Sylvan, who had been away from the office for a few days, not unusual at that time. He gave a sort of grin, she said, and went on tapping his teeth . . .

This did not mean that the US security people were satisfied. We had established that all the ports, all likely exits from the USA were being watched for a possible abduction of Bronski.

"Nor are we above suspicion nowadays," said Archie Struthers lugubriously. "We hoped we might get him into a Navy Yard where ships of ours are still refitting – but it is nigh impossible. Anyway we have nothing due out for some time. The lot we've got over here are total write-offs in my view – scrap them, I say! But the US people are so generous, so keen! They love mucking about with our old *Temeraires*. And, of course, since they are ready to pay for it all, the Admiralty has not a chance! Think how HM Treasury are loving it!"

"So what's next?"

"Thanks to your researches, Tom, we have picked on this freighter, the *Orme Head* due out of Baltimore. We have given orders to the Master – he's a senior RNR captain – to be prepared to receive boarders, and to convey, in greatest secrecy, an important passenger."

"Where to?"

"To Liverpool, his home port. We will make all arrangements for receiving him there."

"And boarding arrangements?"

"That's your job, young man. You've been round long enough to know the scene. Captain Watts of the *Dido* is laid up in Baltimore, waiting for his turn at the Norfolk dry dock. You can't get near his ship, it is in a dock run by, of all people, the US Army Engineers. Now, look, Watts will be at my place tomorrow. I've put him in the general picture. He has some ideas. Come over for a drink after dinner, then you and he can work something out."

The *Orme Head* had been on my original list of possibilities, but there'd been doubt about her port of departure. Now my orders were to get our man out from Baltimore in one week's time.

It was another still Washington night. Flitting shadows under the trees on the steep slope of the Naval Attaché's yard. It seemed wiser to discuss the business in hand behind closed doors, which we did. Captain Watts was a keen sailor. He knew Chesapeake Bay well, and its people. His plan was to bring our secret cargo up to the Baltimore approaches to the harbour in a local Bay vessel, then transfer to his duty boat, which would have business to come alongside the *Orme Head* before she sailed.

What about my end? Where could the cargo be picked up? I had no doubts about this. It had to be Cherwell Cottage, the place Roger had rented on the Bay and where they had told me about how they had spirited Bronski away from New Mexico. There was a small landing jetty there, rickety looking as I recalled but probably serviceable, and I knew of no other suitable place.

A chart was found, Cherwell Cottage identified. Depth of water noted. "Possible," said Watts. And I had a boat in mind. I knew a chap called Hank, who owned one of these Chesapeake Bay schooners. He'd have to lie off about a quarter of a mile, but he had a little dory, a flat-bottomed outboard, that could run into my jetty all right.

A provisional timetable was worked out. We would be leaving the cottage with Hank by mid-morning. We would meet *Dido*'s boat just after dusk, and Bronski would be transferred to the *Orme Head*. She was due to sail with the tide at 9:30 p.m. and Captain Evans would ensure that his passenger was safely disembarked in Liverpool. I would go back in the little boat to *Dido*, and from thence return to Washington.

I got on to Hank at once. He came to Washington and met me at the Fish Market. He took me to a balcony restaurant overlooking the dock with its business-like fishing boats straining against the ebbing river. Hank was half Portuguese, half Indian, and a hundred per cent American. His family owned a number of trawlers and a famous seafood restaurant in Annapolis. Hank had this boat and had long promised me a trip; he cheerfully agreed to help now.

The *Dulcibelle Adams* was one of the last of the classic schooners, so graceful in their lines – the fine sheer, the overhanging counter, the well-raked masts – that had somehow survived into this century. Perhaps it was because of that gentle climate, perhaps the loving attention of generations of owners whose source of income was the business of the Bay. His, he confessed, was not a pretty sight. She had her sails, but a diesel engine was a better proposition nowadays, Hank said. "And we'll need it for this operation," he concluded when we shook hands on the deal.

There were only three days to go. Bronski was still not well. Watts proposed to send along a medical orderly and I agreed. We were now under orders to get this thing done. The departure time of the *Orme Head* was the deadline.

Boots drove Bronski, with the naval orderly in attendance, to Cherwell Cottage. Marcie followed in her Packard. Roger and I were already there; we'd come down the previous afternoon, and Hank had brought his boat in on a trial run. The schooner had come no nearer than three hundred yards, but the dory had worked fine.

I was shocked at the sight of Bronski. He looked shrunken and old. He seemed to have nothing to say. Perhaps he could not speak; perhaps the stroke had already destroyed the essence of the man. Danny the medic helped him to sit on the porch rocker. Having safely delivered his charge, Boots turned his car around and headed back to Washington.

Marcie assured me that Doctor Masudi had told her that Bronski would get better. Also, unbelievable luck, the doctor and his wife were booked on the *Orme Head*. Surely this had been fixed, I asked her. "I don't know who would have fixed it," she said, "it wasn't me. I guess it must be just a serendipitous coincidence. Anyway, it's good that he'll be on board to take care of his patient."

Chesapeake Bay is often subject to summer storms, but we were in luck with the weather today. I'd been up early, and had watched how in the rosy dawn a light mist rolled slowly away, revealing the *Dulcibelle Adams*, her sweet lines silhouetted against the rising sun, whose rays caught and danced on her sparse rigging.

At exactly the agreed time, the dory detached itself and was soon at our jetty. As Roger and I hurried down to meet him, Hank jumped ashore with a hangdog look on his face.

"Gee, folks," he said in an embarrassed apology. "I'm real sorry. The outboard just petered out . . . I guess there's not enough gasoline to make it back to the *Dulcibelle*. Musta forgotten to fill it after our trial run yesterday . . ."

I was trying to absorb this shattering setback when the telephone rang. Marcie was still in the cottage and grabbed the receiver.

"It's Sylvan!" she shouted. "Says the Russians are on their way here right now! Get going. Go!! They may be here any minute! Go! Go!"

Roger's reaction had been a lot faster than mine. Even as Hank was still stammering out his mea culpa, he had run to the garage, and returned now with an enormous jerry-can full of fuel.

"We can't fill that tank from this big baby," exclaimed Hank. "Got anything smaller?"

Roger had anticipated this, and had also found two gallon-sized oil cans. Frantically they started to fill these, not caring how much they spilled. The first was filled but still uncapped when Marcie did an extraordinary thing. She seized the can. "I'll need this. Goodbye all of you. *Dies Irae*! Goodbye! Goodbye!"

Before anyone could move she had sprinted to the green Packard, throwing the can in besides her. Then she was gone, with screaming tyres in a cloud of dust.

Roger broke the spell. "I'll see to her. Now git – quickly! Good luck."

Another pint or two was slopped into the outboard. Danny and I hustled Bronski into the little boat. Thank God, the engine fired, and in minutes we were alongside the *Dulcibelle Adams*.

We were soon away. Hank had his anchor up, and with a puff of smoke from the inboard engine, we turned from the shore, heading upstream to the fork in the bay, beyond which the river would take us up to Baltimore. All our hearts had been thumping wildly. Poor Bronski just sat on the cabin top with his eyes closed, nursing his chest and breathing heavily. I steadied myself with deep breaths of the morning air.

CHAPTER SEVENTEEN

We chugged across the glassy surface of the Bay. Here and there the last streamers of morning mist reached up to the sun and evaporated in its warmth. It was going to be a hot day again.

Suddenly we heard a loud crack. A gunshot? No, louder than that – an explosion? Simultaneously our heads swung shoreward. In the still air, sound carried. It had certainly been some way inshore. Our eyes scanned the shore line, the flat fields beyond, and the little woods where the ground rose to the horizon. We saw above the trees the column of smoke, a flash of fire within, then a thick black wreath of smoke rose straight into the sky.

Marcie! An iron fist gripped my chest. I couldn't know, but somehow I did know that she was involved, that this was her funeral pyre.

Hank too seemed to understand that Marcie was dead. "Guess the lady just gone and blown herself up!" he said quietly.

I turned away to hide my tears as I searched for my own explanation. She could have gone to meet our pursuers. Waylaid them. Bashed into them. Blown them up and herself, her wonderful, vital self, in a magnificent but doomed gesture of self-sacrifice.

Later I found out that that is exactly what happened, but for the rest of that strange voyage I turned the whole matter over and over again in my mind. That she had died, however, I was certain. Goddess, priestess, prophetess, she belonged to the immortals. But the mortal woman I had dared to love was dead. Had died for us.

Hank wanted to show me the rest of the boat, perhaps to stop me from brooding. I moved round with him listlessly. The deck planks lay wide open, uncaulked, shrunk from each other by the long dry summer.

"They take up quick enough when the rains come," Hank explained. "She's a live boat. All that timber is alive still." What paint there had been on decks or doghouse, or varnish perhaps, had shrivelled away into blotchy strips of discolouration. Most of the timber had taken on its own colouring, a soft silver grey, stained here and there with rust from bolts and ironwork. So it was with the spars. The foremast rose like a silver shaft among the wraiths of mist, prodding them from our path through that painted sea.

I sought to wrap myself deeper in gloom and despondency by likening our craft to the doomed hulk of the Ancient Mariner's barque. I pictured the dehydrated crew, lying about the deck, or dead in their shrivelled agony. But the picture would not stick in place.

Only Marcie's image filled the inner eye. I tried to capture the horror of her death, probing morbidly, but of a sudden it was a live, vibrant Marcie who pushed her way through my dreary thoughts. It was Marcie/Athena, Marcie the grey-eyed goddess, and what she was saying was, 'Go. Go on. You haven't finished yet! We had a job to do! It may be quite without point. But do what you have to do *con brio*! Then, then we will talk again, and look for better things.'

So I was a bit more responsive when Hank came aft where I was leaning on the huge tiller.

"There will be a bit of wind coming in from the south east, I guess. We'll get up the sail. Meantime, a little something, huh?"

I followed him down the hatch into the compact, square cabin. When the decks were taken up and the little iron stove was going, it would be quite cosy. White painted, and here the varnished beams on the deck-head, the wainscoting round the single bunk and built-in settees, and on the fiddled mahogany table, shone freshly, as did the brass lamp swinging in gimbals. Coffee was brewing on a small oil burner; there were rolls, cold boiled beef and gherkins. We took all this on deck and called the other two over. Bronski had rested and looked better. Danny, the medic, to whom I had spoken little so far, told us something of what he and his mates had been through before *Dido*, a light cruiser, had been patched up enough to be brought to the US for what promised to be either a virtual rebuild or, perhaps, consignment to the scrapyard.

It had been on the Murmansk run, one of the last actions of the war. Somewhere off the North Cape, the convoy she was escorting was already diminished by successive attacks by packs of U-boats. Then she had been ordered to move off to engage or divert a surface squadron, one of the few sallies by the German fleet from bases in the Norwegian fjords. She had fought till nightfall. Signals over the air indicating a larger British group was approaching was the reason, it had been supposed, that the German squadron broke off the action.

Danny described his job in the medical bay as smashed and tortured bodies were brought down. The crash and sickening crunch as shells were traded by the big guns. It was worse than the more familiar engagement with enemy aircraft, he said, because "our own five-inch turrets were right over head. And cor blimey, they don't half shake you up!"

I could not help comparing his convoy experience with my own; much of the time our patrols had been routine, and on those occasions when we had been in action, despite death being all around I had been spared such up close encounters.

Bronski from time to time nodded his head in agreement but sometimes wagged it from side to side as if indicating the folly of man's inhumanity to man.

"Huh, we don't know what war is, do we?" said Hank. He was much taken with the young man and proposed that they should put out a spinning line, for some fish. This they did, and soon a delighted Danny was rolling in a string of mackerel.

And then the breeze sprang up. Hank sweated up the huge sail single-handed, leaving Danny at the tiller and me to gather in the sheets as the heavy boom swung out to take the zephyr wind. But it was enough to help the boat along nicely. Hank did not stop the diesel, but throttled it back to the softest 'plop-plop'. We were on a broad reach that could well last to Baltimore. The wind backed more to the east. It was now abeam, so Hank set one of his two foresails. And there was now enough sail to give a trembling pressure in the tiller arm. The sensuous enjoyment of handling a great sailing ship banished for the time being the cares of that strange day, and when Marcie came back to me it was as the goddess again, sitting at my shoulder in the stern-sheets, sharing the joy of the wind.

It was a timeless day, but before the hot and copper sun came low, the wind had died away and we resumed chugging. The water grew darker. There were oil slicks, and garbage floated past. The evening light now showed the masts and funnels of Baltimore, its towers and steeples, and the hills rising behind the more discrete, richer suburbs, where lay the Peabody Conservatory and other such monuments to both its merchant and intellectual past.

There were ships inward- and outward-bound in the river: tugs, dredgers and smaller craft. Among them might be some coastguard or harbour police patrol; Danny led Bronski below and arranged a hide for him behind the recessed bunk. We had slowed enough only to keep way on the schooner and were perhaps still three miles off the nearest harbour lights when we spotted *Dido*'s boat.

The little vessel made straight past us, downstream, and so proceeded for a quarter of a mile or so before turning about and nosing up alongside of us. It was now quite suddenly dark. The coxswain had done well to hide his intentions from any watchers there may have been in the last of the daylight.

The coxswain asked for me. "Captain Watts says change of plan, sir. You was to come aboard of *Dido*, I understand, sir, but there's been all sorts of flak flying around at the moment. So he has sent this here bag of clothes you left with him, and you are to proceed in the *Orme Head*, sir."

What, to Liverpool? There was no time to think about or protest this abrupt change in plans. It's OK, whispered the Goddess at my shoulder.

"Very good, Cox'n," I called. "Let's go!"

A quick, warm goodbye to Hank and Danny, then Bronski and I transferred to the Navy boat. Only a few minutes – in what direction I had no idea – and we were nuzzling up against the black hull of the *Orme Head*. There was a door in the ship's side, just a short scramble up a rope ladder let down from it. Bronski and I were heaved through this port into a dimly lighted flat, and our bags, one for each of us now, were thrown up after us.

CHAPTER EIGHTEEN

It was the purser who greeted us. A spare cabin adjoining the sick bay had been prepared for Bronski; there he was taken and put to bed.

"Captain Evans would like to see you as soon as possible once we are under way again. Captain Watts has explained why you are joining us," and here I was conscious of a curious sideways look. "You are not on the passenger list, nor, of course, is the other party. The captain thinks it best if you don't mix with the passengers. He says you are to consider yourself his guest. Take meals in his state room, and you are to sleep in his spare cabin."

The captain's steward, Dixon ("Call me Dicky"), took me to my cabin, which adjoined the captain's own room. "If you want anything, sir, just ask," he said. I settled for a large Scotch, a sandwich and a bath. I had come aboard in no more than dungarees and a sweatshirt, as well as the light sweater that Marcie had thought I'd find useful in the dawn air. The bag I'd left aboard *Dido*, which the coxswain had kindly brought for me, contained only my naval uniform, shirt, tie, socks and shoes. I had been expecting to wear these getting away from *Dido* and back to Washington, as had been planned, in Watts' car. By the time I had had my bath, this outfit was pressed and laid out on my bunk. My Scotch had been renewed and I sipped it as I dressed.

Through the porthole I could see that the big ship was moving smoothly down the length of Chesapeake Bay before making the easterly swing that would take her out of these sheltered waters. I could just make out the low shoreline whence we had come – it seemed an eon ago. Tears welled up as again I thought of Marcie. Another age, another world. When you go through a totally unexpected transfer of scene, as

I had coming on board this ship, bound not for Washington DC (where I remembered I had planned to go to a party that night with Marcie, Sylvan and Roger), but to Liverpool; and with all the events since that dawn, without yet knowing all the facts, there has to be a break. A shadow had indeed fallen between the motion and the act.

While waiting for the call to the ship's master, I tried to collect myself, to discern what was now my part; but still uncontrollable sobs would come. Marcie, Marcie. What had happened? Why did I think I knew she was dead? I pulled myself together by draining my glass of Scotch, just in time, as the steward knocked on my door.

Captain Evans was a small but tautly-built man with bright blue eyes in a wrinkled, weathered face. A Welshman, as was clear from his first few words. He told me later that he indeed came from Amlwch, in Anglesey, where generations of pilots had awaited the shipping at the Mersey Bar, and from whence generations had gone to sea. It was Welsh captains, he said, who had been the backbone of the square-rigger trade round the Horn and up the western coasts of Latin America. Now his first words, after a rather curt though perhaps just business-like greeting, were: "*Dido*'s boat brought me a note from Captain Watts, saying to expect you. He has also got together some picture of today's events which you had better read yourself."

"Marcie?" I blurted out.

"If you mean the lady in the case, yes, I'm sorry to bring you bad news. She is dead. She seems to have driven full tilt from a side road into the oncoming car. There were no survivors."

I took a deep breath and struggled to keep my voice steady. "Who were they? Was it the Russians?"

"One of the men in the other car was thrown clear, so they were at least able to identify his body. He was the junior Soviet Naval Attaché. The others, well, they don't know yet how many even. It was one great funeral pyre, it seems."

"And now there is a flap?"

"Indeed to goodness, yes. A great almighty flap! The Americans were surmising today that the Russkis and us, that is the UK, were having a private game together. But in an American ball park – their own back yard – never was there such a thing! And they suspect that

Bronski is the prize for the winner. The FBI never believed he died in his own car, it seems. And today, really without <u>precedent</u>, I believe," and his Welsh inflexions brought compelling reasons to agree, "the Americans have been quite <u>sniffy</u> about it, making enquiries at the embassy all day. Baltimore, as the nearest port, is virtually forbidden territory at the moment. It is as well we sailed out when we did, or we might not have got away without search parties all over the woodwork!"

"So that is why I'm to come with you? I really am awfully sorry to be a nuisance."

"Nonsense man. It would be <u>your</u> head, not mine, that would roll. We are clear and away now, I think I can say." He went over to a porthole. "Norfolk Roads ahead. You'll feel the bloody old Atlantic quite soon." He peered at me closely. "Look, boy," he said, turning to the door, "you appear to be pretty pooped, if I may say so. Just ask my steward for some Scotch, or whatever you like. You will feel better then. Go to bed, get a good night's sleep and tomorrow, my lad, you have to tell me what in hell this is all about. I'd better get up top and make sure we don't hit some last lingering chunk of America."

Marcie/Athene came to share my Scotch. 'There,' she said, 'now you know what happened! I promise you, I didn't feel a thing. I was just so angry. I had a clear view of the main road. I bet I was hitting sixty when I hit them. Wham! Yes, I was angry with Sylvan. OK, he tipped us off. But who, for heaven's sake, tipped off the Russians? Look into this when you have a moment.'

And who or what had enabled Sylvan to tip us off? I asked aloud, thinking back to the exchange between Roger and Marcie that night we had all met up at Cherwell Cottage. But I was alone. No Marcie. I'd no spirit to face the question. I stumbled to a first slight dip as the ship faced into the Atlantic and fell upon my bunk, to sleep until I was called.

I slept soundly that night, and after a brief interruption for the orange juice that the steward brought in the morning, on through the forenoon. My questions would have to wait. All that mattered for the moment was the safe delivery of my charge. Over a light lunch in his cabin, I gave Captain Evans more details of how and why Bronski and I came to be on board his ship.

The purser had got me a seaman's jersey, company issue, and comfortable shoes that were to prove a blessing. I drew on the rest of my gear to make up a nondescript appearance. Passengers might conclude I was part of the ship's company; crew, who knew I was no such thing, might assume that here was a passenger who liked to look as though he belonged to the sea-going fraternity. For I now sensed that we were not out of trouble yet. Had not Athene said as much, in that final warning? I'd better see how things lay. I had decided to see and talk to Bronski.

I was not anxious to do so. What could one say? And there was in my mind a reluctance, amounting to distaste, to get too close to the man we knew to be a traitor. It seemed necessary, though, to get to know him better. I _was_ involved. I might have to face some keen questioning on the whole Bronski operation. I had no idea what on earth London was going to do with Bronski when he was handed over, but for the moment he did not officially exist. His presence on board must not be discovered. If the Russians had known of the getaway from Chesapeake Bay then they might know also the plan for shipping Bronski out. Might they have people on board the _Orme Head_?

In the late afternoon a message from the captain brought me to the bridge. Cobwebs were for the moment blown aside. There was a keen breeze and some white-caps on the water. It was, after all, late in the summer, and autumn would be here soon enough. But the sea sparkled. It raised my spirits and I was attentive as the captain chatted. The ship was new. Laid down before the end of the war, she had been finished to peacetime standards as a passenger/cargo ship. Her passengers got a better deal in many ways than those on the great Blue Riband liners. The cabins were larger, the service more personal, there was only one class. But it was an eight-day crossing, nearly twice the time taken by the Cunarders and their rivals. Eight days. Time to think things out.

We were now on the rhumb line for Liverpool. We had passed the low coastline of New England, invisible to the west, and were heading for the Newfoundland banks. Whether or not I passed for an amateur sailor, something in me responded to the ship and the challenge of the sea. The fascination for me was that early in the war I had been in the North Atlantic, as a seaman in an old destroyer, convoying merchant ships like this, petrol tankers, shipping of all sorts, which we would pick up off Iceland and escort to the Western Approaches, towards Glasgow, Liverpool or further south to Avonmouth. All this came back, took over a troubled, rather shaken mind. How quickly, and with what healing power, a touch of life can dispel the gloom of death. The sea heaved and scurried by. The big ship hardly deigned to notice.

We were out on the wing of the bridge where you had to shout to converse. This did not suit what had to be said. Captain Evans led me to the lea of the wheelhouse, but still out of earshot of the quartermaster at the wheel and the officer of the watch.

"What is it, boy?"

"D'you think that any of 'them' are on board?"

"Gracious me, boy, you have a persecution complex. How is that possible?"

"If they knew we were on the Chesapeake, they may have known where we were going."

"Well, doubtful. You know we normally dock in New York. Only at the last moment, because of the longshoremen's strike, did we divert to Baltimore – must say, I was impressed. Nice harbour, Baltimore, and most cooperative they were. Most cooperative! Quickest turn-around ever! The point of all that is that they had no reason to suppose that this ship – my ship – would be in Baltimore. Of course, agents know all these things – the Jerries certainly did, during the war. But why should the Russians be alert to a change of schedule like that? Possible, I should say, but unlikely."

"Who joined the ship at Baltimore?"

"Well, everybody. The line had to transfer them from New York. They were brought down by train, courtesy of the Pennsylvania Railroad."

"OK. Yes. But were there any last minute joiners at Baltimore itself?"

"You must ask the purser. I really don't know. And if you are really worried, you had better have him go over the whole passenger list with you."

"I'm sorry to fuss. . ."

"You are quite right to do so, young man. We have all seen some pretty funny business in the last few years. Nothing surprises me any more."

I lingered up there to savour the evening light. The low sun glinted off the flanks and the smokestack of the ship and flecked with gold the straight white carpet in our wake.

The *Orme Head* had accommodation for thirty-five passengers. It did not take long for Mr Jones, the purser, to go through the list with me. About many of them, he knew a great deal. Some had travelled with him before; many were on official business – most, in fact, service people and ministry people. About half were British or London-based Europeans, half American. The only joiners at Baltimore were Doctor Masudi and his wife. Having attended Bronski already, was it really just a lucky coincidence that they were travelling with us now? I asked Mr Jones to arrange for the doctor to come to my cabin so we could discuss our problem patient and compare notes.

Dicky the steward had arranged, unbidden, an attractive tray of canapés and drinks in the captain's own stateroom, which adjoined my cabin, and there I received my guest.

Masudi was a largish, balding man, in his fifties probably, with quick light movements, not so much that of an athlete but of someone fired by nervous energy. He fairly popped into the room as the steward was announcing him, but pulled up short, his hand stretched out in greeting, when he saw me.

"I thought I was to see the captain? You? Yes, I think I know you! It is Lieutenant Davis from the embassy, yes? Yes, but what are you doing here?"

"Why, simple enough. I have to conduct our, er, patient safely to London."

Masudi frowned. "I thought – I fully understood, that I was in charge," he said in a somewhat petulant tone.

"Well, of course you are!" I replied. "You are the professional man, and you have a pretty sick patient. And what luck that you should have booked on this ship!" I was anxious to smooth any ruffled feathers; professional men do not like to have their authority challenged.

"It was not luck, you should know. Your embassy people have strings to pull and they secured this passage for myself and my wife."

That wasn't what Marcie had told me, but really it did not matter either way. It seemed important only to dispel this apparent resentment at my being there too. So I said, "Oh, better still. In the rush of the last few days someone forgot to tell me, I expect. But let's have a drink on it. We are both under orders. You to keep him alive, and me to deliver the living Bronski to his fate – whatever that may be!"

Masudi eschewed the captain's whisky and gin, opting for just a glass of tonic with a slice of lemon. I poured myself a generous Scotch, and we began to talk about the Patient, as we agreed to refer to him. Yes, of course I should look in on him. He had to remain hidden in the sick bay anyway, but it was best, the doctor said, that he should stay in bed. The stroke in Washington had not crippled him, but another before long was inevitable.

The doctor left, amiable enough after our prickly start, and yet, there was something wrong. Putting my feet up, after filling my glass for a contemplative drink, I analysed this.

The origin of my resentment to the poor doctor seemed so petty that I was almost ashamed to admit it, even to myself, but it niggled me! Dixon had given us that large platter – and a platter is bigger than a plate – of canapés. There had been caviar on little rounds of biscuit, shrimps and anchovy and hard-boiled egg similarly mounted, as well as various sorts of unidentified 'spreads'. Masudi had wolfed all the goodies, and left the less-appetizing spreads for me to pick up!

But there was something else, far more ominous. I was myself on edge after all that had passed. Doctor Masudi had doubtless detected my disbelief in his story. He could have found out that Bronski was due to travel on the *Orme Head*; I was sceptical that someone at the embassy had arranged his passage. Why had he really come on this trip?

He was out to beat me, and the prize had to be Bronski.

CHAPTER NINETEEN

It was the morning of the fourth day. In the mid-Atlantic whales were reported and there was a rush to the rails. Yes, you could just spot them, there, there and there. "There she blows!" came the cry, and those with binoculars turned in delight to their companions, to assure them that it was so. Water-spouts rose from the Leviathans. I felt rather alone, not able to share these wonders or to hurry back into the bar to discuss them. But it was time to call on the patient. I could not quarrel with the doctor's wish that he should be left alone for the most part, and that I should only call at hours agreed with him.

The sick bay was low in the ship, but well forward. No throb from the engine-room or the propellers was felt there. Ships are full of noises: creaking built-in wardrobes in cabins, the roar of ventilators, the whip of lashings where the wind slashed at them, wind in the rigging that even a modern ship carries – or did then. Here, though, the quiet was complete. The ward orderly, a strapping young man with the splendid name of William Williams, led me to a small stateroom leading off from the sick bay and introduced me. "Mr Mann," he announced, "visitor for you."

What an ass of an escort I was! It had been left to the sick bay staff to devise a cover name for our Patient. Mr Mann! Very good. Clever chaps! What else had I not done that I should have done? I had passed the last three days in a daze. Surely there was no trouble to be expected until we were in home waters. At Liverpool I supposed there would be somebody waiting to take over. The captain had agreed that there would be some radio message to tell us what to do. I had not thought further into ways or means, or what, for that matter, I was expected to do with myself when I had handed over my charge. I would think through all these things presently. There was plenty of time.

"Mr Mann. Glad to see you sitting up. Are they treating you well?"

Bronski was indeed sitting up, dressed in trousers and sweater over an open-necked shirt. He looked much better than when we brought him aboard. He did not respond to these courtesies. He said urgently, "Shut the door. Now, listen please. You know I have had this stroke. I know about these things – enough to know that the next could carry me off. This does not worry me! It would be worse to be paralysed, unable to talk or write. That is terrifying. I have much work yet to do."

He pulled me down to sit on the bunk with him. In hardly more than a harsh whisper, he added, "There is something else. Let me tell you – let me warn you – these Russian devils are not finished with me yet. You see, I have never given them what they wanted, what they know I have to give. Credit them with that. Your dear countrymen at Cambridge never really got the measure of my work. Do I boast? Yes, maybe I boast. But it is true. Now, they got at me at Los Alamos. I put them off with really harmless, but, I hope, stimulating papers written for my old associate Mikov at Leningrad. They were not satisfied, of course. That is why they were about to kidnap me. It is nothing on paper, young man. It is my mind"– he tapped his forehead – "it is this that they want."

If this sounded like intellectual arrogance, there was reassurance in what he said, for I believed he told the truth. That he had communicated with these people at all meant that they had a hold on him obviously enough; but was that all?

"No, indeed no, they have my family – my wife, my two sons. I have to confess that I had given up hope of ever seeing them or even that they were alive. When I escaped from Hungary – when we tried to leave Hungary we went through Germany. We were caught in a Jewish 'putsch' in Munich. The Nazis, you know. You understand we are a Jewish family. We stayed in Munich with friends. The house was raided. I escaped only because I had gone out to buy some cigarettes – and some wine, yes – for our hosts. I came back just in time to see the dear Katzes bundled into a van – my loved ones were already inside it. I never saw them again. I got to England, as you know. As I had been at Cambridge earlier with Rutherford, my friends there had already arranged for me to work there again. I was so grateful, grateful . . ."

"And the family?"

"These agents at Los Alamos told me that my family had been taken from a Nazi concentration camp when it was overrun by the Russian Army, that they were now in Siberia, and that I might join them – if, if that is, I would work for them. I suppose it is true. I don't know, I just don't know. I had not made up my mind to follow up this, ah, invitation. I temporised. I passed them the material, to keep the option open. It was – it is agony. If what they say is true, do my dear ones know that I am alive, or might come? Probably not, I reason. I hope not. Yes, truly, I hope not. It is nearly ten years since we are parted. Imagine what they have been through! I think and think! I can see only a black pit. That they had survived the Nazi camps would be a miracle; to have survived in some labour camp in Siberia could be a miracle. But what sort of humanity is left in them? I picture them as living dead . . ."

"Come," I said, "you cannot possibly judge. The stories we have all heard of the power of the human spirit to survive these ideological terrors. It's you who are frightened, frightened of facing them perhaps?"

"If you are right, if they live, if they are waiting, waiting to see me, this would be the cruellest of all: they will never see me. I shall be dead."

I tried to jolt him out of this pessimism, though why, I cannot think, as I had no intention of assisting his passage to Siberia or anywhere else beyond the Liverpool landing-stage. A thought he left in my mind, though, is one I have always kept before me since then. In our confused defence of democracy, we had been further confused by the Nazis' proclamation of the supremacy of the 'Volk', which lay at the root of the power of National Socialism. It was the same, my professor insisted, with the Communists, forever proclaiming the rights of 'The People'. 'The People' and the 'Volk' were abstracts, he insisted, in whose name the controlling clique could persecute and kill the individual who stood in the way. True democrats must not lose sight of the individual and his rights against the power of the State.

Marks, the Sick Bay Attendant who was in charge of the facility, stuck his head around the door. "Sorry to break this up, gentlemen, it's time for Mr Mann to have his medications and his nap."

As I said goodbye to Bronski, he begged me to come the next day. My parting question was whether anyone else knew his story.

"One other only," he said, "your colleague – I think he is Mr Sylvan Ross."

I came again the following morning. He said at once, "This man, Williams, the orderly, is my friend. He will deliver some papers to you. You must guard them with your life."

"I thought you said there is nothing you wanted to give away, as you said, on paper."

"If I were to give in and join them, I needed to keep my research work. I planned to send it all to my colleague Mikov anyway, that night when your friends 'lifted' me; then I would recover it later. Now I give my work to Cambridge, yes. I must do this. You must, if I cannot, give them with my compliments to Lord Zender. Not now – I will get them to you. Williams will bring them."

I was not disposed to get involved, whether low melodrama or high tragedy was at hand.

"Tell me, just what is all this about? More particle physics?"

"There is a paper there, yes. But that is not it."

The slightly mad, arrogant tone he had fallen into the day before re-asserted itself. "Much more. What do you know of thermonuclear energy? We go on! I have here"– and again he tapped his forehead – "the secret of the power of the sun and the power to explode the oceans. Yes, there is some of my work on this that will come to you."

"Is that all?" I said, half mockingly.

"No!" He turned sharply and close to me hissed, "I have contributed much at Los Alamos, but I have learned too. You will find little sachets; they are micro film about current bomb construction, which I think your masters do not know about. And I think they should."

The water was getting deeper than I had bargained for. I saw sense in taking charge though, in case anything should happen to Mr Mann. But he had one word more.

"Don't leave anything in your cabin. Has the captain a safe, or the purser? Get it locked there as soon as you can. It will come to you later today. They will search your cabin, ransack it . . ."

"They? Here on board?"

"Go now. Do as I say!" He almost pushed me through the door as Doctor Masudi came in with Williams the orderly.

"Ah, Tom! Our Patient is looking better, isn't he? Two more days of sea air . . . and you've had another chat? Good. Now I'm just going to have a look over our Mr Mann."

With some pleasantry in response, I was glad to slip away to take stock of Bronski's latest remarks. Had he gone round the bend, or was there danger to hand? I realised that I was frightened.

CHAPTER TWENTY

Late that afternoon, just when it would have been pleasant to join the company in the bar, there was a knock on my door. It was partially opened and a white-sleeved arm pushed a laundry bag through, then the door quickly shut. It was the sort of bag to be found outside most cabins most mornings after the stewards had done their round of bed making, changing sheets and towels. I picked it up. There were sheets and towels in this one, but among them several notebooks. A quick inspection showed they were filled with the neatest manuscript – and a string of little bags: the micro film.

I had not been idle. I had made my disposition. Earlier that day I had spoken to Captain Evans. I had told him that I had taken certain top-secret documents from Bronski, and that if anything should prevent me or Bronski delivering them in person they were to be taken by hand to the Foreign Office and given to the Permanent Secretary. Where might they be best stowed? I would like him to take them as soon as I brought them in.

"Whatever the customer wants is right. That is the principle on which this line operates. So yes, of course. Why not take them to the purser? He has a splendid safe."

"I'd be grateful if you will take them as soon as they reach me. I'm afraid – they won't be safe with me. It will be assumed I have them . . ."

"Gracious man! I will do as you say, but what can happen here, on this ship? In mid-ocean? Unless you fall overboard perhaps? You look sure-footed enough. You suspect that someone on board is after Bronski, don't you? I find it hard to believe."

"I don't know, Captain, Maybe something of Bronski's paranoia has rubbed off on to me. He thinks there is trouble. And as for me, well, it's not my job to take unnecessary risks."

It was pure chance the captain was in his cabin when the package came. He was shaving, making ready for his evening's social duties. I was still beset by fear. I had heard, I thought, the voice of my Athene, from a great distance, saying, 'Go on, go on!' I hardly apologised for the interruption. Evans, by training, perhaps by instinct, sensed emergency. Pausing only to wipe his face, he checked the contents of the bag with me.

"I'll put this lot in my own little safe for the moment."

He did so, and pushed the discarded bag into his closet. This done, he said, "Thinking over all this, there is only one real suspect. Right?"

I nodded.

"Most unlikely, but you may know more than you care to tell me. No names, no pack drill at this stage at any rate."

I promised that if I found any good reason to do so, I would come to him. I was relieved and a little less anxious when the next day passed without incident. I visited Bronski'd at one of the calling times agreed with the doctor; he seemed quite relaxed when he knew his papers were secure.

We were still two days away from England and from safety when the captain called me into his cabin and said, "I want to get the measure of your Masudi; you've got me worried. I'd like you to come to a little supper I'm having in here tonight. Just us and the doctor and his good lady. Wholly informal."

So Captain Evans, if he did not altogether share my suspicions, was ready to explore them. This was all I wanted and quite as much as I dared ask of him at this stage. There was nothing concrete to connect my inner fear or Bronski's with the doctor. There was more reason to suppose that our scientist was near to madness, was anyway obsessed with his own deductive powers of reason, and that his unsought confrontation with the world of violence and struggle – the bare mind of science exposed to the cold blasts of politics – had shrivelled him in a shell of resentment and suspicion. Yet even he had not named the object of his immediate fears.

Cap under arm, the captain came through from his to my adjoining cabin. He had some afterthought he wished to pass on.

"I was just thinking –" he began, when there was a knock on my outer door. Evans opened the door. It was the doctor.

"I am so sorry. Had no idea <u>you</u> would be here!" He made to withdraw. The captain stepped out with him.

"Ah, Doctor, you wanted our Thomas? Well, he will be joining us for supper later. Let's go aloft."

I just had time to notice that instead of his usual formal suit and tie outfit, the doctor had on a dark leather jacket and was wearing plimsolls. Just the gear for a game of shuffle-board on the upper deck, perhaps, although I hadn't yet seen him engage in any of the ship's activities.

Dicky the steward was offering his generous tray of canapés to the captain and the other guests when I came through from my quarters at the appointed time. I took a glass of Scotch, the same as Captain Evans was drinking. Doctor Masudi had a large glass of orange juice, while his wife was sipping a goblet of white wine.

I was introduced to Mrs Masudi, who I had not yet met. She was a striking woman, though rather large and going to fat. Her face had a dusky quality. When we had sat down she told me she came from the Lebanon and that she was a Maronite; she had much to say of the hardships of her people, not so much at the hands of the French or the Americans, all of whom she loved and owed much to, but from the warring sects of Moslems who united only to persecute the Christians.

All this was news to me and therefore interesting, but I was distracted by my impatience to hear the conversation on the other side of the table. Evans had used up his standard issue of small talk about the size, speed and seaworthiness of the ship, of storms experienced and records broken across the Atlantic. He was now engaged in drawing the doctor out, making him do the talking. Somehow they had got round to world affairs, and Doctor Masudi, who had changed out of his casual clothes and was dressed in the current American fashion of a rather overlarge loose-fitting suit with narrow lapels, looked and sounded like an American senator with a demagogic bent.

"Roosevelt betrayed us all at Yalta," he declared. "He played footsie with Stalin. He let the Russians run over half Europe. The communists have us by the throat. My belief is that the freedom all those young men died for was sold to the Reds before the war was over."

The captain raised his eyebrows in a way he had and said, "Hurrumph." Normally he would not have allowed himself to get involved in politics while he was on duty, and perhaps he had none, but now he gently provoked his guest to continue: "They fought bravely, though; enormous losses."

"Maybe. So did the armies of the Tzar. Cannon fodder, ignorant masses driven forward by the revolvers of their officers."

"So, what about the United Nations, the Atlantic Charter?"

"Pah! Wishy-washy sentimentalism!"

"But this time we have the Americans – in it up to the neck. Not like Versailles and the old League of Nations."

"The Americans! The Americans are decadent. Yes, decadent. They care only about money, and all the new toys that money brings them."

"Hurrumph!" again from the captain.

"And Great Britain. Great? No more. Now a socialist satellite! Churchill and his like are finished! We need leadership, Captain. Leadership with a will to power, stronger than the money bags of Wall Street. Strong enough to smash the Reds!"

The meal was near its end when this outburst developed. I'd noticed how the doctor had again wolfed the choicest of the canapés beforehand, and my mother would have tut-tutted at his table manners. And he drummed his fingers on the table as he talked, in the most irritating fashion. Altogether, I liked him even less than before. But at least he was not a Russophile. Could all be an act, of course, to cover both his ideal and the reality of his present mission.

Then Captain Evans was called to the bridge. Thick fog, he told us, adding that we were off the south-western coast of Ireland, that we would be proceeding round the southern approaches, through the St. George's Channel, as numbers of mines, broken from their moorings were reported in the north-western approaches. Though the channels were still being swept, shipping had been advised to take the southerly route. "Only one more night, though, if this fog doesn't stop us." He invited us to stay to take coffee and chat till he returned.

Coffee and a silver dish of small confections were offered. When Mrs Masudi had partaken her fill of these and the captain had still not returned, she excused herself. The doctor and I were now alone. He seemed keen to resume his monologue.

"I expect you have heard of Friedrich Nietsche," he said, "he is the western fount of our thinking. He saw that to release the future, the present with all its sickness must be destroyed. This is just what we are going to do." His tone, his very bearing underwent a change as he spoke.

"*Nihil obstat*," I joked weakly. But he went on in a new, low but impatient voice, "And you, young man, you are in the way!"

It wasn't his words but the fact that he had drawn an automatic pistol from inside his coat that made me leap to my feet! "Yes, up you get! We have little time. Into your room please, with your hands up."

He followed me in and shut the door. "Now, the papers of Bronski."

"They're in the captain's safe."

"Well, you were quick. When you have disappeared I might have a word with him about all that." He shrugged. "But it is no great matter. It is the man we want. He will make our bomb."

"Your bomb!"

"Yes. You may as well know. First, Bronski will be taken very ill as he is readied to leave the ship. There will happen to be a private ambulance at the pier, which I shall commandeer for my patient. The official reception party will be told to wait, or perhaps go to the hospital. Not Bronski, though. He will soon be on his way by air to our citadel. I shall be with him!"

"Good of you to tell me," I managed to say. To play for time by keeping him talking seemed the only thing to do. "And where is the citadel, and what then?"

"It is in Africa, our citadel. The great Rommel built it. It was to be a key point in holding up Montgomery in the desert war. Now what you call the Middle East – Islam – is waiting for new leadership. This we will provide. All will rally to our mission, our plan to destroy this – this decadent civilization of yours."

"You'll need quite a few bombs to do that."

"We think not. Two at the most. But laid at the heart of, shall I say, on the high altars of this debased cult of modernity, of this filth – Paris or Rome, perhaps, and New York – terror will do the rest. Come, get out. Time to go!"

It was not Bronski who was the madman on this ship, but Masudi. The doctor had not let his gun waver. "Walk straight down the passageway to our right, down the first steps, through the door and the next door. I will kill you if you deviate or do anything funny."

There was still a moment of time then. He would not want a body on his hands in the passageway. He wanted me on deck.

I was cool-headed enough to think, too, that it was my business not to get killed. I now had a lot to do, so no heroics.

The ship heaved gently, enough to make me stumble. I felt the gun in my back in a trice. The second doors marked "Crew Only" were heavy, double ones. I prised them open. We were suddenly out of the warmth of the ship's interior onto an iron deck. A single storm lamp in the deck-head showed we were in the working part of the ship where the winches and hoists for the rear cargo hold were handled.

The doctor pushed me on out into the open air. The fog swirled round. We were at the ship's side, and I stumbled against one of the great bollards that took the mooring lines. We must have been just about over the propeller on the port side, and through the openings of the hawsepipes the foam and spume of the wash seemed near and full of sound. So did the air. Two great ventilators roared nearby, and the ship emitted a mighty blast on her foghorn. The noise filled my head. There was no room for thinking, only that the time I had bought was spent. I could say nothing. No word would form on my lips. I could not get my breath, could not raise my arm to strike back, however uselessly.

CHAPTER TWENTY-ONE

"You are a poor, pathetic fish," sneered the doctor, almost having to shout above the cacophony. He pressed close against me – I could feel the gun sticking into my ribs. "I knew you would not stand in my way for long. I don't even need to shoot you. Here, you just fall overboard! Up now, up on that mushroom thing. Come! Up, up!"

He half lifted my sagging body onto the bollard, and like a circus dog I obeyed. But I moved sluggishly. I had felt the slow roll of the ship. My last chance. The side we were on, the port side, was heaving out of the trough of the roll; and was it Athene or the Good Captain who had ordered a slight shift in the course, which accentuated the upward movement?

I sprang fully upright onto the bollard with a foot on the ship's rail. Had the list been the other way I would have been carried over the side! A half turn and I could hurl myself feet first at the madman, taking my chance of surviving the inevitable shot.

I firmed my footing; the ship's movement held and helped me. I turned to spring. In that instant it was the doctor whose body came crashing at my feet on the bollard. I could not check my own spring, but it was into the arms of another shadowy figure. We slithered on to the deck together. It was Bronski.

We pulled each other up, and he pointed wordlessly at his victim. A fireman's axe was stuck fast between Masudi's shoulder-blades. I could not find my voice. Nor seemingly could Bronski. We gawped at each other. Then Williams was at our side:

"Cor, professor! You give me a fright when you go walkies like that. What you two gents up to? Some mischief, I'll be bound!"

Bronski pointed again, pointed at the body. The startled Williams took a look, produced a torch and became the professional he was.

"Dead orl rite," he pronounced. He waggled at the haft of the axe, then had to give a hard tug to remove it. He sniffed, unnecessarily, at the blade. "Have to give that a good clean up and put it back where it came from."

"What do we do?" I said dully.

Williams straightened himself up, eyed us both in turn.

"Over the side, if you agree, gents. That's the simplest. Then I'll hose down this lot."

I was ready to be sick, as, in the torchlight, we saw what had to be hosed down. Williams was in charge. He located a hydrant and ran out a length of hose. The gun lay in the scuppers where it had fallen from Masudi's hand. He whipped out a handkerchief protruding from the dead man's pocket, picked up the weapon and wrapped it carefully. "Here, you take this, sir, and you'd best get Mr Mann back to the sick bay. First, give me a hand with this here."

I took the legs, Williams the shoulders. With difficulty we got the heavy body on to the rail, and it was gone. Williams took one look at his white jacket, now fouled with blood, stripped it off and threw it overboard too.

I was emerging from my own paralysis. "Thanks, pal."

"Never mind that; just get <u>him</u> away. He looks bad. I'd better get back to the flipping captain."

Bronski was leaning against a bulkhead, his arms dangling, his breath rasping through his open mouth. No words came as I led him away, supporting him with an arm. It was late into the night and fortunately we met no one before, after several wrong turnings up blind alleys or locked doors, we reached the sick bay.

I got him into his cubbyhole and on to his bunk. He was shivering. I covered him with blankets. Then he tried to raise himself. An arm came out from the covers. His fingers felt for and locked on my shoulder. He was trying to speak. I looked round for some water, but there was nothing within reach. The stricken man's hand held me firmly, half on my knees beside the bed.

"It's OK," I said. "You are safe. Safe now. Thank you . . . thank you, old chap. You saved my life, I reckon."

Still no words, But the grip tightened on my shoulder. Then the sagging face tightened. The skin drew back, baring the teeth into the semblance of a grinning mask. Something like a chuckle came, that made him choke. The grip let go. I felt all tension drain from Bronski's body as it slumped back on the bed

Gingerly I put my fingers to the inside of his wrist; there was no pulse, nor any movement of his chest. Bronski was dead.

For some moments I did not stir from where I was kneeling. I was shaking all over, the outward sign of the turbulence inside me. I took a deep breath, then another, and another. Gradually my body relaxed. I rose and found some water; then joy – a bottle of brandy, kept obviously for medicinal purposes.

I still had no inclination to leave. Someone might be along shortly. I must sort out in my mind a coherent picture of what had been happening these last hours. Hours? I looked at my watch. It was less than an hour since the captain had left his table. It was too much to take in. I let it go. I felt the gun in my pocket, and put it on a side table. It might be important to prove that it had been the doctor who had had the gun. Clever Williams.

I went back to Bronski's bunk. His face had relaxed; it looked younger, smoother, and at peace. I remembered that the thing to do was to close the eyes, then cover the head. I did these things, but I did not like the effect of the blanket I had drawn up over the head, so I drew it back again. The now-peaceful face was better company than the shrouded corpse. I just straightened the body a bit and arranged the arms and hands decently.

I settled down at the desk in the sick bay, the brandy beside me. I would wait here, while I sorted things out. A warming glow suffused me. The uppermost thought was that I was alive.

'Hooray for that'. There was the voice of my spirit goddess, Marcie. 'Nasty business, wasn't it? But the best possible ending.' I had to think about that. Best possible? My charge was to deliver Bronski safe and sound to our masters in London. I started to my feet. I had missed the central point. I had failed, failed in my mission! Not the Russians, not the Americans, nor the mad doctor and his, so far, apocryphal associates, but I, his guardian, had brought him to his death! I beat my fists on my head and wailed aloud. What had I done? What had I left undone?

It was now Marcie's hand that seemingly fell on my shaking shoulder and led me back to my seat. 'Calm down,' she was telling me. 'Think. What could our people do with Bronski? We have no desert in which to hide him, and frankly, you can reckon his best work has been done. He was a great scientist, very great, but he was burned out. Wasn't that your impression?'

"Yes, I suppose so."

'And I think you will find that the great men of the Cambridge and London scientific establishment will agree.'

The thought lifted some of my gloom. Perhaps the FO people would not be too sorry, whatever the dirty tricks lot thought about it all. They might even be pleased, since they had been left out of the plot from the beginning.

I caught sight of myself in a mirror. A bruise was beginning to spread round my left eye and at that side of my nose. My jacket was filthy. There was blood there, but nothing like as much as had been on Williams; the dark cloth didn't show it up. The bruise, that must have been from Bronski's knee. I remembered now. As I plunged, right over the doctor's head, I had landed on Bronski behind him. His knee, or something had come up as I bore him down. God! What had that fall done to him? I had straddled him on the iron deck and his head must have hit it. Had it been me who killed him? I slumped under the weight of this new load of guilt, nursing my head in my hands.

I did not notice when the doors swung open until the captain said, "Thank God, here's one of them, anyway. Tom, Tom! Wake up! What has happened?"

There was the captain, the purser, and the sick bay attendant, Marks. I said the first thing that came into my head. "That's Masudi's gun on the table – he tried to kill me! Can we check it for fingerprints?"

"How would we know if any prints were the doctor's?" asked the purser.

I made a mental picture of the scene at the table. "He had a glass of orange juice at dinner, the only one. The rest of us drank wine."

Evans was quick on the uptake. "And he drummed on the table all the time he was talking. I'll see that nothing is touched. Now, Tom, what's this all about?"

At that moment Williams came in, spruce and clean as a whistle. I was glad to have his support as I sketched the main points of the story.

"Then you chucked him over the side? That was rather stupid, wasn't it?"

Williams pitched in. "We was only thinking of you, sir. Very awkward to explain to the judge why your passenger ended up with an axe in his back – and it was a mess, too, sir."

Evans raised his eyebrows.

"Hurrumph. Now what about Mr Mann?"

I pointed dumbly to the open door into the little cabin. Marks stepped quickly in. The others crowded round to look over his shoulder.

A brief examination followed. "Heart failure, almost certainly," said Marks. "Not surprising, given his history – and his exploits tonight! I'll take a closer look later. What about you, young man?"

Time to cool off and a bath was all I needed and it was so prescribed. Late as it was when I had cleaned up, Evans demanded a more detailed account. I did not know how he was taking it. He remained impassive; so I was relieved when, at the end and after keen questions, he said, "It was all for the best." He would deal somehow with Mrs Masudi.

Then he added, "I think I should bury Bronski at sea. We are still well outside territorial waters. I'm thinking about these various reception committees. It will save a lot of pother. And, of course, he is not on my manifest – manifestly not!" He smiled slightly at his own joke.

"You could, I suppose, tell the lady that her husband has had a fatal heart attack, and would she mind if we put him overboard." I was aghast at my own callousness.

"Excellent idea, boy! Seriously, yes. Let us see. You say she left my table early? I had the impression that they were not a very devoted couple, did you?"

"Yes, she seemed rather resigned to following where he went. She said she hated leaving Washington, that he had not confided to her their future plans. She seemed bored by the whole thing."

"Right, I will break it to her that her husband went on deck and appears to have had a massive coronary . . ."

"And fell down a companionway."

"Yes! Marks, in charge of the sick bay, will be with me. He will confirm that it's best she does not view the remains."

I put it down to hysteria and exhaustion that I laughed uncontrollably.

But so it all turned out. Mrs Masudi, shocked but under control, gave permission for a sea burial, declaring also that she had no wish to see the body. Marks confirmed that Bronski died of cardiac arrest and that there was no mark on his body that would suggest damage from the fall with me on top.

Toward noon the next day the engines were slowed in an oily calm; we were now away from the Atlantic swell, somewhere near the Fastnet, with the southern Irish coast on the horizon. The ceremony was ostensibly for Dr Masudi, although unbeknown to all but a handful of the watchers, it was Sergei Bronski who was buried at sea. Captain Evans was at his Welsh best as he intoned the tingling words of the service: "We therefore commit this body to the deep . . ." and concluded, in ringing tones, from Psalm 130, *De Profundis*:

"Out of the depths have I cried unto Thee, O Lord,

Lord, hear my voice; Let Thine ears be attentive to the voice of my supplications,

If thou, O Lord, shouldest mark iniquities,

O Lord, Who shall stand?

But there is forgiveness with thee . . ."

Not only for Bronski, but for all of us – for me, for Sylvan, for Marcie, for the troubled world –did I join the sturdy chorus of "Amen" that came from those of the ship's company required to be present.

CHAPTER TWENTY-TWO

The *Orme Head* did not come to the floating landing stage with its pavilions where, in another age, the bands had played to greet or to send off the legendary Cunarders and White Star liners: the four-funnelled *Mauretania*, *Aquitania*, *Majestic*. And before them, *Lusitania* and *Titanic*, and their smaller sisters *Franconia*, *Carinthia* and *Samaria*. It was now about twenty years since I had stood on the same landing stage with my Dad to watch the *Samaria* move out. As a boy I read all there was to read about these magnificent ships. I made clumsy models of them. I loved them, and still their names are printed in my mind. The sight of any of the surviving vessels is heart-stopping.

In the past year, when the Naval Attaché had sent me to New York on various errands, I always made time to go down to the Hudson River piers to see the great liners, now in their uniform of battleship-grey paint. I had never actually been on one, though on convoy duty earlier in the war I used to watch for hours as some of the smaller sisters ploughed alongside tankers loaded with petrol and smaller cargo steamers zigzagging their way home. The "Greyhounds", the *Queen Elizabeth* and *Queen Mary*, survived without recourse to convoy escort, relying on their speed. I travelled in them both later on. They, too, are gone now, but their memory is indelible.

We woke to a grey, still morning to find the *Orme Head* anchored in the river. Passengers were already crowding the staircases and the flat where the iron doors in the ship's side would open and they would be embarked on pinnaces to take them ashore. As I was not on the passenger list I was to stay on board until Captain Evans went ashore to report to his agents. A signal was also expected telling him what to do with me.

What indeed? What next? The ship was silent. In the passengers' quarters, stewards collected and sorted laundry. The pleasant Verandah Bar smelt of last night's parties: the stale, morning-after smell of beer, spirits and loaded ash-trays did not stop me from slumping down into one of its leather-style club armchairs. For the whole of the crossing, the past eight days or so, there had been no conscious effort to think what this escapade had been all about. I had made no decision of my own. I had simply acted out the part assigned to me. Of the many still moments in a leisurely sea voyage, there had been none when I had dared to let my mind pan over the fantastic web of events in which I was caught up.

There had been many hours of just watching the sea, the gulls playing over the ship's wake; moments on the bridge with Captain Evans, who passed me his binoculars to see schools of distant whales spouting. I remembered the comfort of a sea water bath, with massive gouts of water gushing from the outsize taps into the rust-stained tub, the kindly and knowing stewards, the conscious enjoyment of good food. I had, I concluded, shut out, refused to listen to the beatings on the doors of my mind. Had I been pumped up by excitement, or had I just existed in a state of shock, in a trauma as they now say of people brought to hospital after motor accidents and things like that?

Now, now indeed it was the morning after. The fact that I was taking stock seemed an indication that this phase was passed. Now I felt chilled. Thinking first about myself was natural enough, I suppose – and my first thought was how to get back to Washington. I supposed I was still on the books at the embassy and would be sent back – indeed, I hoped for this. Checking to ask myself why, the answer came that, after all that had passed, I shrank from facing the norms of English suburban life, from sharing my times with family and friends, from the questions: "So what's with you lately?" "Did you have a good trip?" "How's Washington?" What with time at sea, then Washington, I had not seen my family for five years, except for that rather hurried weekend as the curtains fell on the war.

They had had a rough time, with bombs and shortages. They had lived without a window in the house for three years – and they had never told me! "You've had a cushy billet," they would be thinking, and I would feel guilty because it was so. As for explaining the last few months – it would be impossible, the more so as the whole affair was subject both to secrecy and no doubt to a very sticky enquiry in the (to me) still unknown corridors of Whitehall. I was a stranger in my own land. A quick return ticket, please!

My first need was to sort it all out with the survivors of our adventures in that once arcane but now familiar world around Massachussetts Avenue. Before any enquiry I wanted most to go over it all with Sir John. Some of the embassy staff thought of him as a bit stuffy and old-fashioned, but he had been in this thing up to the hilt; he had trusted me. I could confide in him as a fellow conspirator. The Naval Attaché, the RAF man with whom I shared a tiny house in Georgetown, others who knew, to whom I could unburden myself. And, of course there was Sylvan.

I now longed to talk to all these people, to tell them what had happened on the voyage. I was at once reliving these past few days. It was this most recent series of shocks that I found myself trying to describe to myself. I had been a participant; I was also a witness. I would need to fix the details, the times, what had been said. Soon I must write it all up. I would be cross-questioned. Must write it as it really was, for already I caught myself embroidering – picturing how these events might have taken different turns. How I might have been the one to go overboard, and how Doctor Masudi would have explained this to Captain Evans. How would Evans have decided to act? As I had not been on the passenger list, it might have been more convenient to hush it all up.

Then my mind focussed clearly on the dead man in the scuppers, the gun handed to me by Williams. I saw the axe, the blood on the iron deck, Bronski dying and Bronski dead. These details were fixed like flies in amber. I could detach myself from them, yet it seemed that there was still some block in my mind that prevented for the moment any recall of my own part in them or of my own emotions. There had been tension, fear, revulsion, I knew, but for now I could not re-assemble them. I puzzled over this; I warned myself to expect a reaction later. So, detached, my mind travelled back to the penultimate act of this bloodshot play – to Marcie.

"Marcie!" I cried aloud to the empty room.

It was then that the chill and stony dyke inside me burst open. Choking tears welled up as my body struggled to expel all the internal pent-up forces. Once I would have disparaged such an overt show of emotion as unmanly, but now I just let the feelings wash over me. I sat there, slumped forward with my head in my hands, till a clatter of movement stirred me. A vacuum cleaner began to hum, stewards were collecting the empty glasses.

"Sorry to disturb you, sir, we got to clear this lot away, but here, take this," and someone thrust a discarded glass of brandy at me. "Looks like you need something."

I drained it and rose. I calmed down. It may have been the drink, but Athene had also spoken. I had heard her at the moment we were interrupted. 'There's still Sylvan,' she had said. 'There's not much you can do for him, dear Tom, but do what you can.'

I went out to the after rail. With the tide on the flood, the stern faced up river; the tired and battered lower quarters of the city were still shrouded in mist. Higher, the sun was breaking through. The nobler towers and spires of Liverpool glinted; the faded gilt on the great Liver birds turned to gold. 'Flames in the forehead of the morning sky' was the line that came back to me from schoolroom struggles as to what Milton was on about, which left me cold. Now the beauty of the words sunk in.

'For Lycidas your sorrow is not dead . . .'

Nor then was my Athene. I caught again at the sound of her voice. I would obey her command, whatever it meant, whatever it took. Drifting into an excess of mawkish sentimentality I gripped the rail, made a final sententious stab at recollecting the blind poet – 'Tomorrow to fresh woods and pastures new' – twitching my mantle about me and shutting out the unsorted farrago of events, violence and voices from the so recent past.

A tap on my shoulder. It was Dicky, the captain's steward.

"Ah, found you, sir! Sorry to interrupt your reverie, but Captain's compliments, and will you join him as soon as possible please. This way, sir!"

Evans greeted me with a smile. "Hello, Tom, I've received your marching orders. I'm going ashore in one hour's time. You'd better be ready to come along too. You are to report to the Naval Officer-in-Charge. He will kit you out, advance you some cash, and give you a rail warrant for, er, let me see, the 5:35 to Euston. A room is booked for you at the St. Kilda Hotel. You are to present yourself for some sort of debriefing meeting at the Cabinet offices at eleven hundred hours tomorrow."

"Where's that?"

"I don't know. Just ask a copper. I know the St. Kilda is just round the corner from Whitehall."

"Am I to take Bronski's papers?"

"Yes, I've had them done up in a security bag. Heavy it is – made to sink if we have to chuck the ship's papers overboard. So if you are chased by the Reds or mad mullahs round St. James Park, just chuck them in the lake. They are bound to sink!"

Evans stood up as I did. He grasped my hand.

"Good luck, boy. You've been through a lot. Don't let those fancy pants get on top of you! One other thing. I've done my own preliminary report. You can take a copy with you. See you at the gangway in – yes – forty-five minutes."

I reckoned that the train journey would be the chance to prepare myself for tomorrow's meeting in Whitehall. I rehearsed this and that approach, but nothing seemed to serve. I practised my opening remarks: 'Gentlemen,' I would begin, but there might be ladies, even lords. My thoughts trailed off. I still could not concentrate. A drink or two did not help. I ordered dinner, glad of the distraction. Swaying along to the dining car, I wondered about the loco at the head of the train; certainly we were rollicking along, and I enthused over the great steam locomotives hardly less than over the great liners. Anything at this stage to keep my mind off the business in hand.

The dinner helped the distraction, it was so awful. After some tinned grapefruit, there was what I assumed was beef, close-grained and grey, with greens and potatoes floating in a thin gravy. It reminded me that Britain was still under rationing; that these people I was going to meet and the folks at home were probably more concerned with their domestic problems than with any yarn I was going to tell them. It was for me to be forbearing and gentle. There was no need for me to try to put on a show.

The coffee was as bad as the rest of the meal. I set it aside, then opened and read Captain Evans' report. There was nothing I would wish to add, for it gave an account of my part in all this that would free me of any need for heroics or for undue modesty. It was the answer to my problem! I would invite the Whitehall people to read it and then be ready to answer questions. Hugely relieved, I ordered a double Scotch and snoozed the rest of the way to London.

CHAPTER TWENTY-THREE

I had decided to get Evans' report into the hands of this committee before I met them. The next morning, after a surprisingly good breakfast of bacon and eggs, toast, marmalade and a pot of tea, I called the number on the letterhead of the instruction note that had been given me. Consultations followed on the other end of the line, then, "Yes, good idea. A messenger will be with you in about twenty minutes."

As well as the report I was glad to hand over the cumbersome canvas bag. The messenger, a bull-dog of a man (ex-marines, he told me) looked as though he knew how to take care of himself, and it. He also showed me how to get to the Cabinet offices. I had thought I would probably be directed to the door of No. 10 Downing Street. It was just the opposite – the back door in fact.

I ordered some more tea and lit a cigarette. Sitting back in a deep armchair in the Edwardian foyer of the hotel, I tried once again to prepare myself for the meeting at eleven o'clock. Nothing sensible came to mind, yet I was not worried as I had been earlier, rather I felt quite important. All these grand people coming to meet me. Evans' report would tell them more than I could have possibly said about my own part. A pat on the back at least. Perhaps they would offer me a job, and a good one, as I had nothing but my temporary engagement pay in Washington, and if I had to stay here there were lots of things I would need; not least a decent car, I thought, as I watched a neat little Alvis two-seater draw into the courtyard outside the foyer window.

Mad! Fool! Snap out of it! I did. There was less than an hour to go. I felt frightened again. Ass, I told myself. Think big! Perhaps a secret service sort of job? Lawrence of Arabia, Hannay's Greenmantle . . .

when they came to realise all that I had been through . . . but exactly what <u>had</u> I been through? I had planned nothing, contributed no ideas, I was but a small cog in the machine. I could no more plan a campaign or devise such a mad scheme as Sylvan had than play cricket for England. I was small beer. Ass! I addressed myself again. Pull yourself together!

It was time to go. I told myself that there was nothing to worry about. I was shaking a bit. Some sort of reaction was setting in. Just calm down. But again I felt frightened, and cold about my midriff.

I found myself in St. Anne's Gate, and hurried down the steps into St. James Park. I was now too early, so I warmed myself with a quick walk to the lakeside, checked that the pelicans were still there, and on to the war memorial opposite Horse Guards Parade. It was chipped all over from bomb blast, as were most of the frontages I had passed. Just across the road from the St. Kilda there had been the evidence of an enormous explosion. The wheel of a bus had imprinted its mark on a shattered wall two stories above the street. A porter at the hotel had told me this, and how not a house, office, church, water main or sewage pipe had been undamaged, how bombs had fallen the length of Whitehall and on Parliament, and how it had been much worse in the East End, in Whitechapel where he came from. It helped to calm me down, to think what these people had been through. I remembered air raids on Portsmouth before I ever went to America. They had turned my stomach to water. These people, porters and cabinet ministers alike, had been through years of it.

Thinking of others did the trick; I straightened my back and took a deep breath. The morning sun now broke through the low clouds, gilding the cupolas of the Horse Guards and the Admiralty building and turning to a golden russet the creepers that had begun to establish themselves on the grim walls of the fortress building at the Mall end of the Parade.

Time to go in.

You pass along the back of the garden wall of No. 10 Downing Street and look for a tunnel-like entrance into and under the adjacent offices. There was a glass-paned door through which a messenger was to be seen, sitting in a booth inside, sucking his pipe and reading a newspaper. Particulars were taken and a phone call made. I was expected. Another messenger was summoned to escort me.

These, then, were the Cabinet offices, with access to No. 10 at an upper floor level and to a myriad of other offices in the Old Treasury Building which fronts on to Whitehall. The whole was a warren of offices and it was at the Downing Street end, not in the great Fortress across the square, that the Prime Minister had his underground war-room.

Any sightseer to London is familiar with this exterior scene but few, unless they work there, have a picture of what goes on behind those tall windows and stone facings, blackened with a century of London soot and fog; now doubly forbidding with sand bags and bricked-in basements. Of all the world citadels of power only the Kremlin, surely, had a greater reputation for secrecy than Whitehall. Ordinary people had no clue, beyond the comings and goings of people in black jackets and striped trousers and carrying brief cases, a picture of Whitehall perpetuated by the cartoonists. I had never entered here. I knew only its voice, from the daily flood of telegrams that came to us in Washington. It was going to be very different from Pennsylvania Avenue, where I had attended meetings in several departments of state and indeed at the White House.

And different it was. As different as taking tea with the House Master and his family after the school cricket match is from waiting outside the Headmaster's study for a wigging. As my warder/messenger led me up stairs and along corridors, I checked myself in these reflections. Was it a wigging I feared? Why the sense of guilt? I was accustomed to a sense of guilt, an unease that had possessed me since getting these instructions to report to this office.

As we approached the door, I longed again to be back in Washington where, in encounters with the Americans, it had been so much easier. And Americans spoke up. This was important to me as I was a bit on the deaf side. The embassy people, most of them anyway, seemed to have taken on this States-side colouration. There a warmth in relationships prevailed, which I had not known hitherto, even in my own family, although our family relationships had been happy and normal by the standards we accepted before the war.

My messenger opened a door and ushered me in to a high-ceilinged conference room whose details I was to explore only as the meeting proceeded. My immediate attention focussed on the dozen or so men seated at a long table whose deliberations were not in the least interrupted by my arrival. I stood with the messenger by the door while some document was read out. My worst fears were realised: I could not hear a word. After a few further exchanges there was some sort of break and with gentle pressure on my elbow my escort pushed me forward.

"Ah, come in. It's Lieutenant Davis, right?" said a voice from the top of the table.

"Sub-Lieutenant Davis, yes, sir."

"Now, sit down. You were very sensible in forwarding the Bronski papers and Captain Evans' report this morning. The papers are already on the way to Professor Lord Zender, who, let me say, is extremely upset about Bronski. It appears that he held the key to the development of this, er, even bigger bomb, this two-stage something-or-other that is supposed to make the Hiroshima thing seem like a mere squib. But that is for the experts. None of us here know much about it. Let's hope the Bronski papers contain this key. You may, on reflection, Lieutenant Davis, think it quite amusing that since you landed yesterday, you were carrying one of the world's most terrible secrets under your arm! Now, Evans' letter, which has been circulated to this committee and which we have already read. Do you wish to add anything? I assume you have read it yourself."

I could think of nothing. I saw only alien faces. At a US meeting there would have been introductions. I did not know a soul round this table. A mumbled "No, sir" seemed to be the safest answer.

From down the table a sharp-faced man addressed me, but did the courtesy of explaining that he represented the Attorney General. "Young man," he said, "you are credited in the captain's report with some splendid heroics. But let me point out that you have a lot to answer for. You were responsible for the safe conduct to this country of this Professor Bronski. You have failed to deliver him. Then there is a respected physician, whose professional services were sought by your own Ambassador in Washington. It appears from the Evans' report that, if you did not actually kill him, you assisted in his disposal – overboard."

I began to stammer out a reply. This was cut short by the Chairman, a tall man with fading reddish hair and clipped moustache; well turned-out, in a double-breasted waistcoat with a thin watch-chain across it. I could take this in because even before he spoke I had noted a twinkle in his lined face and sensed that relief was at hand.

"Lieutenant," he said, "you must have realised that your involvement in the deaths of these two men would be the subject of a searching enquiry – if, that is, there was to be an enquiry. You may be relieved to know, however, that just before you came in, we concluded – that is, we have decided to recommend to the Prime Minister that there should be no enquiry. Unless you have some more horror stories for us. Anything you want to say, Lieutenant?"

I was pressed to check a few points in Evans' account. Particularly I was pressed on who else among the crew had had any part in all that had happened. There was Williams, of course, the other sick-bay orderly, Marks, the purser, the captain's steward Dixon. There must have been others; the burial party – and who had sewn up old Bronski in his canvas bag, to be committed to the deep as Masudi? The pit of fear had opened again, nor was I the only one for whom the alarm bells were ringing. To hush it up and then to have the story break could do more harm than any enquiry. "You can control an enquiry in all sorts of subtle ways," someone said, ". . . but you can't control the press," added someone else, turning to the Attorney General's man.

For a time the debate went this way and that before the chairman said, "Frankly, I don't think the burial party gave a damn as to which of the passengers they buried. Not many were involved. I propose to have MI5 get on to Evans right away to check out and interview any who might know about it." He glanced over at a rather insignificant-looking man sitting in the far corner, who had contributed nothing to the discussion so far. The man nodded, and I guessed that he must be here to represent MI5, the domestic security service. "Perhaps our Lieutenant here had better go along too," the chairman continued. "If anyone has to be squared, let him be squared and cubed too if need be. This matter should not, must not, go further."

"I agree, Walter. Hell, man, we've done it before. Remember that Polish chappie. Spain?"

"Yes, Colonel. Yes, indeed. It was war-time, of course, and that made it a bit easier."

General agreement followed. Secretaries were sent out to rough draft a submission to the ministers involved. Some of the men around the table stood up to stretch their legs, and there was a pause marked by the tapping-out, filling and lighting of pipes.

CHAPTER TWENTY-FOUR

Just as I was wondering if there'd be any chance of getting a cup of tea or coffee, a voice from halfway down the long and narrow table called out, "Tom!"

Concentrating so hard in the last few minutes to catch what the speaker of the moment was saying, I had not seen him. It was Sir John Portent himself.

"Tom, I've flown over for an inquest on this whole affair, going back to the original plan to lift Bronski from Los Alamos. I have confessed to my masters here that the whole plan was hatched in my room at the embassy. It was endorsed, you remember, by Sir Gaspard Jebb here, whom you have not yet met – he runs the Foreign Office – and by Sir Walter here, your chairman and Secretary to the Cabinet. So it is not just you and me who may yet be shot for its, dear me, failure."

Sir Walter intervened.

"Steady on, John! Not a failure at all. A success! Bronski was not lifted by the Russians, nor, in the nick of time, was he exposed by the FBI, or whoever, as yet another British-sponsored traitor. Pity about Bronski, though. What loss his death may be to science, I've no idea. Zender will tell us all about that, and meanwhile he has the papers which Bronski obviously thought important –"

I interjected, "It's all to do with the thermonuclear hydrogen bomb. This much he told me before he died."

"There you are then, gentlemen. Jolly important stuff! Great success!"

Sir Gaspard spoke. "As you now know, the whole thing was masterminded on the spot by our man Sylvan Ross. I needed Walter's endorsement because frankly, it is unusual – very unusual for the Foreign Office to involve itself in . . . er . . . practical work of this sort . . ."

"The dirty work," someone guffawed.

Sir Gaspard ignored the interruption. "There is, as you know, the secret service. What was MI5 or MI6 up to? Were they not in the act?"

Confirming my speculation about his affiliation, the man in the corner cut in: "It was most irregular. The Director was – still is – furious! Not all of you may know that Ross was under our instructions – control, if you like." Several startled faces looked up. "His task is to watch this new CIA set-up and to keep close to certain individuals in the US scientific community. We were not consulted. Why? We would still like to know!"

"If you must know," said Sir Gaspard, "it is to do with our historic relationship with the United States. Your people have built up our intimate relationship with the American security service. I don't know just how close to your lot is that little plant of British spooks holed up in New York – they are said to have a line to the Prime Minister. I wouldn't know about that," throwing a quizzical glance to the Secretary of the Cabinet, "but I gather they work closely with and for American intelligence."

"You mean that they were hardly qualified to take the pants off the CIA and all that lot?"

"Yes, just that."

The M15 chap, as though to retrieve attention, stood up. "To cut the story short, Mr Chairman, we have reason to have some doubts about this Mr Ross from the Foreign Office. We have put in a request that he should be recalled, now, as soon as possible."

Sir John also stood up. He seemed not to respond to the MI5 man, for it was to me he half turned and said, "You will be sorry to hear, Tom, about what happened after you left with Bronski and – er – Lady Marcia was killed in that terrible accident. That night, Sylvan went berserk. He smashed up his office in the Chancery, got thoroughly drunk, smashed things at home. He frightened the daylights out of Bella and the children; she's taken them away with her to stay with her mother for a while. We got him into a private nursing home and he was diagnosed as having a serious mental breakdown. Now he is on his way home, on the *Queen Mary*. Frankly we needed no advice from M15 on this. We will move him as soon as the doctors allow."

The chairman now declared that new ground was being broken, not the business of this meeting. "Our sole purpose today was to establish an agreed position on Bronski which we can ask ministers to endorse. Let me remind you that Bronski's disappearance was all over the press weeks ago. It is supposed that his remains were eaten by eagles or whatnot on the mountain slopes of New Mexico There is nothing to connect us with his – repossession."

The discussion was allowed a further extension.

"Yes," said a man whose name I hadn't caught, "but what about the press? The story is still limping around. Only last week the American papers were speculating again that the Russians had got him."

"But, interestingly," said someone else, "*Pravda* issued another firm statement denying any knowledge of the British professor, while other Soviet sources declare that American capitalist circles had done him in for obscure reasons of their own."

Walter turned to Sir Gaspard. "You remember at Yalta, how Stalin's people were always looking to drive a wedge between the Brits and the Yanks? They are still at it. That's all, friends! No story! No press! A hope rather than an edict, but so far, the press in this 'sceptered isle' are not as sharp as the American press. We will probably get away with it."

The way the meeting had gone, one might have expected some after-chat, a few comments, a word of encouragement, enquiries as to how I was feeling now, that pat on the back – but, no, all these great men had just hurried out. Two only remained; the M15 man was talking to Sir John at the other side of the table.

As I moved to the door I felt again useless and resentful. Good there was to be no enquiry, but this shattering event in my life (this was the first time I had so defined it to myself) was to be forgotten; there was to be no release in retelling the tale; no recognition. Then Sir John called me over.

"Tom, I want you to come and have lunch with me. First though, Symes here wants a word."

We were introduced, my proffered hand being met by a brief nod. Symes went on speaking to Sir John as though I were not there. "– so we want Lieutenant Davis to report to Leconfield House at 2:30."

"We will be lunching at the Travellers," said Sir John, looking at his watch, "and it's a bit late already. I suggest you have a car for him at the Club at, shall we say 3 o'clock?"

As we emerged into the sunshine of Horse Guards Parade and walked through St. James Park, the angry resentment evaporated and warmth flowed back. It was, of course, due to the civility of Sir John. I had no status; he had reinstated me. I had no recognition (and if we prod ourselves honestly we find we all want to be recognized); Sir John had recognized me. And as though he had read my thoughts he said, "Sorry all those chaps had to dash off, I'd like you to have met some of them. But everyone is so busy these days. I'll bet they all had another meeting to attend before they got to their muttons."

It was indeed a mutton chop, cabbage and potatoes, with a flask of Club claret that warmed my still chilly insides and further calmed me down while Sir John filled me in on Washington. He told me about Marcie's death, confirming what I had already guessed.

Roger had been the only one more or less on the spot. It seemed that she had sped back about half a mile from the Chesapeake cottage, then had backed into a side lane, up a bit of a rise. The road back to Washington was unmetalled so she had probably noticed the dust of the on-coming Russians, and from her elevation would have seen about fifty yards of the road as they approached the junction. Roger had been over the spot carefully to make a reconstruction. He had said that the tyre marks suggested she had let in the clutch at full throttle and had torn head-on into the Russian car. Her open petrol can might have contributed, but the force of the impact must have led to the explosion that engulfed both cars in the ball of flame and fire we had observed from off-shore.

"It is all quite horrible," Sir John said. We fell silent for a moment, then he continued, "You know, she was rather fond of you."

I'd have wished him to say that again and again, but denied myself more blushes by countering, "She really loved Sylvan."

"Ah, well, maybe. But you realise, I hope, that she was older than either of you."

"But she died for him," I said, "or at least for his crazy plot. Sir John, I have dared to think – just played with the idea – that Sylvan was, or had been, working for the Russians. Then he gets this idea of – of sort of redeeming himself with a sort of counter-plot, counter espionage, you might say. And was Marcie also a spy? No, I can't believe that. Forget it, sir."

"Tom," said my host, "drop the 'sir' business. It's never good form, except with the cleaners and clerical staff. Sorry to shock your egalitarian tendencies, but that is how it is in the Office. I have been thirty-five years in the Foreign Office. I had hoped to retire with a decent ambassadorship, but now it is too late. And this latest escapade will do nothing to prolong my career as Minister at HM Britannic Embassy in Washington DC. Now, you were saying about Sylvan and Marcie."

He looked carefully round the almost deserted dining room before confiding *sotto voce*, "The spooks think he was."

"A spy?"

"Yes. They have built up quite a dossier. They know, apparently, that there is a traitor in their own outfit; indeed, they believe there is more than one. They just don't trust each other. Sylvan, as I knew, was working for them. Several pretty bright Foreign Office people have been enlisted on secret assignments. Even their own bosses aren't privy to these, and I really did not know Sylvan's task until that loathsome chap Symes spilled it out this morning. So, they think Sylvan may be a great catch for MI5; they think exposing him as a Russian agent will get both MI6 and the politicians off their necks because, as the world knows, there have been scandals enough."

"MI5 I understand to be the counter-intelligence wing; and MI6?"

"The active side of intelligence gathering."

"So, poor old Sylvan was spying on the Americans and feeding stuff to the Russians . . ."

"And then, as you put it – rather a good scenario – seeking to redeem himself by shooting down both his task-masters in flames!"

"No wonder he got drunk. Yes, it all fits together – he was being torn apart. Er, John, I've got to meet these MI5 people this afternoon. It will be all about Sylvan, I'm sure. What am I going to say?"

"Nothing. We all learn to say nothing, even if it goes on all night. They may be tough but remember they are not a court. Just keep them guessing!"

"It must be time to go, but what really do you think about Marcie's part in all this?"

"I don't think. I don't know. We shall never know. We agree she loved Sylvan. She may therefore have known something of his secret activities. She was wise –"

"Wise as Athene," I interjected.

"What? Yes, indeed, very wise, and also fey. She had a sort of second sight and a fey is one doomed to die."

"I believe she was determined to save Sylvan. She saw his redemption in his mad plan and resolved to die, if it would help his salvation – even if that meant no more than saving his career in the Foreign Office."

"Strange woman. I will miss her too."

A club waiter came to say that the car was at the door.

"Well, goodbye for the moment, Tom. I'll see you again. I've asked the office to send you back as soon as possible, and by the way, you are still officially in uniform. If you want to join us for the long term, you'd better sit one of these Foreign Office exams. I'll see what they can arrange. Off you go. I will stay a bit. Certainly we don't want to waste the rest of this excellent claret. Besides, Symes may be in the car; don't want to meet him again. Good luck, and don't let the bastards grind you down!"

CHAPTER TWENTY-FIVE

Symes was waiting in the car. I got in the back besides him.

"Leconfield House, again, Jimbo," he said to the driver. The driver wore dark glasses, was fair-haired and wearing a light-coloured jacket and, as I could see from the driving mirror, a soft shirt unbuttoned at the neck, so his loosely-knotted tie served no purpose unless it was to advertise his preference for busty girls such as the one screen-printed down its length.

Symes had nothing to say. I measured him up for the first time.

I had only the vaguest idea of what a secret service man did but to me he certainly didn't look the part. Not at all sinister, even a bit foppish. Pin-striped trousers, black jacket and a carnation in the lapel; a small moustache on a fattish face, really too large to carry it; black and rather greasy hair; collar and cuffs of shirt were also grubby. And he smelt. A familiar smell of sweat. When you rode the London buses in those days, it was a smell distinguishable without undue sensitivity from the pervading smell of cigarettes. In America, everyone had seemed so clean; Londoners seemed dirty.

Wait, I mentally chided myself, where is your compassion? These people had been at war for six years. Soap was scarce. The King had led the nation in water economy by drawing a line in the Royal bath five inches deep above which the hot water might not rise. This tendency to judge others! I had already judged the pathetic Symes as not quite a gentleman.

"Nearly there!" said Symes, and after a pause, "Sorry to have had that slight contretemps with your old buffer. I hope he gave you a good lunch." I nodded and he continued, "You see, we are all so busy these days. The Director has altered his schedule though; he is anxious to meet you. Ah, here we are!"

We had carved a way through the narrow streets of Mayfair and now drew up at what appeared to be some sort of back entrance to a largish brick building that might have been a private residence in grander days. As we waited for the door to open, I asked Symes if he too was from the Foreign Office.

"No, not actually. King's Messenger. Carried the Diplomatic bags all over the place, all over the world."

There was a hatch in the door, like they had in the old American movies about speakeasies in prohibition days. A panel slid back. We were admitted to a small foyer giving directly on to the open cage of one of those old-fashioned lifts with sliding lattice-work doors. It does not go if the doors are not properly engaged, a sensible enough safety device, but one which reduced Jimbo, the driver, who had now joined us, to fury and curses I had not heard since I had first joined up as a seaman. Symes took over.

"Not very mechanically minded is our Jimbo! Here, let me do it!" I saw Symes as a dog-handler. In this small act he handled the other man as he might a fierce guard dog. As the lift clanked upward, Jimbo was panting heavily. I assigned him a rather nasty role in this company of spooks, as better men than I had dubbed them.

The room we now entered was a comfortable one, well carpeted, well furnished, a sitting room rather than an office. Three or four armchairs and a sofa were mostly occupied by men who got up as we entered, but there was a small desk at the end of the room where a largish, balding figure stayed seated. Symes made the introductions. I was introduced to the director and the others – most of their names are forgotten now, except for one.

"Now, here's a Foreign Office man for you and, of course, he is in intelligence too: Philip Kimball."

I won't forget Philip Kimball's easy smile, his firm handshake, his lined features in a young-old face, nor his restless eyes. I got the impression that he was someone important.

"Haven't got for ever; let's get on," said the director.

His large frame, exaggerated by a loose-fitting double-breasted suit, seemed to bulge out and overflow the small desk. He took time to relight his pipe, then said to Symes: "Good work, Jack! I should have got to that meeting this morning but you did all right. Thanks for phoning in your report. I've put everyone in the picture. And now you have brought us this, er, Lieutenant Davis?" Turning to me he said, "I think you can tell us something."

"About what, exactly?"

"Now look here, Davis We've done a quick shufti into your history. You don't appear to have been much involved – except in losing this Bronski for the nation – but obviously you knew Sylvan Ross. That is why we are going to ask you a few questions."

There was a shifting of chairs; the soft afternoon sun had filtered through the Venetian blinds, but these were now closed and a light switched on. I was ushered to a seat in the middle of the room. Jimbo grabbed the light, a table lamp on the desk, and directed it full at me. I raised a shaky hand to ward off the brightness.

"Turn that thing off, Jimbo, you're blinding the poor chap!"

"Don't mind, me," I retorted, "this is just what I was told to expect from our NKVD."

"All right, Lieutenant, let's all calm down. Jimbo here tends to the histrionic. Back to your kennel, boy."

Jimbo, still wearing his dark glasses, smirked and took station behind the director's chair.

"Now, Mr Davis, what do you really know about Sylvan Ross?"

What a stupid opener, I thought. I could hit that for a six!

"Why, sir," (I decided a 'sir' was in order here) "you must know more than I do since he was working for you."

"What? Who told you that now?"

"Mr Symes told the meeting so this morning, It caused quite a sensation. I certainly knew nothing of this."

The director frowned. "Jack, is this true? I'll have your guts for this! But never mind now. We are in the last act, so you may as well know, Mr Davis, that our American friends have some leads on Ross. They have concluded that he is a Russian agent. Yes. He has worked for us, actually told us more about the Americans than the Russians! We can't

137

confirm the American evidence yet, but we have had our own suspicions. But the Foreign Office," and here he turned to Kimball, "have protected him like he was their darling child! All our enquiries there end in a ball of cotton wool."

He turned to another of the men in the background, who'd been introduced to me as Mr Bright. "Peter, you started this in-depth enquiry business. What do you want to ask our young friend?"

"Well, Director, we didn't need the American experience to conclude that we had plenty of Reds – communists – under our beds. Martin Dies' congressional committee may have done harm by going too far, and now the House Committee on Un-American Activities has been made a permanent fixture, but they had the right idea. With your permission, Director, we need to cut through the old-boy crust. OK, Mr Davis. About Mr Ross – we know now that at Cambridge he was already a Marxist. Were you aware of that?"

I wasn't, but leapt upon its irrelevance.

"He may have been," I said, "but so what? Marxism is, to this day, a perfectly respectable interpretation of history."

"You mean then, that you too are a communist?"

"Well, Mr Bright, the communist system under Stalin, which sounds pretty terrible, does not invalidate Marxism as a philosophy of world history. Consider the history of Christendom. Are we to suppose that the awful aberrations of the Inquisition totally discredit the glorious tradition of Christianity?"

Bright was not diverted. "While still at Cambridge, Ross came under the influence of dedicated communists – of Stalin's people – please note."

"A lot of us did. There was plenty we wanted to change in our benighted, class-ridden society before the war, and plenty who survived still do, as a matter of fact." I added somewhat sententiously, "Many, of course, went out and died for King and Country." I grappled in vain to recall anyone in particular lest that provoke the next question. Mercifully the ferret-like little man avoided any diversion.

"You appear to take the Foreign Office view. Have you talked to anyone in the Foreign Office?"

"I only landed in Liverpool last night," I replied, " and if you must know, I've not yet even seen the inside of the Foreign Office."

"So, Washington then. We will be looking into your history, Davis, what vetting you had, who placed you there."

"Please do, but when I enlisted as a seaman, I never took an Oath of Allegiance. I believe there was to have been some initiation ceremony but it was cancelled because of an air-raid warning."

"How come, then, that you were engaged in this atomic work?"

I sensed danger here. "You know the embassy is short handed. It was a local arrangement. With the war running down, and Washington still full of British missions – and admirals – the Naval Attaché Office was a bit surplus. I was released to assist Professor Hopkins. He in turn was our channel for discussing with the Americans our post-war collaboration on – and indeed world control of – atomic energy."

"And this was quite unauthorised?"

"Well, there were signals to and from the Admiralty who released me temporarily for these duties, at the Ambassador's request – I have never been discharged."

"But you might be anybody! Here were you, with access to the most secret work in the embassy and, as we now know, an intimate friend of this Ross. Good grief! Mr Kimball, is this arrangement possible in the Foreign Office?"

Kimball had so far not joined in the discussion, though he had clearly been following it intently. He now spoke for the first time.

"As Mr Davis – that is, Lieutenant Davis – says, it was a local arrangement. I understand that you were given the rank of a third Secretary – locally engaged. Right?"

"Right."

"So he is not really on the Foreign Office books as yet, but we often take on people locally in this way. Have to take 'em where you find them. Er – sorry Lieutenant Davis," he said with a charming smile, "but you know what I mean."

"Director," said Bright, "we have waited too long for a response to our paper on the need for positive vetting throughout Whitehall. We must get that authority soon from the Prime Minister, and starting with the Foreign Office!" He glared at Kimball.

I intervened. "You must have a very big outfit here, it seems." Then, remembering what Marcie had told me in what seemed like another lifetime, I added, "I think you will find if you look hard enough that there's already a file on me."

The director cut me short. "We are getting nowhere. This is about Ross. Get on with it, Peter."

"I'll come to the point. First – you liked Ross?"

"Well, yes, of course. Everyone likes him. He's a first class administrator and a most helpful sort of chap; helped me in lots of ways."

"So I suppose that is why you assisted him in this mad Bronski scheme? We have a copy of the embassy's preliminary report. It seems from what Sir John – the Minister, you know – wrote, that you were one of the very few people involved. You saw him in action. Did you not guess he was working for the Russians?"

I tried to contain my anger. "Can you imagine a more patriotic act than snatching that poor man from both the Russians _and_ the Americans?"

Bright continued without looking up from some notes he had in front of him. "How did you come to know that the Americans were closing in on Bronski, that they were expecting him at a letter drop in that mountain bar?"

"Why, Sylvan, of course. Ross, that is. Working as he was for your lot he found out about this and, then, well, he pulled a fast one on the Americans – knowing what a stink it would cause HMG if they exposed Bronski."

"But odd, isn't it, that he did not tell this office? But now, let me ask you this. How did you conspirators know that the Russians intended to lift him, and the exact hour?"

"I haven't really thought about it. I was not with them in New Mexico when the signal was given. I only had the story second-hand when we got back to the Chesapeake. Incidentally, I've not actually seen Sylvan, since, dear me, weeks ago, when we were planning the shipping-out operation."

"But you heard from him?"

"I – I don't think so."

"Oh yes you did. Who phoned that morning to say the Russians had wind of you all and were coming?"

"Marcie took the message. Yes, I think she said it was Sylvan."

"Of course it was. Who else could have known? This double traitor – he was at the centre of the web. No one else – unless you have some explaining to do about your part in all this? Think, man. Just how else could you have known all you did know?"

I knew the answer, of course. It had to be Sylvan. I remembered now Marcie's defensive tangle of doubt. 'How does he know?' she had said to us. And I remembered what John Portent and I had almost concluded at lunch only an hour or so ago. Perhaps he had done the unforgivable, but, with Operation Bronski, was looking to make amends. That was nothing that these people would buy. Even so, I began to offer this explanation, but checked myself.

"You were going to say?"

"Nothing."

There was a pause while the director relit his pipe. Two matches were needed before a satisfactory smoke signal emerged from the bowl.

"So, no answer," he said. "Well, I think that is enough for the present. We aren't out to extract some confession from you, Lieutenant. No! Nothing like that. The case against Ross is not yet complete. We are just trying to build up a clearer picture of the man. You can't contribute much, as far as I can see, but your silence is a factor, quite helpful actually."

The meeting broke up and I was even offered a car back to the hotel. I preferred to walk.

Setting off towards the parks, in the fading dusk, there was an opportunity to think. The interview had not been so bad; I had expected some sort of third degree. The director and Kimball too, I thought, had not really been very interested in me. Recalling John Portent's remarks one could suppose that they were more worried about traitors in their own bailiwick, fantastic as it might seem. Only this niggling Bright person had seemed determined to catch his man.

I was now determined to defend Sylvan's good name, assist in this wonderful plan of redemption. That surely was what Marcie had wanted: 'Help him, Tom . . .' she had said.

CHAPTER TWENTY-SIX

Waiting at the hotel was a message for me to call on Mr Hacket, Personnel Department at the Foreign Office, Room 76(a) at 10 a.m., if convenient.

This was an enormous relief. Someone was going to take charge!

I had spent a day – my first day in this alien land – thrashing through a dark forest on whose floor were thorny growths and clinging brambles, with no sense of direction. Now there was a sign-post; something to make for. But it meant another day, probably, before I could do what I must do – face the family.

I had not yet had time to call them since I'd got back. I did so now, still not knowing what to say. Both Ma and Dad came to the phone. I told them I couldn't talk for long, but that I'd call again after I'd reported to the Foreign Office in the morning. I had to make it brief because, once again, I was beginning to choke up. They must have felt a bit shaken too, but seemed to understand that this was no time for questions. Dad just had time to ask jovially if I had been sacked and for me to assure him that I hadn't, not yet anyway.

But why this curdling inside, this choking with tears? It must be this trauma business. At parties in the States, people talked about their traumas, describing their latest visit to their psychologists. I could analyse myself quite well, thank you.

Three deaths: Marcie, Masudi, Bronski. I had been a witness, an accessory to each of them. No wonder I was in shock. Then there was the threatening cloud surrounding my friend Sylvan. Only that afternoon, in a totally unrehearsed performance before those MI5 people, on a day when I learnt just how serious was his position, had I discovered that my mind was made up. I would fulfil Marcie's injunction to help Sylvan, though it was hard to see what I could do at this range.

Soothed by more Scotch, sleep came quickly. But I started up in the dawn light as though a star had burst in my head. A traitor! A spy! Case not yet ready for a prosecution but what else had these people been on about? Not only MI5, but John Portent too had known it was only a matter of time. What was I doing? Had I not known? Known all along? But wait a moment! Only yesterday, at lunch with John Portent we had revived the notion, rehearsed with Marcie and Roger, of an act of penitence. Sylvan, at enormous personal risk, had defied his Russian masters, if such they were; broken whatever hold they may have had on him. Had he not won forgiveness? In the chapels, the old soak who breaks with the bottle becomes the show-piece of the Temperance people. In the church up the road, the penitent intones: "Bless me, Father, for I have sinned . . ."

Then, and after confession, an absolution is pronounced. Is not this the heart of the matter, the essence of our faith? We do dreadful things and yet, if we confess them, that surely means really acknowledging them and trying to make amends – we can start again the next day. The complicating dogma that Christ has taken all our sins upon himself cannot obscure this central and psychologically proven fact – that redemption can follow a contrite act. All the pomposities that encrust the church cannot obscure its promise of the availability of salvation to those who seek it.

A traitor was he? A spy? Well, no longer! Sylvan, I was determined, had exculpated himself, performed his penance, and done so rather more effectively than by reciting a string of Hail Marys.

So I was to report to the Foreign Office. The night before, it had been a relief to know that someone was taking charge of me. I'd need to look presentable, but the only clothes I had landed with were my naval uniform, thrown aboard the *Orme Head* at the last minute, with a shirt and tie. On the ship it had all had been cleaned and pressed, and for the journey I had been kitted out with an assortment of jerseys and trousers suited for the official stowaway I had become. Now the shirt was grubby, my shoes were scuffed, and I felt a proper fool at being in uniform at all. There was just time on the way to buy a new collar and, fumbling with the studs, to put it on, in the 'Gents Outfitters' I had noted in Tothill Street. From there it was only a short step along Storey's Gate to the rim of St. James Park and the back entrance to the Foreign Office.

My instructions were to present myself at the King Charles Street entrance. King Charles Street is the twin of Downing Street. It is reached from the St. James Park end by a flight of steps. Almost immediately, on your left, there is an inconspicuous door, a sort of back-door to the Foreign Office to which the main entrance is on the other side, facing No.10 Downing Street. This door was an entrance to the old India Office.

An aged messenger led me up stairs and round the gallery that overlooked a once-splendid central court, open to a glazed roof high above. Now there was no roof, only a scanty web of scaffolding draped over with flapping sheets of tarpaulin. This last relic of imperial grandeur must be low on the list of war-damage priorities – that India, the Jewel in the Crown, was well on its path to independence might be the reason for that.

The way led through corridors lined with shelves of books. These, too, were half open to the sky; there was a smell of rot and mildew.

"Part of the Old India Office Library," explained my guide. "Shame, really, very precious some of them old books – historic too! Pity they can't decide who should have them. Give them back to the rajahs, I say."

Hacket, whom I had come to see, gave me a cheerful welcome. He struck me at once as a warm sort of person, and shrewd. I felt him sizing me up, even as he was speaking.

"You will have a lot to tell, but not to bother about that now. John Portent rang to ask me to see you as soon as possible. He wants you back in Washington, but you'll have to stay here for a while to see out the next phase of this astounding – I don't know – what do you call it?"

"Security operation," I responded, straight-faced.

"Yes, that will do. He suggests you be given a few days to write up your own report on this – er – security operation. We've absolutely no room here, so perhaps you could go home – take some leave – for a few days. Then he suggests we might find you some departmental work for a bit. Everyone is screaming for extra hands, so that should not be difficult. And, one more thing, he suggested that you might as well sit one of our entrance exams. Post-war 'special entry' and all that. They are a piece of cake. Good idea?"

I nodded with no show of enthusiasm, for the very idea of exams still gives me nightmares.

"Right, we'll fix you up."

Hacket's desk was only one of three in a large but overcrowded room. He now led me back to the door.

"Let's get out of here for a moment. There is something else."

He took another route back to the India Office balcony, through a maze of temporary offices, thrown up with hardboard partitions, festooned with telephone wire and cables, loud with the clacking of typewriters. We then emerged into the cool, sad silence of this great ruin. We stood leaning our hands on the marble rail, chipped and blasted by the bomb, as were the Corinthian pillars that rose to the gaping ceiling. Along the balustrade were ship models – exquisite models of the Viceroys' steam yachts, Hacket explained – mostly battered and half out of their shattered glass cases.

"I'd like one of them," I said.

"Good God, whatever for?"

"Just to repair it," I replied. "I hate seeing them like that. You could have it back, of course, after I'd fixed it."

In that instant I knew that sitting in the old shed at the back of the garden at home, working on these lovely models, was what I wanted to do. To hell with the diplomatic service!

Hacket did not hide his look of amazement – or was it just amusement. Had he made a note of less-than-total dedication in his prospective candidate for a hard-nosed service? But what he said was, "Now come, Tom. It is Tom, isn't it? Look old chap, from what I've heard so far, you have been through a lot and I don't want to press you, you know. But a quick word about Sylvan Ross. The *Queen Mary* docks on Tuesday. We will arrange to meet Ross. He is a very sick man." He went on to confirm all that John Portent had told me.

"How can I help?"

"The spooks are after him, but they have not as yet told us a thing. The American CIA – I think it is called – have a man named, unbelievably, James Jesus Angleton. He and his lot are convinced that the Foreign Office is a branch of the Kremlin. They seem to have passed to MI5 a dossier on Sylvan Ross and are crying for his blood. But my department has been told nothing! MI5 – they are the ones I call the spooks – have the papers. Philip Kimball, who sort of liaises with them, tells us to keep cool and that it will all blow over. But enough has leaked about to make me really worried. So, tell me Tom, honestly, was Sylvan Ross a spy?"

I decided not to air the Prodigal Son analogy. After a pause, I said, "The best way of answering that is to pass on what I do know, and all of that is what I have learned here in London in the last forty-eight hours. I can give you no answer based on the Washington experience."

I told him what had passed at the Cabinet Office, including Symes' slip in revealing that Sylvan had a secret assignment working for MI5. Then I told him about my own session with MI5 where they had assumed Sylvan's guilt, where the word 'traitor' had been bandied about.

All this was news to him, Hacket told me.

"Kimball was there, you say? I'm sure he will give us a report."

"What can you do – to help Sylvan?" I asked.

Hacket threw a sharp glance at me. "Help? I don't know, Tom. Personnel Department is quite peripheral to all this. We are told to expect a pretty sick man. Various reports on him should be with us shortly and when we have seen him, then we will discuss what to do next. A further assignment, perhaps? Certainly sick leave, and, from what we hear so far, probably a spell in hospital, maybe a mental ward. But help? Any misdemeanours obviously have to be noted, and if criminal charges follow they have to take their course. But you are onto something there. Naturally we will protect our own just as long as we can."

"I hope you will," I said. "He might decide to take his own life."

I don't know from what deep wells we come out with such unrehearsed remarks, but remembering that long-ago conversation with Marcie about a suicide pact, I thought I might be right.

Hacket did not appear to take my assertion too seriously. "Well, Tom, thanks for putting me in the picture." he said. "We must get weaving. I am horrified that M15 were on to you before we had the least sight of you in the Office here. *Mea culpa*! We really must tighten up the screws! Now you had better take the week-end off as leave. Let me know where to reach you. And Tom – others have been before the inquisitors at Leconfield House. They really are worse than the Kremlin. Just a tip, old lad! From what we know they are likely to keep a tail on you, the spooks do that to our people. Just watch your rear-view mirror. Unbelievable, isn't it, in our victorious democracy?"

CHAPTER TWENTY-SEVEN

Hacket sent me along with his PA to collect an advance of pay and by lunch time I was free.

There's nothing like a roll of notes in your pocket to make you feel good. The advance seemed a lot at the time so, after calling the family to say I'd be along later, it was just a matter of buying them some presents in Jermyn Street – a pipe for Dad and one of those large red handkerchiefs with polka dots, also from the pipe and tobacco shop. For Ma – difficult. Finally, an imported luxury at the cheese shop, a healthy-looking Camembert – she had always liked those. But there seemed to be nothing to buy that related to the indescribable world across the Atlantic that they would all want to hear about. The best answer seemed to be a bottle of bourbon and the ingredients for an Old-Fashioned and also for a Manhattan cocktail, including the cherries. They probably wouldn't like this, but I would, and I might need a few stiffeners.

A light drizzle had passed and it was quite warm. In the garden of St. James, Piccadilly, a tidied heap of fallen masonry offered a seat from which to take in the ruin of the church. It was not the ruin that set off the blubbering and choking with tears again, it was still this traumatic condition that I'd already diagnosed. Best let it all come out, so I decided to stay a moment, and try to read something in the ruin before me.

Someone had made the point that in every town and hamlet in the land, indeed, throughout Christendom, these churches still stand and had stood for centuries; matrices, wombs, giving form and foundation to the faith of their builders. They might rebuild this church; it was an important landmark – tourist attraction – in the heart of the West End. But would new stone, bricks and mortar, new carving and gilding, revive the message it had been dedicated to carry? And were a thousand churches up and down the country, untouched by bombs, any less dead than this one? Still, there they were. Some day, surely, someone must repossess them, proclaim in new terms the message this astonishing network had relayed through the world. What was it now? Salvation? But no one wanted to be 'saved' today. Or they say they don't. Perhaps it is the language, with its pietistic connotations, that gets in the way. We do want to be saved – from our dead selves, from our awful yesterdays – before we are floored by the weight of our past. We want that now so as to go on living, not when we are dying. We don't want to be saints or angels with harps and wings. We know we are sinners; so did the old church. Cranmer's priests still say before the Confessions, "If we say we have no sin, we deceive ourselves and the truth is not in us."

Next Sunday, and every day at Evensong, the same words will be said, the same forgiveness promised. So, even after repentance, confession, are we still sinners? Does that make it a sham? Perhaps not. The formula has worked through the centuries because the wise old church recognized us for what we are, caught up in a web of our own and the world's awfulness: not a community of saints, of the saved, the elect, as latter-day sects had proclaimed, but of sinners, just ordinary folk. What it offered in its services was relief, an aspirin to get us through the night to come and the next day, and perhaps something more: for those strong enough to do it, to perform an act of penitence that will expunge from the record the hateful thing with which they were burdened. This way not only would there be rejoicing in heaven, but self-respect and fellowship would be restored.

Thus, I was determined, would it be with Sylvan. Never mind the final outcome of the Bronski affair; Sylvan's act witnessed his intention to break with his Russian masters and do a service to his country. It is not given us to know how God disposes of His ever-lasting mercy, but, surely, in the community of sinners, he has done enough to win his release?

Would they take him back? I had to doubt it. His appeal had to be to the world of the self-righteous, the press, the politicians, the Pharisees, not to the ordinary chaps – his fellow sinners. A dejecting prospect.

I crossed the Park, past the Palace to Victoria Station, gateway to the southern suburbs I knew so well. As the train lumbered towards Clapham Junction, the same morbid curiosity that compels passing motorists to slow down at the scene of a smash-up drew my eyes to the close-packed acres of streets and terraced housing, now criss-crossed with the trail of bombs and sticks of incendiaries, the gaping sites, the roofless little homes. Nor had the bombers followed the line of the streets; the whole area was sliced this way and that. The target must have been the ganglion of railway tracks converging on the Junction itself, the nerve centre of the Southern Railway.

Do we forgive the Germans? Since in the end we gave them more than we got, we'd better; and hope, too, for forgiveness for ourselves. Was this perhaps the meaning of 'Original Sin'? That we are all caught up in it; that the brave, even saintly acts of which people are capable will not free them from the web of awfulness mankind has woven? May well be, but what about free will? Can we not choose a better way? Perhaps. Perhaps that's what religion is all about: a set of rules for individuals living in a jungle world, so the soul doesn't die but is daily renewed by confession and absolution. Here was a first glimpse of what the Church in which we had been cradled should really mean for us. Pity we can't do something about it.

It was drizzling again. The slate, tiled, and tarpaulined roofs glittered like the surface of a wave-tossed sea. Riding the waves like a whale was the grey roof of St. Simon and St. Jude, a Victorian monstrosity, or so I regarded it; I had never actually been inside. Perhaps it was bringing the renewal of life to this stricken neighbourhood? I had no idea, but this latest attempt to analyse the seeds of faith had dispersed my black mood with the thought that after all, all things were possible: Sylvan had to be forgiven his trespasses.

Now for the homecoming. For the past forty-eight hours, propelled into the grey yet somehow exotic world of Whitehall, there had been no fear, just bemusement. But this was familiar ground; as the train pulled into each station, I knew where we were without looking out of the windows. The fear grew of the familiar: of the suburban round, tennis parties, cinema outings, Sunday church. I had felt on that lightning visit last year at the end of the war that things had not changed much while

I'd been away. There'd been no time then for resuming family intimacies and, anyway, I was immersed in a job important enough to have brought me and my chief across the Atlantic by air, which was itself quite something in those days. But even then, it had been a relief to get back to Washington. I recalled that leisurely awakening in Georgetown that Sunday morning when the Marsden affair – his murder, I now knew – had started the trail that led to this homecoming.

I might still get back to Washington; John Portent had asked for me. Hacket had encouraged me to sit the Foreign Office entry exam. But it was the life, the friends, the excitement of America that called, not the work. This now appalled me.

While involved with Sylvan's affairs – the subject of this narrative – my own work had seemed all-important. It came to include responsibility for the UK side of the discussions on the future international control of atomic energy. When the Foreign Secretary Ernest Bevin had come over to the US, I was the one who had to explain to him our policy before he went on to meet his American opposite, who wanted to discuss these matters. London had provided no brief for him! He was at the Waldorf-Astoria. There, the huge man sat at a card table in the middle of the bare reception room of his suite. On one side of the room sat his wife, knitting. On the other, a portable bar, its shelves bare of the usual – only a pitcher of iced water stood on its counter. I outlined the American plan for a world development and control centre, told how I was backing this. Under whose instructions? There were no instructions from London. (No one had taken the scheme seriously, I was to discover. They had left it for a junior official to play along with the Americans until the thing petered out, as they assumed it would do.) But, as I spoke, the Foreign Secretary seemed to swell across the little table finally to explode, as it seemed to me.

"You mean you are trying to put us under this control thing? What is it but an American scheme to corner the world atomic market! Who else now has the know-how, the men, the plant? We are going to have our own nuclear power plants, my lad, and our own bomb!"

Thereafter the delegation to the fledgling United Nations in Lake Success, New York, which I had been advising, was given a sharp steer away from the course I had in my innocence set them. The new line was the Russian line: of course there must be a world organisation, but each country would preserve its sovereign rights, would be responsible for its own controls. But the British team never said "Nyet" like Mr Gromyko and his successors, nothing so crude; they just kept the ball in play for another twenty years until it was safe to drop it, on account of Russia's unflagging resistance.

If Secretary Bevin ever bothered to report this encounter then future progress for me in career diplomacy was unlikely, but it was the moment that a shell of idealism cracked. It had survived the war. The living thing within it had kicked with life in the glow of Roosveltian liberalism, even in that nest of self-seeking go-gettism and corruption that America was taken to be – even, cheerfully enough, by so many Americans. It was the moment that I knew that half-baked idealism was not the stuff of foreign policy; that clear-eyed pursuit of the national interest was the proper role of the Foreign Office; and that this was both beyond me intellectually and also repugnant.

As yet, though, it was not time to give up. Here was this United Nations right in New York which, with our UK delegation, I had already been visiting. I could work for the UN itself! I had not broached this with Hacket; perhaps a missed opportunity. He would still expect me to pass his wretched exam. He'd almost certainly noted my lack of enthusiasm for this and perhaps for the whole business. What <u>was</u> I going to do with myself?

And that was one thing the family would be sure to ask once the preliminaries were over; but first would be the banal questions like: "How was Washington?" "Did you have a good trip back?" and so forth. How dreary! There were all those books after the last war telling how men could not speak of what they knew, not only of horrors, violence and death, but of the comradeship in the trenches, of women behind the lines when the battalion rested. I could no more tell them of the good life in Georgetown than of the horrors of the past weeks or of the unsolved enigma of Sylvan Ross.

It would not be difficult to play this recent past as very hush-hush, for such it was. But anyway, the parents had been given to understand that the reason for my spending critical years of the war across the Atlantic was highly secret work. My regular letters to them would have done nothing to sully that impression. War-time censorship of letters from serving sailors, soldiers and airmen had greatly extended the art of sounding interesting while saying absolutely nothing, and that was but an extension of our usual pattern of family intercourse. The strength of the English bourgeois family lay in not probing the deeper questions, in confining conversation to the weather, the big match results, or the morning's news . . . dull, yes, but the family got by; arguments were avoided. I could recall no conversation in my own family, in the years of growing-up before the war, that had had any lasting significance – one sharp reproof perhaps, for not having written a thank-you letter after a week-end with rather posh friends of my mother. So a veil could be drawn over the past, and perhaps over these unresolved prospects for the future too, supposing the family convention of non-communication had persisted.

It was well before the rush hour; the little train, almost empty as it neared the end of the line, hummed and rocked along as it sped towards Belville, our station. As my parents had told me in their letters, this too had been bombed; a temporary shed still served as a booking office and shelter. There was not much other damage round about, but they had told me that there had been doodlebugs, the spluttering little V1 rockets, in the neighbourhood and that one had fallen on open ground not a hundred yards from our house.

CHAPTER TWENTY-EIGHT

It was less than ten minutes walk home from the station. The hedge and the grass were uncut, the front garden littered with soggy, decaying petals washed from the overblown roses by last night's rain. The house looked deserted, unpainted for years, with swathes of pebble-dark plastering fallen away and still partly windowless (some windows boarded, others covered with sheets of some transparent material). A sinking feeling made me hesitate before ringing the bell, but the door was thrown open anyway. Ma almost jumped down the steps to embrace me. We had never hugged or kissed since my babyhood! The warmth of it and her kisses to either cheek was not the stuff of our pre-war relationship or of that one leave from Portsmouth in early blitzkrieg days, when we had sat through a close air-raid, each in our own chair, unable to reach out and touch each or in any way give comfort or share our fear, trying not to cringe when bombs whistled down. This was indeed a new beginning. We went in happily, arm-in-arm. It was the same with Dad, now confined to his chair in front of the sitting-room fire by the illness that had forced his early retirement. He too reached out for a kiss. Never before had we kissed.

There was tea, jam, bread and butter, and the spicy little Welsh cakes that had been a favourite of mine when I was a boy. Although she had lived in England all her married life, my mother had always prepared for her family the treats that she herself had enjoyed as a child growing up in Wales, and I knew she had made these specially for me. Ma had always liked her teas. I was quite out of the habit of it, and in my so recent cold-inside mood, could easily have pained her by refusing or taking no more than a token nibble – even said, "No thanks, I'll wait for a drink." But no, I gave myself back to these old parents, took two cups of tea, polished off the Welsh cakes, and ate the last slice of bread and butter over-loaded with home-made strawberry jam.

The tea things barely cleared away, Dad turned on the huge old wireless set at his elbow for the five o'clock news. "He has his routine," said Ma firmly, refusing my offer to come out to the kitchen to help wash up. There was nothing on the radio I wanted to hear. I lit a pipe and gave over to thinking through this new relationship.

My brother, who was older than me, had joined up just before I followed him. Our parents had begged me not to go. Only now could I understand their feelings. At the time, they had not registered; nothing was put into words.

I had gone to University but never fulfilled my father's hopes for a professional career, as the coming war postponed any need for decisions. Only now did I come to terms with my own, what would be a fair word for it – fecklessness, perhaps – the feckless relief I had experienced at the prospect of the war, of joining up so that decisions about a career could be postponed *sine die*. Also with the seeming truth that one does not change. That is, one may rise to given occasions, do things you never thought you'd do, but, without pressure, you revert to being what you are – feckless, mediocre, or whatever.

No escape? No being 'born again'? Think of all the wonderful converts! St. Paul himself! Well before the Road to Damascus he was a known busybody and zealot, and so he was afterwards, even though the bearer of a new and wonderful message. Today's converts seem to be over-endowed with zeal and self-righteousness, a trait which the Jesus of the Gospels blasted away at without mercy. The righteous could take care of themselves. It's the rest of us, helpless sinners, we have to worry about. Then I thought of this new understanding of forgiveness – redemption, not in some future world but here and now. The idea that anyone, if he can examine himself, can make amends for that day's folly and start afresh the next day. A warming thought, and one I should like to have related to my own condition, but somehow I could not do this.

My mother had returned and Dad turned off his wireless. While never in the past having discussed anything more serious than a railway time-table with my parents, I now outlined my redemption theory. They heard me out with attention, my mother with bright-eyed delight. Dad said, "I'm glad you seem at last to have caught up with the essence of the Church's teaching. You remember I wanted you to aim for a career? I did not exclude the Church. Never really discussed this, did we? But when you went up I discussed it with your Dean. The college had quite a name for its clerical output, including bishops, and, yes, one archbishop. Pity we didn't go into it more fully."

"I would never have been strong enough to be a good priest," I replied. Sensing the naked truth of this insight, I covered it by adding, "OK, but the Church seems to require a submission that today seems quite out of place. That you can only be 'saved' by paying your entrance fee. What about the millions before and since the Church got going? Had they no way to grace? And its promise – always a pie in the sky! Can it really help us sinners now?"

Ma joined in. "I know you are on to something good here, Tom. But we mostly know our own weaknesses. For most of us they include a lack of just that discipline you are demanding of us – that daily introspection. Now, surely, that is what faith is all about – Christian belief. Our church is there to keep it before us. Of course the Catholics endow their priests with the powers of absolution much better than we do; we Presbyterians are a bit wet, really. But you are right on the central matter. Unless we can put our awful pasts behind us from time to time, there is no hope for us in this life, let alone the next. We've seen it, you know: people cracking up, going to drink, break-up of home, suicide."

"I'm sure you're right," I said. "But I've tried, and I don't believe. Don't believe in anything! But think of this. Supposing you have done something really awful. You know it, and you make a sacrificial and astonishing act of expiation. Have you redeemed yourself?"

"Oh, probably. Yes, why not?" We'd never had such a substantive discussion. As if embarrassed by her own unaccustomed earnestness, Ma quickly changed the subject: "I know you are tired, Tom dear. Go and have a clean up. You'll find your room just as it was, you can sort out some of your old togs. Margot and her new husband will be here for supper. Now, go and expiate yourself!"

Throughout our childhood my brother and I had shared this room with its dormer window looking over our modest strip of downland.

Each of us had had his own chest of drawers. I looked into my brother's. All his things were there, neatly folded. Then into my own. It was the same. Ma had washed, ironed and tidied everything away.

For all that strange coolness that had marked our years into manhood, this motherliness had been there all the time. Our tidy room, our carefully folded clothes were the signature of her love. Again, choking tears began to well up. Again I chided, pull yourself together! You are still in shock!

After a short lie-down in my old bed and a good wash in the bathroom on the floor below, which the family had always shared, I chose an old cricket shirt, grey-worsted flannels of generous cut and a sweater – unfashionable clothing, perhaps, but comfortable and comforting. Then I descended, bearing my small gifts. Dad eyed his pipe lovingly. Ma accepted the Camembert with cheers and another kiss. Then to the drinks. A decanter of sherry, with glasses, was laid out along with a plate of cheesy biscuits. Margot and her husband Ifor had come and we greeted each other in a casual way.

I now said, "I'd like you to join me in a libation – American style, to celebrate tonight!" No dissent. Glasses were found – not the right thing but small tumblers that would do. And, of course, there was no ice! I prepared five Old-Fashioneds. All were accepted, and Ifor helped by proposing a toast: "To the sailor home from the sea."

"Well, from DC!" interjected Margot (I had forgotten her gift for deflating family exchanges). Glasses were raised, and lowered with varying degrees of distaste.

"Very nice, Tom dear," said Ma. "Supper will be ready in fifteen minutes!" There were no more orders except for me. I poured a second stiff one, and found time for a third while the others chatted before we were called to the table.

We all ate well. The family chatted away with unexpected animation. It was, I know not how long after, that I overheard my mother talking to Margot in the kitchen: "Poor Tom. He is flat out! I knew he had been through something pretty awful as soon as I looked him over. But we haven't asked him about it, what he has been doing and all that. I expect he will tell us in good time."

"Just living it up, I bet, the way they do in the States," I heard my sister reply.

I went to bed. I did not understand what Margot, who was older than I, saw in her husband Ifor. He struck me as a bit of a cad. I declared these views at breakfast the next morning.

"You are a silly boy," said Ma.

"And a snob," said Dad. "You despise him because he wasn't in uniform. You don't know, do you, that he has been working on radar, all through the war, and that the boffins think he is quite brilliant? His students at the Poly, where he now teaches, think the world of him. A little less judgement and more charity, my boy, if you are keen on this redemption thing."

I was at a loss and duly humbled. Dad went on, "And he has done a good turn for you, my lad. As you know, we have no car now. We let the big old Austin go to war; I believe it has served with distinction as an ambulance. But Ifor has restored Margot's old Austin Seven. Rebored, rewired, new tyres, lots of things. He knows a place up at the Elephant and Castle with a complete line in Austin Seven spares. It's practically a new car! They don't actually need it, so it's in the garage here. I've kept it licensed, ready to go. If you hadn't been so drunk, we would have made it over to you last night as a homecoming present! Still, there it is. The body still needs attention – pretty ropey; but it's all yours, Tom – if you want it after all your high life."

No Buick, Cadillac, Oldsmobile, Packard or Pontiac now seemed as desirable as this little fellow As soon as thank-yous were over and a promise given to call Ifor when he got back from work that evening, I was lugging back the doors of the lean-to garage at the side of the house and had the little car on the road. My only ungenerous thought was to wish it were an open tourer, especially as the mildewed cloth headlining of the saloon dangled in my hair.

CHAPTER TWENTY-NINE

On my first day in the office Hacket took me to meet the head of the Cyprus desk where I was to be attached for a time. My new boss was tall, with pale blue eyes, flaxen hair, and dressed in a soft shirt with a loose cardigan. His jacket was on the back of his chair.

"Thanks, Hacket," he said, "You know we are quite desperate for extra hands. Has our friend any useful expertise, even experience?"

I was about to declare my total ignorance when Hacket broke in: "You are the luckiest of men, Pepper; Tom here has been doing secret work for us and I'll ask you not to probe him about it. He must tell you nothing – Official Secrets Act, Defence of the Realm, you know, all that sort of thing."

I warmed to Hacket. It may have been his way of selling a pup, but he had given me a face behind which to hide my total confusion in this unknown world of Whitehall. Prompted to banter, I said, "Well, I know Greek; that is, I did Greek for a bit at school."

"Well, we'll get on fine," said Pepper. "Do you know anything about Cyprus?"

"Where the Minotaur was? The Bulls? And where that German chap found the Mask of Agamemnon?"

"Sorry, chum, you are thinking of Crete. Cyprus is where we are trying to hold things together in the face of the government, the communists, the Orthodox Church and Uncle Tom Cobley and all."

"A thankless and probably vain task," said Hacket.

"Maybe, maybe," said Pepper, "but you must know, my dear chap, that our task is to uphold the dignity of the British Empire, and ensure we are not driven out in a shower of rotten tomatoes."

"Do we have to be there at all?" I asked.

The other two looked across at each other with what I detected as gently mocking grimaces at my simplicity.

"You will learn," said Pepper. "We have important military installations on the island. They are vital for keeping tabs on the Palestine situation. The Greek Cypriots are agitating for reunification with Greece, to which the Turks are bitterly opposed. It's bound to lead to trouble sooner or later. We are engaged in a race between some sort of political patch-up, which this Office is set on, and MI5 who want to get in there and assassinate the ringleaders."

"Is MI5 in this too?"

"Yep. With all this secret work you seem to have been doing you probably know them. You might help there too. Frustrate their knavish tricks, you know. Here is a file. Read it up. It will put you in the picture."

Hacket rose, ready to go, and I followed suit.

"One moment," said Pepper. "Here's the first job. We are to have a visitor. The Prime Minister has been given word of some quisling priest. One of these bishops with chimney-pot hats, you know. My instinct is not to trust him an inch. The RAF are to fly him over pretty soon. Dear boy, you are quite presentable in that uniform. You can arrange his reception. As this is a wheeze of the PM, we'd better put on some sort of show."

Hacket said, "It's only a lieutenant's uniform, RNVR too. Hadn't you better get someone more senior?"

Pepper waved the idea aside.

"Nonsense. Put on a couple of extra stripes if you like. Indeed, why the uniform anyway? I thought this was the Foreign Office?"

"He's only just arrived," said Hacket. "No time to demobilise yet."

I tried to explain that I had been released for Chancery duties in Washington and that the Admiralty signal agreeing to this had concluded 'Officer to retain his rank'; that I had had no further word about demobilisation; that I had a cheap American summer suit that was ill-fitting and far too light for this chilly English weather and that, so far, I had not had a moment (or the money) to get anything else.

It was apparent the other two were not greatly interested in these particulars. Pepper said simply, "Get a suit. Try Montague Burtons. Off the peg, but as good as you will get. Cheap too. Certainly good enough for this dubious bishop. Off you go now!"

I stood up. "Is everything in this file?" I asked. "Can you give me a bit more to go on?"

"Oh yes," said Pepper. "Where were we now? Yes. The prelate is to be ferried to RAF Blackbushe within the next week. You had better go down and see the Commandant. I don't think a red carpet is needed, but he might muster a small Guard of Honour – just a little one. Might make His Holiness feel good. Then you bring him to London. Try and get a Rolls or something. At least a Daimler. Then – no, not Claridges; consult the Government Hospitality people about some half decent hotel. Fairly central, and a suite I think. We can afford that if it is not Claridges."

My new desk was only a few doors away. Hacket came with me.

"So you have your Marching Orders. Think you can cope? You seem quite pleased."

"Yes, I'd almost forgotten how to smile. I like it," I said, "I like it because I like being told what to do."

"Sounded a bit like a Ruritanian farce to me, but I warn you, Pepper is tougher than he looks. He was in Greece a couple of years ago with the Resistance there. You wouldn't know it, would you?"

"No, I thought him a bit of a fop, if I may say so. Anything for me after all this treachery and killing and, if it is all slightly fanciful, what a relief."

Hacket rose to leave but put his hand on my arm as he said, "Try and forget all this Washington nonsense, but this is still a dangerous game, Tom. Be careful."

I could only nod a promise to be good.

"Just take your time and settle in," he continued. "Look, they're serving coffee over there."

He introduced me to one or two people who were queueing up at the coffee ladies' trolley. "Must get back to my muttons – good luck! And try to forget Sylvan Ross and all that. Not your problem any more." With a pat on the shoulder he left.

I was alarmed to have to make conversation with strangers, all probably expert at their jobs. But one man to whom Hacket had introduced me was friendly enough.

"So, you are new to all this?" he said. "I have one piece of advice. All Whitehall is thought to run on a nine-to-five – nowadays nine to six, seven or eight – basis, with all the chaps at their desks. Now, I ask you, what is a desk? It is just a prison, dear boy, with the happy adjunct of a telephone to the outside world. Don't let it ever grab you. Promise from the start to spend no more time at it than you must. The enlightened Mr Hacket, who has just left us, appreciates the danger. He awards Brownie Points to all who get away from their desks."

I did not care for this line of talk. I had always found in my short public service career that your superiors expected to find you at your desk and that it was as well to be seen there. I had just been assigned a desk of my own and that had been a comfortable reassurance. I returned to it, as soon as I had put the coffee down, for a first read of Pepper's file. Given my immediate assignment it would not appear that I would be at my desk very much. Nor, of course, had I been exactly desk-bound since the start of the Bronski adventure. Perhaps this chap had been right, and not merely decadent as I had begun to suspect some of my new colleagues to be. Perhaps public service was not just a matter of writing minutes, studying or writing reports. Perhaps you could and should actually get out there, do things, talk to people.

The PA attached to Hacket came to see what help I needed; provided me with four new pencils, writing paper, scribbling pad and a packet of government-issue paper clips, then took me out to lunch at a canteen behind Storeys Gate. She was a lively, well turned-out woman, a Cambridge graduate as it emerged. She filled me in with pictures of the work-mates I was yet to meet. I was coming to sense that the Foreign Office seemed to draw on a pool of women whom I can only think of as 'the better class', discernibly more interesting than those to be met in other government departments. I told her about my suit problem. She said at once, "Monty Burtons up in the Strand. Come on, I'll take you there."

We walked up to the Strand. I was content to let Brenda (she told me that was her name) fuss around and finally to choose a suit; clerical grey worsted, double-breasted. But I had to try several before she was satisfied with the fit. Once the suit was bagged up and paid for, I said, "We'd better get back to the office."

"Why on earth? Let's have a coffee somewhere! Come on! Fortnums, I think. It's more or less on the way back!"

We crossed Piccadilly, past lesser establishments, then Jacksons and then into the Aladdin's cave of Fortnums. Frock-coated gentlemen walked the floor and attended counters loaded with exotic foods, delicacies from all over the world. Even in New York I had seen nothing more extravagant. Here, in still-rationed London, it was repulsive. I was not to know then that this opulent facade concealed little that was substantial.

We passed through to the Coffee Room, facing on to St. James's Street. It was pretty full of elderly ladies with their fur coats and younger women with their shopping bags at their feet as they poised on high stools at the counter.

"Your deal," I said. "What do we order?"

"Coffee Schlag and a Wienertorte," Brenda replied.

I ordered the same for myself and we moved from the counter to a vacated table. I was clamming up, I know, simply because of the price of this extravagance, which would be much more than the cost of the excellent meat with two veg and apple tart we had had in the canteen and where, anyway, she had paid for herself.

I was clamming up, too, because, as we had walked over, this Brenda was revealing in her remarks something about herself that I had never cared for. She had been chattering on about Foreign Office people obviously of some seniority, using their Christian names only, and in the maze of relationships she retailed I sniffed gossip as being the meat and drink of Brenda's existence. We all enjoy the glow of warmth that can come from contact with the great or even the merely important; we seek to come to the notice of such people, to be in their company. So put, it sounds contemptible, but we know it happens. What really is not done is to make a display of these borrowed feathers before your fellows in the mess, the canteen or at a dinner party.

"I really don't know who all these people are," I said. "These Arthurs or Berties – I suppose you are telling me they are all very important?"

Brenda pouted. "I'm just trying to help you. These are the people you must get to know. They are the ones you are working for – and with." She lit a cigarette before continuing. "I'll tell you something else. They are all on edge. The spooks – these MI-whatsit people – think the Russkis have some agents, pretty top people, in the Office. Did you see that Russian film of *Ivan the Terrible*? That sense of watchfulness, fear and, well treachery . . . maybe I am overdoing it."

"So what?"

"Just this. I have seen your file, and" – she looked around furtively for any eavesdroppers – "you are being investigated!"

As I had supposed that this must be the case, I registered no shock. If I were to be a candidate for the Diplomatic Service, that was only right – and I said so. She persisted. "Investigated as a suspected traitor, I mean. That's what made me mildly interested in you."

This was more to the point. "What else have your researches disclosed?"

"I've seen the Sylvan Ross files too. George Hacket is holding off the spooks for the moment but it looks as though they have Sylvan by the short hairs. But all the evidence so far comes from the Americans; even MI5 realise that is not good enough."

"Why are you telling me all this?"

"Because you get a mention in Sylvan's file too. That's why they are after you."

"Well, I suppose I have to thank you," I said. "But what are you up to? I take you, frankly, for a bit of a gossip. Is this quite the thing in your job?"

Brenda turned quite fiercely on me.

"You are a slob and an ass. I couldn't care less about you or what happens to you. But as you are already involved, you have to know. Sylvan must not be caught. Sylvan's business is not yet generally known about the office but it soon will be. No one knows yet about you except the personnel people and some of the high-ups who have been involved. My idea, Tom, is that you can somehow help Sylvan."

Phew! I allowed a small gasp. "Is this FO policy or a scheme of your own?"

"Obviously the Office hopes Sylvan will vanish, just die, for God's sake. George Hacket has said as much in my hearing. After all, Sylvan is said to be pretty sick. You've got to get him out of this; lie, cheat, swear black and blue if you must."

"But why, Brenda; what's it to you?"

"Because I love him, that's why. I have loved him since we were at university together. He must not die! They still shoot or hang traitors, don't they, but just think of it, Sylvan in the dock, sentenced as a traitor. I couldn't . . . we must get him away!"

Once again I was in awe of Sylvan's ability to inspire such devotion in these bright, strong women.

"I'm glad you've told me all this, Brenda," I said more gently. The place was emptying. "Come on, we'd better go."

It was well into the afternoon. As Brenda said she would not return to the Office, I took her home in a taxi to a block of flats near Baker Street, careless of the extravagance – for I had never before hailed a taxi in London. I took the tube back to Piccadilly Circus, and set out to walk across the park to Victoria, observing the operative principle that seemed to be in force – don't be at your desk unless you have to be. Not without some misgiving though. Suppose someone had summoned me? Craven, this sounds, but I could not kid myself that I was otherwise.

CHAPTER THIRTY

It was misty, but still quite mild as I made my way down Lower Regent Street to the Duke of York steps leading into the Park. Two men, arm in arm, had just staggered up the steps and turned left into Pall Mall. I did a double-take. You can recognise people more easily by their gait and posture than by facial reconstructions. From his walk and bearing I was sure that one of these was Sylvan. I had to follow. If I were wrong I could get to Victoria just as quickly via the next gate, by St. James's.

The two men passed the Athenaeum, then the Travellers, then, at the Reform, one of them darted up the steps. The other turned to meet me. It was Sylvan.

"Tom! Come in here a mo'!"

He glanced up and down the street before ushering me up the steps. We removed our coats and mounted the broad staircase to the balcony. The Club was quite deserted, it being only just on five in the afternoon. We sat down on the faded buttoned-leather chairs at one of the small tables behind the grand balustrade of honey-coloured marble between columns of marble flecked with agate. You had to peer forward to see the floor below.

Before any introductions, Sylvan's companion summoned a waiter from the dark recesses. I took a Scotch. Both the others took gin with something in it I had not heard of.

At last Sylvan said, "Spotted you as you came across from Lower Regent Street. What luck! Just the man we need!"

"Please do explain, Sylvan, I was just going to catch a train . . ."

"Sorry, my dear chappie. All a bit sudden, what? But it is just a chance, a chance in a million. You could help."

"Fill me in," I said.

"I landed last week. The Office met me with an ambulance if you please! Quite delightful that! I was half expecting a police van. They've put me in a clinic at St. Thomas', you know, across the river. I'm OK, as you see. All sorts of treatment and I'm in bed mostly. Psychos too. But there seem to be no rules against my slipping out from time to time."

As he spoke, I looked over my friend. Still the bow tie; his suit was rumpled and he needed a hair cut. But his face – it frightened me. The eyes seemed lifeless and deep sunken; the always prominent cheekbones stood out above hollow cheeks. "I've not been to the Office," he went on, "but that nice Hacket chap has been over and filled me in, given me the full story. What a time you have had! Sorry about Bronski though. Clever chap that I am, I always suspected that shifty fellow, Masudi. The Ambassador wouldn't hear a word against him, of course; he loves all Arabs."

"You'd better come to the point, Sylvan. First, am I allowed to meet our host here? Is he your – sort of minder?"

"Oh, yes, excuse me! My minder, good idea. Yes, this is Guy. You must have met him when Bevin was over in Washington. We were at Cambridge together. Somehow we both got into the Diplomatic, but he now big man! Private Secretary to the SOS, the Secretary of State for Foreign Affairs."

"SOB," said Guy, otherwise merely nodding his how'd'ye dos. He was not a prepossessing figure: a well-cut suit with double-breasted waistcoat and expensive-looking shirt only added to the aura of decadence. His rather ugly patterned socks struck yet another discordant note.

I turned back to Sylvan. "Sylvan, I had thought this chapter in my life was closed. I'm now under new instructions. But I can't forget Marcie's last orders to me. They were to try and help you, I can't think how, but I told her I would do so."

At the name of Marcie, Sylvan's face fell forward into his cupped hands. "Marcie, Marcie," he burbled through a spasm of tears. "We killed her. It wasn't worth it." He continued to weep, his head cradled in his hands.

Guy said sharply, "Pull yourself together, Sylvan. She killed herself. Jolly decent of her since she wasn't one of us."

Not one of us? Meaning? But Guy had left the table to order up another round of drinks.

Sylvan recovered himself quite quickly. "Sorry about that. Tend to lose control from time to time." He wiped his eyes before saying, "Tom, my dear wee chappie. You know more than most now with your MI5 grilling – God, what a lot of wolves they are!"

"So, what is this all about?" I asked gently.

"Tom, you must have put two and two together by now." I nodded. "So you must know that we – I, that is – have worked for the Russians. Your kind heart may have refused the idea and – so far – so have our kind nannies at the Foreign Office."

"Well, yes, that's about it," I allowed, "and yes, this is the first time I've let myself think about it – in this way."

"Fact is that Angleton and his CIA goons have got a pretty water-tight case and they are over here now to rub your public-school noses in it."

"So you are going to give yourself in – make a confession?"

"Nothing of the sort," said Sylvan quite sharply. "If they want me they will have to come and get me."

"Will 'they' at this stage be the police?"

"Yes, but they aren't fully in the picture yet and MI5 can't go about arresting people on spec, thank God, not in this dear land."

Guy, who had returned as we spoke, said, "And the charge will be treason."

"You can still be hanged for treason?"

"I think so," said Guy languidly.

"There might be worse fates," Sylvan proposed.

"Nonsense," said Guy, "Think of the stink it would cause."

I knew very well what he meant: the shock to Anglo-American relations, suspicion that all was not yet revealed, witch-hunts, let alone all the personal and family grief. But where was I in all this?

"For God's sake be quiet for a moment!" I interjected. "Why don't I turn you all in?"

Guy said, "Because you are Sylvan's lover-boy, I am assuming. Can't think why else he pounced on you just now."

I stood up and crashed my glass on the table. "Sylvan, that's a damn lie and you know it! Just tell your friend, will you, that that is a lie!"

"Hush, dear laddie, you'll upset the waiter. But, yes, Guy, that is not true, so just forget you ever said it."

"OK. Then why should we trust this character?"

"Quite simple," said Sylvan. "Tom here and I are both Celts, and you, you Saxon moron, may not believe it, but he has pledged the goddess we both adore to do what he can for me, so he will!"

"I hadn't reckoned on this super-cargo," I said, indicating Guy.

"It involves no extra charge," said Sylvan. "And another thing, Guy, this little fellow is loyal to the Foreign Office, and our plan – damage limitation, no more – is just what they want. Right, Tom?"

I could have backed out even then, but instead I muttered, "Right".

"So how do you fit in?" I said to Guy.

"Me? My plan is to change the world. I don't look like a social reformer, but nor did lots of them – Tolstoy, Bukharin and the rest. They just had the brains to understand that the System could not survive. Sylvan here is the romantic. I am the one who recognises that the state of Britain is rotten, the City full of dirty tricks, and Parliament futile. I could go on, but I too am about to be exposed. A sad day for Britain's best interests!"

I voiced the suspicions passed to me so recently of other informers in high places. "With you two put away, will MI5 and all that lot be content?"

Sylvan joined Guy in suppressed laughter.

"Communists in the public services?"

"Yes. Lots of brave men. With this war over they want a clean start here."

"But why communism?" I went on.

"OK, Uncle Joe Stalin is a terrible chappie," said Sylvan. "But you've got to understand he is an aberration. Just think how the Church has survived those wicked popes, the Grand Inquisition, and those witch-burning puritans. No, ideas may be corrupted by their professors, but they survive."

As ever, I found myself half drawn into Sylvan's camp. I did not see how Marxism would help in the least but, as in the US, my instinct was to share his fears for the state of American or our own democracy. I did not know about Guy, but Sylvan, surely he was in the tradition of Blake or Wordsworth: 'Our England is a fen of stagnant waters . . .' Why, oh why, had he got himself into this mess? This was the stuff for politics – not treason.

"So," I said, standing up again. "What have we to do?"

"So we won't –"

"What won't you do?"

"We won't wait – look, we must get out of here."

The club was filling up. Tired civil servants drifted in; groups assembled at the bar in the court below. Some were coming up the staircase.

"Tom," said Sylvan, "get your coat. Go first. Meet me by the bridge in the Park. Yes," looking at his watch, "yes, ten minutes from now."

Mists of light cotton-wool swirled over the lake. Ducks floated about aimlessly with occasional tired quacks, signifying nothing. Others lined the bank, several in repose with heads tucked under their wings. How some of them managed this on one leg revived for a moment my interest in the mad but marvellous world we had inherited. Its survival would be more important than all our awful national fetishes. This was the straw I grasped at as I justified my unrehearsed entry into a plot to evade the course of justice – come off it – to help this pair of traitors. No clear avenues gave direction to my battered mind. It too was in a fog.

I looked away from the lake where the darkness was relieved only by the orangey glow of the Victorian lamps on the old bridge and strung along the lakeside footpath. The bright lights of cars in the Mall – flash, flash, flash between the almost bare trees – were blinding, but against them I saw the silhouette of Sylvan, hurrying towards me. He propelled me by the elbow back along the lakeside towards the head of the water where there is the unkempt island. A steep retaining wall above shuttered out the view from Buckingham Palace. It was too dark to see each other or to be seen.

Pulling me down to a bench, Sylvan now spoke quickly. "Guy is watching for us. We are safe here. Now look, Tom, we are not going to wait for the police; we are off – skedaddle! Never mind where. It's the only thing to do. It's best for everyone, best for the country too. If I don't go now, Tom, I will kill myself before they get me. It would be better than going to prison," he added in a flat tone.

"You might get off," I said hopefully. "I would testify that you are a patriot, so would John Portent. All your friends."

"What a hope!"

"Honestly, Sylvan, even when I was pretty sure you were up to something with the Russkis, I had to square this with your Bronski plan, which fooled the Russkis and the Yanks as well and certainly saved HMG from a ghastly embarrassment. It was, I thought, an act of redemption."

In the darkness I sensed a grin on his face. His hand fell on my knee. "Dear old chappie, what a lovely idea – a redemptive act! Yes, you are right. Yes, dear chap, yes – but I had been too deep in this other thing for the Law ever to forgive me. But, yes, the idea was to do something for this stupid old country of ours, and to break the hold the NKVD have had on me for all these years. Even if it cost me Marcie. Yes, it had to happen. An act of contrition, a search for redemption – I like that!"

"So you've broken with the Russians?"

"Dear boy, they don't let you do that. I am of no use to them now. They may kill me, but they will never let me go. I know too much to start with."

"Sort of blackmail?"

"Well, on their side, yes. You may as well know that they had some sort of hold on me at Cambridge. I had done something that seemed rather awful at the time and they kept me on a string. They never let me forget; but it was not until Washington that they pressed the button to activate me. God, it's been hell! Whatever comes now, that is past. I didn't really do anything horrendous, you know; it was all this atomic thing. The Russians were so far behind I fooled myself into thinking that if they caught up a bit there would be a sort of balance of power between East and West, and that might sort of, sort of be the best way to keep the peace. The Russkis know the strength of the Yanks and they wouldn't be so stupid as to start a fight. They wouldn't have an earthly! Nobody seems to remember that they were our allies and that without them we might well have lost the war!"

"Maybe, maybe," I said, "but what now. Are you telling me that the Russians are going to kidnap you, lift you, or whatever they do?"

"Right. This is it. You remember Captain Sodkin, the Soviet Naval Attaché in Washington? Well, old Sodders is here now, but he is in civvies and he is in charge. Good chap, Sodders, if they hadn't got his wife and kids under their bloody thumbs he would defect – dozens of them have, you know. They know the whole system is rotten, that Stalin is a sick man who must surely die soon, and then it will begin to break up."

"But you still want to go?"

"All the more reason – perhaps there will be a chance of pushing things along a bit – from the inside."

"So, what's the plan?"

"I don't know. Sodkin and some of our friends at the Office are fixing it up. But God! Why am I telling you all this? How can I trust anyone, you or anyone, now?"

I felt he was shaking again. He withdrew his hand and fumbled for his handkerchief. "Are you going to help?"

"Don't worry, Sylvan. Marcie, the goddess Athene, directed me to help."

"Our Athene?"

"Yes. She came to me as Marcie. I've told you all this before. Her orders were quite clear."

Against all sense I reassured this troubled man. Only later did I try to sort out my motives. Was it devotion to Marcie, or more immediately, love for Sylvan aroused only now at this strange encounter, or was it cowardice that had prevented me from telling these two idiots where they got off, or from reporting them at once to the authorities?

But Sylvan had recovered and was speaking. "Can you drive?"

"Yes."

"Have you got a car?"

"Well, sort of, yes."

"Good, that is what Sodkin wants. I really don't know much more but give me your address. Sodkin will know tonight how to reach you. Still on?"

"Yes, I said so, didn't I?"

"Right, wait for a word from him. We must go."

He gave a low sort of bird-like whistle and Guy was quickly with us. We parted silently. I walked briskly the short way to Victoria Station.

CHAPTER THIRTY-ONE

I was now living at home. Season ticket – thirty minutes to Victoria – at my new desk at the Foreign Office by nine.

The post seldom came before I left for work in the morning, but on Tuesday there was a letter for me on the mat. Delivered by hand. The note paper was unheaded; the message, would I be at the Mercury Restaurant, Wardour Street, Soho, that evening at 8 p.m.?

As my Dad did not get up before noon, my mother took up a light breakfast and had it with him. I got my own breakfast as a rule. That morning it was a mercy that I was alone, to think out what I was letting myself in for. No answers came, though. I gave up. I knew it. I tried to peer left and right but a tunnel enclosed my vision. As before, I could only follow orders.

I called up to the parents that I was just off and not to expect me before pretty late. This was the form more often than not these days. Indeed, the working day seldom ended before 7 or 7:30, and seemingly for more senior people it never ended. As had been usual during the war, camp beds were kept handy in their offices. Now, the last hour or so in the office was often the best; a time for informal planning and the floating of ideas or the exchange of gossip, perhaps in the office of the Section Head, perhaps with the Minister. It was the 'Happy Hour' for the 'in' people.

For me, that night, it was just a matter of clearing my own desk before setting out for Soho on foot. I had done a 'recce' in the lunch interval. The Mercury proved to be a surprising survivor from pre-war days. Red plush curtains, suspended from a brass rail, covered the lower half of its high-windowed front. They formed the backdrop to a row of atrophied dishes set on glass stands under their glass covers. A peep inside showed cold lights hung from a high ceiling. A few potted palms broke up the squareness of the room, furnished with square tables with chequered table-cloths. Set to them were hard-looking bent-cane chairs. There were no customers.

Returning in the evening I felt I was in another world. Soho concealed its scars under winking neon signs and strings of hanging light-bulbs and the glow of restaurants and honky-tonk joints.

And there was animation in the streets; lots of people, lots of noise. The shored-up buildings, the gaping ruin of St. Anne's church, the depressingly tawdry shop fronts and side alleys, the piles of rubbish that repelled the daytime visitor, were now masked behind the bright and restless foreground. Pubs, cafes and restaurants drew in and disgorged hosts of cheerful clients, taxis honked and the people in the narrow streets were out to enjoy themselves.

The Mercury, too, had shared in this transformation. A row of coloured lights swung above its window front. Inside, the tables were mostly full. There were lighted candles on the tables, and the savour of Mediterranean cooking, cigar and cigarette smoke garnished the air.

It was just on eight when I pushed open the door and took in these details. Almost at once, a very elderly waiter shuffled over to greet me. Thin, greying hair was plastered across his scalp; a drooping moustache sketched in miniature his drooping frame. Over the arm of his faded tail coat was a clean napkin. His feet flopped outwards too. The Walrus in *Alice in Wonderland*, I thought. But a sharp eye had looked me over. "Lieutenant Davis? This way, please."

He led the way to a curtain-covered door at the rear of the dining room, ushered me through and up a steep and narrow staircase, then knocked firmly before leading me into the upstairs room. It was smaller than the dining room below, well carpeted, lit by shaded wall brackets and shaded table-lamps set on the dining table ready laid. There was a low coffee table further in the shadows. The walrus withdrew without a word, and only then from these shadows did my host emerge to greet me.

"You may not remember me, but we met at our embassy in Washington."

"I do, indeed I do," I said, accepting his handshake, but peering hard at him in the dim light, for Captain Sodkin was now clean shaven, whereas as Naval Attaché he had had a moustache, something which never looks well with any naval uniform. Nor was he now in uniform, but in a smart grey suit of English worsted.

"Let me introduce my, er, companion – Boris, you may call him. He is really in charge of all our plans. First though, a drink."

He led the way back to the low coffee table where the vodka and caviar were waiting.

"Spacibo!"

"Cheers."

"You will have a meal with us, yes? But first, sit down here for a word about this business."

It was now or never that I had to make my stand, put my cards on the table. I had to show these people the limits of my commitment, that I was still my own man – but, on the instant, I recognised these as the very points I had struggled unsuccessfully to clarify for myself.

With the recharging of glasses after that initial swallow and the lighting of the proffered cigarette, I shaped my opening gambit, still clueless as to where it would lead.

"As to this business," I said, "you are assuming a lot about my involvement. I must make it clear at the outset that I am not . . ." I faltered for the second it took to ask myself what it was that I wasn't; not long enough to consider what I was or what I was doing here. "I am not," I blurted out, "I am not, shall I say, one of your people."

"My dear Lieutenant," said Sodkin, "if you were, as you say, 'one of our people' you could not do this job! The police have files and profiles on every one in this game, including myself I'm sure. Boris here is perhaps different. He comes and goes." His broad smile revealed his white teeth as he put out a friendly arm to the shoulders of his companion, seated on the sofa beside him. "His English is not all that good, so we keep him out of sight as a rule."

"So," I said, "that is why you want me to do your dirty work? Why do you think I am the man for this job – whatever it is?"

"Come, Lieutenant, I will explain in a moment that you are invited to share in an act of great patriotism, a service to the United Kingdom!

I am not alone among my countrymen in that I have developed a real love for your country, and for its way of life." He waved aside an attempted intervention and went on. "But first; why are <u>you</u> here, young man? I shall give you three reasons. Number one: our friend Sylvan Ross. He is now a broken man, but I have always trusted him, and it was he, of course, who sent you to me tonight. Second: we know you better than you might think. We have what the Americans might call a psychological profile on you as also, incidentally, on everybody involved in the Bronski affair. Shall I tell you about yourself? Briefly then. You are a good soldier – sailor, I should say, who does what he is told. You obey whoever commands you. In the war, in your Royal Navy, you knew where you were and it did you good. Then in this so-called peace, this cold war, you have been less certain. Like one of these nuclear particles, whizzing round at random until it finds its mate or master. For you it was Sylvan Ross. You were his to command."

"Nonsense!" I interjected. "It was Marcie – it was Marcie who told me to . . ."

"Ah, that tragic lady. Wonderful woman. None of us know the half of it. But it was our NKVD people at the embassy; it was their idea and my assistant was fool enough to go with them – and he died! It was all a cock-up, as you say."

"It was because Marcie loved Sylvan that she told me to . . ."

"Yes, it is as you say. Lady Marcia loved Ross. Like you, really, she would do anything for him, even to looking the other way when –"

"Nonsense again!" I said. "Are you telling me that she was a traitor too? She never –"

"Calm yourself, my friend. OK, she never . . . but by doing all she did for Sylvan she sailed pretty near the wind, as we sailors might say, eh? Yes, she loved our Sylvan. And you, young man, you love Sylvan too, and that is why you are here and why you will help him now."

"Sylvan used to tell me of this web in which your people had trapped him. Are you telling me that I am in it too, this web of – of treachery?"

I knew I was long since caught but fought to preserve the notion that what I had to do was a duty, a duty to Sylvan and to Marcie. My histrionics were a last lunge on the line by the hooked fish.

But Sodkin only smiled broadly across at me as he said again, "Keep calm, Tom, if I may so call you. You are no traitor. You are loyal; you are a patriot, not a traitor! What you are going to do is an act of high patriotism. Look at it this way. You may have realised that Sylvan planned the Bronski affair as an affirmation of his ultimate duty to Great Britain. Here was a man deeply compromised by his work for the Soviet authorities, which he did without pay, because – exactly – he was caught in this web. Believe me or not," he said, rising and standing over me, "I hate it as much as you do. It has terror at its centre, its threads are made of fear. It cannot last. I and others hope it blows away before we die, even if, needs be, in its dungeons."

I looked up wide-eyed at this Russian agent. "D'you mean that you are working for us – MI5 and all that?"

"No. I could wish it. But like your Sylvan I am entangled in this web. So also is my friend Boris here. If we are caught with one foot wrong, then" – he drew the side of his hand across his throat – "zonk! and our families too."

"But you are going to sneak Sylvan and this other chap out of Britain, presumably to this horrible fate in Moscow?*

"Oh yes. There we are just obeying orders."

I could only gape as he continued. "Look, old chap. What is best now for Britain? That he is brought to trial, a trial that will make Britain the laughing stock to her allies? To the Americans an ally they can no longer trust? You need them now as much as in the war. It's not only these atomic things, but her money. You know how, right now, she is propping up your economy with her dollars."

"And Sylvan? He's the sacrifice?"

"No, no. Think about it. First, he can never be readmitted to that society in Britain he loves so much. Here, there is nothing but disgrace, even prison. I don't think you are hanging people much now. But Sylvan would rather die than live on here."

"But what better fate can be expected from Stalin? Prison, torture, third degree – we've all learned what you can do to people."

"Stalin is a monster. He is seriously ill, though; he is never far from his doctors. He may be dying – it is hard to find out anything about him lately. But let me tell you, in the Russian House are many mansions! You think of us as a monolith. So we must appear. But believe me, all up and down the country there are cells of dissent, even in the highest places. When Stalin goes, you will see. Here in the security services we too have these cells – and perhaps you don't know this, but it will come out before long, dozens of our agents in the west have sought asylum. Military men, too. Anyway, take my word for it. Sylvan will be in the hands of one of our cells; a prisoner superficially, but in some quiet spot. A university perhaps; probably with his own dacha. He will be freer than he has been for years, in soul if not in body. Probably write text books for us – on how the West was Run, perhaps!"

"I have supposed Sylvan to be a communist," I said, "are you?"

"Well, I think so, probably yes. You don't have to follow Stalin to be a communist. To me it is just that I have the ideal of justice and fair deals for all. For all its exciting charms I never really cared for the American free-for-all way of life, with devil take the hindmost."

"You continue to amaze me, Captain Sodkin; this was the ideal of socialism in this country – particularly of those wonderful Christian Socialists of a hundred years ago, and it has survived in the hearts of socialists today, even under all this Marxist nonsense."

"I have seen that. I am sure that in this country of yours the goal of social justice still stands; perhaps it will be Great Britain's last great contribution to show that social justice and capitalism can co-exist."

Between the vodka and the wine with the meal that followed, my confidence grew that I was doing the right thing. What had seemed yet another drift into an unplanned and unsought venture became a duty to perform; no drift but destiny, a manifest destiny as someone had said – the goal to be reached without fumbling and at whatever cost. Yet it was simple enough – such a little task.

Sodkin produced a sheaf of notes and a map. "Now then. Passports, tickets and everything have been prepared for our friends. They cross to the continent from Newhaven. You will drive them there, at least to a rendezvous quite near the harbour."

"If you say so!" I said airily. "But where do I pick them up? At the Foreign Office, Downing Street entrance?"

"You will have your little joke. No. They will converge from different directions at Wimbledon."

"Wimbledon?" I chortled. How prosaic! I had expected something a bit more exotic than Wimbledon Station – some lonely moor, perhaps, a deserted airfield or haunted churchyard at dead of night.

"Wimbledon has both main line and suburban trains, and the Underground, that is, the District line. Guy comes by District, Ross will come up from Hampton Court where he is now on medical leave at his mother's house. Guy should be there to meet him off a train arriving at 3:30 in the afternoon."

Other details were outlined. I was to meet them in the concourse then conduct them individually to my car, which would be in the temporary car park adjoining the station. Missing only was the day. This would be signalled at no more then twelve hours' notice. Then I was escorted out through a service door to an alleyway that eventually gave onto the Tottenham Court Road. Mingling with the crowd, I assessed my assignment.

Timing was the first worry, as I was now fairly deeply involved in the Cyprus business arranging for the reception of this highly political prelate. It was not by any means a desk job. I was calling on various Greek factions in London and on the Orthodox hierarchy (though they did not seem keen on the planned visit) and even on the alarming people in MI5 as they too had a finger in the Cyprus pie; for, while the Colonial Office and the Foreign Office were trying to promote some sort of concordat between the Cypriot factions, M15 thought that the thing to do was not to mollycoddle but to assassinate the trouble-makers. The issue was whether MI5 should be allowed into the act at all. I had no knowledge of the pros and cons, but, cravenly, allowed them to pressurise me into helping put their case in Whitehall. It seemed sensible at the time to be and to be seen to be on the right side of the security services.

So it was that I was not forever at my desk; this gave me some room for manoeuvre. I would phone the Office if away for long.

Two days after my rendezvous with Sodkin I was told that there was a call from Leconfield House. Would I come to a meeting that afternoon?

CHAPTER THIRTY-TWO

It turned out to be a routine meeting. The Cyprus thing was the first item on the agenda; I was to leave when it was disposed of. It was about done; I heard the Director thanking me for my efforts, felt a spread of warmth inside – not because one could ever like these MI5 people but because it was always pleasant to be accepted, to be one of the group.

But the Director was interrupted by a messenger. He asked for me. Would I come out to take a telephone message? A call from the Foreign Office. "Put them through on my phone," ordered the Director. "He can take it in here!"

I'd rather have left the room, of course. This could be less of a courtesy than another MI5 trick to keep tabs on everyone. I rose, went to the desk and took the phone, taking care to press it close to my ear. After the usual clicks as the connection was made, I heard, "Tom? That you? Good. Tomorrow, 3:30." Frozen, I kept the phone close and said loudly, "Yes, yes! Shall do. Half an hour then," and put down the receiver. I pulled out a handkerchief as though to stifle a sneeze.

"Nothing wrong, I hope?" asked the Director.

"No, no, really." The eyes of all present were on me. "Flu coming, I think."

"The call – everything all right?"

"Oh, that. Yes. I'm wanted at a meeting in half an hour, so will you excuse me, Director, gentlemen?"

"Of course, off you go. What a busy chap he is," said the Director approvingly, it seemed, to the company at large, and as he waved me away added, "At least you've got shot of that Washington business. And thanks again for your help. Oh, yes, and about that Sylvan Ross business, you may as well know that we've got the rabbit in the bag just about – any day now!"

I fled. I could only think, the nerve of the man! The call had the marks of the old Sylvan but it had not been his voice; it had been Sodkin. It was from Sodkin's people that the call to action was to come. I took a cab straight to Waterloo station and took a train from there. As I flopped into a carriage I could think only of my next move.

First a reconnaissance at Wimbledon station, which was on the Waterloo but not the direct Victoria line, and then I must get home and check – once again – that the little car was provisioned and ready to go. I reflected briefly that there was something I had to do for the Office tomorrow, but whatever it was it would have to wait.

Only one stop to Wimbledon. I was soon climbing the stairs from the platform to the concourse overhead and chose a position from which I could spot my men as they came through the ticket barriers. Then into the street, turn left to the car park. It was pretty full. It was before the rush hour and would be the same tomorrow.

I spotted a vacancy; I would reserve this space. This was a rough-and-ready sort of car park, just a piece of no man's land in front of the entrance to a builders' supply yard. From a pile of waste at its gate I took two discarded planks and two small oil drums and lugged them back to form a barricade. Back in the station, I bought a thick crayon and a large pad at WH Smith, Stationers. 'Reserved for Ambulance' I wrote, propping the pad on my barricade.

"Ere, watcha a doin' of?" It was the night watchman from the builders' yard. Had it been a policeman I might, in my then state, have done something stupid. As it was, I explained that there would be a sick and disabled relative arriving tomorrow and that I was anxious to reserve space. The pound note I proffered as I spoke was probably unnecessary. "Orl right Guv. Just put that stuff back when yore done."

It was too early for the pubs to open, but the chill in my guts was spreading. It was not flu, it was fear; fear and excitement. The fear was not for tomorrow's adventure, it was that silly old fear that I would be missed at the office, that someone had wanted me and I was not there, and there was something else I had to do tomorrow. To this I firmly shut my mind. Across the way was a brightly lit cafe, a beacon in the gathering dusk. I had a pot of tea and two hot buttered crumpets with jam. That was better. More tea was available and to prevent my mind wandering up other distracting channels, I fished out my paper and folded it to the crossword.

But it was no good. The very first clue I answered at once: 'Revolutionary sets out – flyers.' Answer: 'Redstarts'. At once the sluice-gate in my mind opened to release a trickle of new thoughts about our plans. If my flyers got away, and I supposed that they would, where would this leave me? Was I playing the hero or was I a traitor? Did commendation await me, or disgrace? But then another thought: if tomorrow was a success there was no way in which my part could be made known. It would have to be my secret, to carry to my grave. I'd have to tell someone! One gets by through suppressing one's instincts. My instinct would be to brag about it, but that I could never do. Perhaps I might share it only with my pillow, perhaps with Marcie poised there, to stroke my brow and say, 'Well done.'

But think again. Some one knows already. The Russians know. Could I trust Sodkin's word that I was not now one of 'them', that I would be left alone? One interpretation of that had to be that I was quite unimportant. A useful pawn for this one move? A mere cog? I didn't care for that. But if they thought I was of potential value they would come back at me, blackmail me, as they had Sylvan for all those years. Perhaps there was some money in all this? I had no capital and was living off a temporary arrangement of allowances until I was properly established. This was a wicked thought to be dismissed at once.

But it led to another: not money, but recognition! To be hailed as the pioneer of better East/West relations! Did we not all dread conflict between the West and the USSR? There was a chance of bridge-building. That insight Sodkin had given into the cracks of the Eastern monolith, and that young Tory MP who, in the Foreign Secretary's own room, had said, "Why are we all so terrified of the Russians? They will break first – their system is so rotten." And then, on our side, with all the wonderful achievements in science, in industrial organisation, what was it being used for? To turn the world into a hamburger heaven, watered by Coca-Cola? Someone had to give a lead to bring together the creators of seemingly limitless wealth with the socialists and old communists and

Christians and so forth who all want the earth to blossom but also to ensure that its fruits are shared fairly.

So this was my destiny? To Save the World? Me? Day-dreaming like this? Ha, bloody ha.

But I was not laughing. Again one of those uncontrollable bouts of sobbing took over. I sat with my elbows on the table, moaning softly, till the waitress came and touched me on the shoulder. I paid my bill and went out into the night.

CHAPTER THIRTY-THREE

By the time I got home my parents were asleep. Apart from Dad's bottle of preprandial sherry, they didn't keep any liquor in the house. But I took a slug of Scotch from the bottle I kept in my room (as my mother knew very well), then another.

The die was cast. As I got ready for bed my only thought should have been how to accomplish my mission for Sylvan and this other chap with efficient precision. But I tossed half the night on my bed, going over in my head, as in a courtroom, the arguments for and against my involvement. Cold comfort came with the thought that I had merely a walk-on part in what was for the others a life-shattering drama, yet there I was, worrying about an entirely insignificant role – the messenger, the coachman – neither patriot nor traitor worthy of the hangman's rope. Thus cut down to size, I dropped off to sleep rehearsing my checklist and timetable for the coming day's adventure.

Dawn was showing through the window when I started up. Like a star-shell in my head had come the realisation of what I had forgotten, or had refused to look for earlier – my official duty for that day! This was the day I was supposed to meet the Greek cleric, to drive to Blackbushe in the official car, to do the honours! There was no choice: Sylvan came first. So my brief career in the Foreign Service was over almost before it started! Broken and stupid, I'd get what I deserved.

But wait. Had I ever actually consented to this farce? Was not my duty now to end it, turn in Sylvan, reveal his Soviet contact? Gosh, think of the headlines! I could do it now, this morning. They would trap Sylvan at Wimbledon as he arrived at 3:30, while I would be doing my stuff for King and country at the airport. The bishop was to arrive at that very hour!

Cold and clammy and hating myself, I took a bath, mercifully hot. And through the vapours came my Goddess, my Athene, Marcie. 'Pull yourself together, Tom. You know what you have to do. And you promised me. I will tell you what will happen. In time they will all come to their senses. This atomic thing, don't forget – it hangs like a dark cloud over the Russians just as much as over us. Russia will change, the way Sodkin hopes. Sylvan can even help him, even if that is hardly the issue at the moment. So think straight. Just call the office as soon as someone is there and say you have 'flu, bad back, anything. You are not indispensable. They will find someone else to meet this Greek chap – he is a villain, by the way, and will be of no use at all to HMG.'

The fog cleared from my head. Once you have your orders it is a wonderful release. You know what you have to do. So it had always been with me. I would wait until about nine when there was sure to be someone in the office who could take charge. I'd call Hacket.

Ma was already in the kitchen and had put the kettle on. She said she knew I had not slept and that I looked awful. I told her that I feared it might be 'flu, there was a lot of it about. She suggested I'd better stay in bed; I said I'd think about it but I had a job to do that afternoon. Then the phone rang.

"For you, dear, Foreign Office."

It was the Head of the Personnel Department, Hacket himself. "Ah, Tom, glad I caught you at home. His Holiness is not coming today, after all. Technical hitch. Sometime next week is all they can promise."

"Thanks for letting me know," I said. "Sorry if it messes up your plans, but frankly, I think I have 'flu. Mind if I take the day off?"

"Not a bit. You do that. You've had a busy time lately. Never see you in the office – good sign, that!"

It was left that I would try to get in on Monday but that it did not matter. They would be working on alternative plans – "and, after all, laddie, you need not get involved. You are only the taxi driver. Just be ready when I hail you! And yes, we'll deal with the hotel and the reception. At any rate, the Hospitality people will do all that. Get well!"

Obediently I returned to bed and accepted a couple of aspirins. And slept till my mother came up with a bowl of soup.

"You're looking better," she said, "I was quite worried about you when you came down this morning!"

I <u>was</u> feeling better and said so, and made to get up.

"But you had better stay in," she said.

The last deceit had to be played on my own family.

"You heard us on the phone. I've got the day off. Ma, I have a plan. There is a Washington family just over. They are in Chertsey. I'll call them and see if I can visit."

I dressed casually. My mother was upstairs and well away from the hallway where the telephone was. I made my bogus call. She came down as I rang off.

"Such nice people," I said. "That's fixed. They suggest tea and then that I should stay for a local amateur dramatic thing in the early evening – I'll think about that."

I got out the car and busied myself with a last check, and to pass the time even polished up the windows and passed a rag across the bonnet. But the lie nagged me. I returned indoors.

"Look, Ma, it really is all OK," and taking her by both elbows I kissed her forehead.

As she looked up at me with a puzzled smile, I said, "I did not quite explain, and it's not actually Chertsey I'm going to, but there are people I have absolutely got to meet – in just an hour's time."

"So your cloak and dagger stuff goes on then?" Her smile closed into a frown.

"Yes, Ma. But it's the last chapter. It will all be over soon, even tonight perhaps."

That was as close as I came to clueing her in. Then it was time to go.

I blew her a kiss. "Wrap up well!" she called after me.

I was glad to have done that much. If all went wrong – if the evening news reported that the whole party was under arrest, this exchange would at least reduce the shock. The half-truth would be easier to reflect on than the crude lie.

It was barely twenty-five minutes' drive to the Wimbledon station, allowing for average afternoon traffic. It was windy. Short sharp showers rattled on the roof. I had time to turn aside at Morden Underground terminus where there used to be a cafe. It was still there. I bought three ham sandwiches and three cans of soft drink. I had whisky in the back, but it might be ages before we had a chance to eat again.

I was soon turning into the yard adjoining the station; no gates, no attendant, rather muddy. It was separated from the tracks only by the huge track-side advertising hoardings at the approach to the station. It had not yet graduated to the class of tidied-up bomb sites and vacant lots that were later to become the basis of some big fortunes. Now, nothing to pay. I passed up my barricaded reserve area, which was right up against the hoardings and close to the tracks. There were other spaces available today, better placed for a quick get-away. I parked nose out, right by the exit.

On the station concourse, the clock showed that there were five minutes before Sylvan's train was due. Guy was to have come by then, but he had a choice of trains; he aimed to come early, then melt away, and present himself only when Sylvan arrived. I bought an evening paper from Smiths and found a spot where I could watch the exits from the platforms below.

The concourse shook as the great expresses thundered through below. There was the slamming of doors, the whistle of guards, and unintelligible announcements over loudspeakers as the stopping trains came and went. Dribbles of passengers came up from the District lines. No Guy. But at the stroke of 3:30 there was Sylvan, presenting his ticket at the barrier at the top of the stairs. The ticket collector squinted at the proffered season, but did not look up.

Sylvan glanced around the concourse; our eyes met, but once I knew he'd seen me I didn't look at him again. Peering over my newspaper I saw him go to the kiosk. He bought a magazine and some cigarettes.

The agreed drill was that if only one of the travellers showed up, I would lead him to the car then return and wait for the other. Minutes ticked by, then I moved off. Sylvan followed me into the street. "No Guy?"

"No Guy. I'll show you where the car is, then I'll go back and wait for him."

But as we turned into the yard we pulled back. A small knot of people were gathered round my improvised barricade; with them, my night watchman. He saw me, and ambled over. My instinct was to run, but I came forward to meet him. "Hey, what's up?"

"Cor! Fair terrible. They shot 'im dead! He shot first though. I saw the flash, but that big train came through. Then, bang! Bang! – and they shot 'im."

"What 'they'?"

"Secret p'lice, I suppose. Plain clothes, yer know."

Two men were still crouched round the body. From where we were, I could only see the legs. The body was thrown back over an upturned oil drum. I could see the socks and obviously expensive, new-looking shoes. It was undoubtedly Guy. I had noted the socks when we met at the Reform Club, a rather garish black, white and red tartan pattern.

The men were getting up. "Better clear orf," said the watchman, "the rozzers are on their way."

I returned to Sylvan in the shadows, propelled him quickly to the car and took off. As we turned into the street, the flashing lights of police cars were approaching. I accelerated away in the opposite direction.

CHAPTER THIRTY-FOUR

I knew the area pretty well and was soon back on the Morden Road heading for the Sutton by-pass leading to Reigate and the Brighton Road. Only then did I say, "It was Guy, of course."

"I knew it," said Sylvan.

We were now clear of the built-up areas and humming along the bypass at all of forty miles per hour, before Sylvan said, "Tom, do you want to give up?"

"It's up to you. You are on your own. Do you know the way?"

"Yes. I'm the one with the instructions. I'll push on, if it's all the same to you."

"I'm yours to command," I said sententiously, but it was the truth. If Sylvan found himself in the dock, I'd be beside him.

"Sylvan, that was pretty close. I guess they are after the pair of you?"

"Oddly, no. I think not. They have no reason to link me with Guy. And anyone who knows us at all knows we are not – were not – fond of each other. Truth is, Guy was a paid agent of the NKVD. MI5 had him clearly in their sights – without any help from the Yanks. Guy was their real quarry. It was Guy who Sodkin was ordered to get back to Moscow. It was his idea to put me in the same package for my own good. I'm not all that important to the NKVD but Guy . . ."

"How come?"

"He's the real pro. He's given Moscow the names of tons of our agents. He directs a raft of their agents here, and, sitting as he does in the Minister of State's Office, gives his masters a running commentary on Foreign Office thinking – such as it is."

"The sod."

"Frankly, I thought so too. You see, I know nothing of that side of things."

"So you guess it was our spooks who got him, not the Russians?"

"Frankly, again, yes. Not those fancy boys you meet in Leconfield House, of course. They'd never soil their lily-white hands, but they have their thugs in the basement; hoods, if you like."

"But I don't see how it helps to have killed him. Who is in charge of that anyway?"

"To your first point, no. I think it quite possible that Guy may have shot first. When that happens even the police, when armed, shoot to kill. They have no option. A wounded boar can still rend you. On the second point, it was the Prime Minister – but that is a farce. I always say the Secret Service should be fully accountable to Parliament. When the estimates are presented, you know, £x for y number of assassinations, £z to maintain a squad of compromising dolly-birds, and so forth."

I wondered at his capacity for banter at such a time, but silence followed. In the close proximity of the little car, I sensed a growing tenseness in the man besides me. I had tried to share his initial sang-froid, but now I, too, shared this tension. Delayed shock, perhaps. I saw again Guy's sprawling body. My stomach was as water, my hands on the wheel felt numb and cold.

"Let's pull in for a minute," I said, and bumped the car over the kerb into a gap in the furze-lined highway high on the North Downs. It was a crossing place for golfers for a course that lay on both sides of the road. A rickety sign-post pointed to the tenth tee. Sylvan got out and threw up over the nearest gorse bush. I dared not move lest my insides fell out, but after a moment felt in the back for the whisky bottle. We both took a swig.

We stood for a moment looking back over London. A fresh wind gave a clear view to the horizon where, below the fringes of driven clouds above us and against a washed-out sky, you could pick out the dome of St. Paul's, Big Ben, and the up-turned legs – the chimneys of Battersea Power Station. I pointed them out to Sylvan. "A last look," I said. Sylvan threw a swift glance to where I was pointing and turned to get back in the car. "If you think you can, Tom, we'd better push on."

Still on the crest of the North Downs, we headed for Reigate Hill. I thought it better to talk, chat about anything, rather than dwell on the awful start to this adventure and what might happen next. Perhaps it was different with Sylvan, but before long I asked what baggage did Guy have – my God, tickets, passport?

"Just a light travel bag. Same as me. But don't worry. We were told to have no documents on us at all. His people were to provide passports, money, tickets when we met."

We began to slither and slide down Reigate Hill. The Austin brake mechanism tended to pull the car to one side and took some controlling. Sylvan grasped the dashboard in front of him with both hands and his face showed a happy grin. "Tom! Keep her moving!"

Sylvan had always responded to excitement. He had enjoyed the Bronski exercise; perhaps he was enjoying this last escape, though obviously hardly less shaken than I had been by Guy's death. Perhaps it was part of his madness. For my part, my head these past months had rung with alarm bells.

For all the butterflies in my stomach, I tried to respond whenever Sylvan's spirits seemed to revive.

"You're quite mad!" I said, with a feeble laugh. "But here we go!" There was little traffic and we fairly bounced along what was now the Brighton Road proper. Then Sylvan gripped my knee, tightly. "Steady, old chappie; police car behind."

I saw it, still way back, but with lights flashing. "What do you want me to do?

"Keep going. Just trundle along."

But he had slipped down as far as his long legs would allow and snatched the rug from the back to cover his head like a shawl. The police rushed by and were soon far ahead. Whoever they were after, it was not us.

CHAPTER THIRTY-FIVE

As the lights of the speeding police car disappeared down the road ahead of us, I wiped sweat from my forehead. Sylvan stretched and rearranged his cramped limbs. He was quite calm.

"As I had thought when you re-emerged on the scene, the perfect car for the job! Even if they had been after us they would have passed us up in this little bus! Had you come up with a Maserati, or even a Jag, they'd have stopped you, probably, simply on principle."

"But I guess that they are after us by now?"

"Guess all you like, dear laddie. I have calculated that they will have no reason to miss me until midnight, when I hope you will be safely tucked up in bed and this little baby back in its garage."

"I hope so," I said dismally, "But why?"

"It's not really your business, but this is the score. I think you know that I am now staying with my mother at Hampton Court – one of those Grace and Favour houses. Really very nice. Of course, I am watched – but only part time. The M15 blokes check my movements with the guards at the main gates, and most days I go over to the railway station, take the train to town and attend this damn clinic. I set off that way this afternoon. It will not be before midnight, when they check at the gates – they do that, creatures of habit – they will find I have not yet returned. Then they may start to worry . . ."

"What about Lady Ross – your poor mother? Does she know, does she know everything?"

"Poor Mama, as you say. She has been quite wonderful about it."

"Do you want me to go and see her? Can I help?"

"Tom," said Sylvan quite sternly. "You just stay right out of this. It's best for you to know as little as possible."

I held my silence for a moment but I had a right to be angry. Yet again, I was being used; I was just a pawn in this conspiracy.

"Oh, of course," I said, with a mock show of resignation. "I suppose it doesn't matter what happens to me at the end of all this."

"Ass! There will be some dreary enquiry, and you may well be caught up in it. That's why it is best for you not to know the full story; best for us, too, of course. If things go wrong now – but they won't – well, we've thought about that. Sodkin will fix you up. He was very taken with you, by the way."

I relapsed into a gloom of my own. No, I would not take Guy's place on the Russian run. Yes, of course there would be an enquiry.

"Hey! There was a turning there – Burgess Hill and Lewes. Shouldn't you have taken it?"

I had indeed missed it, and it might have been better, but I knew this road and I said so, and added irritably that getting him there was my job so leave it to me.

"Don't get fussed," said Sylvan, "there is another thing. We know that the police are still not involved in this. But only yesterday the Yanks persuaded the Foreign Office that they have to make a move. So far it has been all MI5. We now know that the police will be briefed tomorrow and charges prepared. Hence the rush."

I swerved dangerously at this chill reminder that I was aiding and abetting the escape of a criminal. When you can't face thoughts requiring incisive thinking, you grope for any distracting thought. I had latched on to a roadside name, Pease Pottage. How in heaven had they thought up that one? Then I thought of Ponders End, Picketts Post, Sollers Hope – somewhere in the Forest of Dean, wasn't it? As also Symonds Yat, the Point of Air! They did not seem, like Babblecombe and Billingshurst, rooted in the English countryside. They suggested distant outposts where Pickett or Scaler Symmonds had staked their claims, raised the Flag, or been eaten by cannibals.

These irrelevant but soothing reveries melted away as the motor began to labour up the incline of the gap in the South Downs. In the old days, as Dad's car crested the rise between the rim of the Devil's

Punchbowl and Ditchling Beacon, we used to think we were almost there, for a day by the sea at Brighton; but I knew there was quite a way to go yet. And now, for all the light traffic so far, there were two heavy vans labouring up the hill ahead of us. No chance of passing, and other cars were coming up behind. We were down to bottom gear and the engine was running hot.

"When we can, we will pull off."

"Can't stop now." Sylvan was peering up through the side window.

"Must," I said.

"Keep going!" Sylvan insisted.

"Must, or she'll blow up."

We were at the steepest part of the rise, between bare downland. I swung the car into a picnic spot, a small plateau, with a viewing point for visitors and a waste-paper basket. I got out and with a rag in my gloved hand, gingerly unscrewed the radiator cap. It would all have to cool off before I refilled from the water can I always carried in the back.

And then with a cataphonic clatter, a helicopter swung low over us. It landed not fifty yards away, but out of sight, below the rim of our plateau.

I had done with the radiator. I leaped back to my seat ready to drive off.

"Stay," ordered Sylvan. "Sorry Tom. Maybe my calculations were wrong. Guess they've caught up with us. It's a helicopter!" In his lap was a revolver.

"For God's sake," I hissed. "Don't start shooting. OK, we can't win, but shooting the police – that's for the gallows."

"It's not for them, it's for me. I won't go back." He added almost brightly, "What about you, Tom? Do you want to come with me? I've six slugs in here. Shoot you first, if you wish."

"No! No, please!" I grabbed the gun. Sylvan offered no resistance. He slumped back into his seat, his knees against the dashboard.

Two figures approached over the rim of the plateau. One was a girl; a white coat covered long, trousered legs and strands of golden hair blew across her face. The other was Sodkin. He ran the last few steps towards the car and was rapping on the closed window.

I could only flap my hand back at him. Sylvan did not stir.

Sodkin soon had us out. We both leaned against the car till we got our breath back.

Sodkin's first concern was why we had stopped. Had it been a breakdown? Assured that we could get going as soon as the car had cooled down, he said, "Glad to have found you. Losing Guy is terrible."

"So you know what happened?"

"Yes, we had men tailing both of you. Guy arrived at the station too early. He saw they were closing on him – there were three of them. He seems to have panicked and bolted. They followed him into the station yard, fanned out and could not find him at first. You, Tom, must have arrived about then. Guy had holed up behind a sort of barricade. One of the hoods found him. It all happened very quickly. Our man thinks Guy drew his gun first – but they got him right between the eyes. Silencer perhaps, but with trains rushing through that station it probably didn't matter. Anyway, they emptied his pockets and one of them cleared off with his things. The others simply stood around, waiting for the police, no doubt, whom they must have alerted, because they soon came."

"Phew!" I sighed. "It might have . . ."

"What happens now," asked Sylvan, dully. "Do I go on?"

"My dear Mr Ross, it is entirely up to you. We have tickets, passports and lots of money – francs, lira, even dollars – always valuable travelling across Europe nowadays. Enough for two. Perhaps Tom here should join you. But come, we have a moment. You are actually ahead of schedule."

He led us out to the viewpoint, with its handsome parapet of stone. We looked towards Ditchling and the points of the Downs beyond. A low shaft of evening sunlight cast gentle shadows in the folds of downland, glinted on the white scars of a chalk quarry and on the roofs and spires of the villages of the Sussex Weald below. A brisk off-shore wind spun streaks of cloud into a cavalcade of galloping horsemen with burnished shields and helmets, their banners and pennons flying gold and purple. Seaward, the sky was black.

Sodkin introduced his companion, Anita.

"Yes, she runs this taxi service. Couldn't move without her. As you know, we are limited in our range of movements round your country, but Anita's whirlybird lifts us above the Law. We had her on stand-by today, so after this Guy business we decided to check your progress."

Anita was gorgeous. Her white coat was made of leather, surmounted by a high collar of fur, bear or seal. A valkyrie, though the effect was rather spoiled as she responded in a depressingly South London accent, "Pleased ter meet chew."

From fear and the edge of defeat, from the dreary buzz of the little car, to this fantastic vision of uplift in the champagne air of the Downland, with the helicopter grazing like Brunhilde's Grane on the well-cropped slope below us, was like the transmogrification from pre-dawn darkness to daybreak sunrise.

I took Anita's arm and whisked her round to join the other two who were in earnest conversation.

"Let's go!" I cried. "Let's all go off in this lovely whirly-bird."

I met a stony look from Sylvan.

"My dear Lieutenant," said Sodkin, "it is only a two-seater, I fear, and your job is not quite finished yet. Mr Ross and I are just considering the odds. Unfortunately they have moved slightly against us. I was about to say, Sylvan, I have no orders to get you out. Your Mr Kimball thought it would be best for all concerned – and I certainly thought so too. You are, as they say, my baby. But it was Guy they wanted back in Moscow. He is – was – one of 'them'. He held senior rank in the NKVD. He knew the apparatus inside out, our agents, our codes – and, of course, yours. My orders were to get him home. I was allowed to add you as part of the baggage. So now they have lost him, they may lose interest in the future for you, may even parcel the blame for losing him on to you, and on me too," he added with a gesture of self depreciation. In his low-key way he was signalling that he was almost certainly for the chop.

"So?" said Sylvan, "Go on?"

Sodkin continued, "I think you should still go ahead. The arrangements are in place. The machine adjusts only slowly. Stalin is out of circulation, and, believe me, there is a ferment throughout the hierarchy. I know some of the men ready to take over, smash the system – and they will, in time, – but right now the Berias, the secret police, with no clear political direction just watch everything and everybody. I still hope, dear Sylvan, that our friends there will get control of you, enlist you to prepare the tinder for the new revolution, help shed a little light over the desks of our powerless intellectuals. I know there are many, waiting to help."

There had been little speculation about what would happen after Stalin. What there was concerned which of those grim over-coated figures lined up besides him on the Kremlin wall in photographs of the May Day parades would take the dictator's place. Keen Kremlin watchers noted who stood nearest to Stalin, or who might be absent. The Molotovs, the Vyshinskis – one or two like that had made their own marks on the page of history, but mostly they were unknown, grey faces, one of whom perhaps had been ordained to maintain control of this monstrous monolith of the USSR, others who might be liquidated if they stepped out of line.

It was only in talking to Sodkin that one had even glimpsed other possibilities. There were perhaps 250-300 million people in this grey prison, and its walls contained no less than twenty separate republics. Ukranians, Georgians, Usbeks, Tartars all had ancient histories, languages, ethnic and religious cultures, and so it was simply against all historical precedent that this heaving mass could be held down for ever by the instruments of modern terror. There must be a running cancer of discontent fed by nationalists, romanticists, religious bigots and martyrs; and among them all, idealists, writers, thinkers, secretly working for the day of liberation.

We knew so little history, and alas, as Sodkin had said to me, the usual pattern of revolution is for its pioneers to be consumed in its flames. Now the tinder was not yet dry enough for the critical conflagration. Perhaps he and Sylvan, like others before and others to come, would perish, but not before they had put their crowbars into the clefts in the great rock, and sooner or later it would crack apart. And then? I had asked Sodkin about this.

"Then," he had said, "then, God knows! Can you just try and see what replaces the USSR? Frankly, I can't. But that will be for others to worry about."

"Capitalism?" I suggested.

Sodkin gave a short laugh. "Heaven knows what your capitalists will do when there is no communist bogey. Hegel, you know – thesis, anti-thesis, and synthesis. A synthesis will emerge."

I had no reason that day to suppose that all these things would come to pass in our own lifetimes – mine at any rate.

CHAPTER THIRTY-SIX

That meeting on the Downs was our last.

Sodkin looked at his watch. "Time to go. Old Boris – whom you met, Tom, at the Mercury, is in charge. He has everything you will need. Same place as arranged, on the sea-front road, the promenade, at Seaford. He was expecting you to come down from the Lewes road. Now you will be coming in the wrong direction. You'd better turn the car round, then wait for the taxi that's coming to pick you up. He will flash his lights twice as he passes. Good fellow, local man, and they all know him at the Docks."

Sodkin embraced Sylvan, kissing him on both cheeks. He did the same to me. "Go now, there's nothing in sight on the road."

He turned to follow his pilot, Anita, who was already on her way to the chopper.

We drove on, into Brighton, each with his own thoughts as we said nothing. Then I asked banally whether he knew the area at all, and getting what appeared to be a negative grunt, I pointed out features as we passed: the Pavilion, the Aquarium, then along the coast road in the now gathering darkness, Roedean, St. Dunstan's, Peacehaven where the Downs were ploughed up and sown with ribbons of houses, straight lines of them, which took no account of the gentle contours of the hillside. I rattled on about all this while planning in the back of my mind what else to be said at our parting, and how to say it.

It was dark as we crossed the river at Newhaven. A strong wind was blowing off the sea. There was a glimpse of the ferry steamer in a pool of flood-light. A car was being hoisted aboard by crane. The ship itself was 'all lit up' as Woodrooffe said in his famous radio gaffe.

A few minutes further on we were out on the sea front. I chose the spot and swung the car round.

"We're here!" I announced "Minutes to spare. Not bad, eh?"

Sylvan straightened himself up in his seat.

"Tom," he said, and his voice was choking, as with one who had been crying inwardly. "Tom old laddie, thank you for everything."

"Not a bit," I said awkwardly. "Here, let's have one for the road," and I felt behind me for the whisky bottle.

Sylvan swallowed deeply, then had another.

"Look out for the taxi chappie, lad. I'm going to have a pee."

He shut the door against a blast of wind and crossed over to the promenade.

I stayed in the Austin, the windows wound up tight against the wind. With its light springs, the little car shook to each gusty squall.

I could just make out Sylvan, leaning on the rail of the promenade, partly silhouetted against the white breakers that covered the nearer sea. Beyond that, sea and sky merged in total darkness. There was no horizon.

Then the flashing lights. I flicked on my headlights in return. The taxi-man was quickly with me.

"Any luggage? You're to give it to me. Where's the bloke?"

"Just taking a pee, I think. I'll get him."

I crossed over the sea front, bent over in the gale and stumbling on pebbles strewn across the promenade by a recent storm.

Sylvan was not there. I glanced in both directions. A few yards to the right was a break in the rail with concrete steps leading down to the beach. I made for them. Useless to call out his name over the roar of the wind and the rising tide.

I stumped about on the heavy pebbled beach before I found him, spread-eagled, face down, under the sea wall.

The ugly bullet wound left no doubt that he was dead, but I turned him this way and that to make sure. I don't think the taxi-man heard my howls of pain, *Eloi . . . Eloi . . .* but he was there at my side, and with a torch. He spotted the revolver, slipped on the safety catch and pocketed it.

"C'mon, feller, just make sure we've left no tracks. Nah, better gimme a hand." And we pulled the poor body a few yards nearer the line of the surf, as close as we could get to where the incoming waves surged against the shingle.

"It's spring tides, the sea will take him away," said the taxi-man. "He'll be happier to go with the tide."

Wet with the spume and spray, we made our way back to the promenade.

"Now you git, young feller. I've got your man's bag in the taxi already. I'll get back to Boris. Now go 'ome, mate – go on 'ome!"

CODA

I drove home like a zombie, without incident. I let myself into the house well before midnight, and fell on my bed.

That was the Friday.

Ma woke me, late in the morning, with a cup of tea.

"Heard you come in last night. Not so late, after all. I was so relieved. But look at you! It must be 'flu, or worse! You stay right there in bed. I'm going to take your temperature."

She did. There wasn't one, but I did stay in bed, and for most of Sunday too. I dozed, but listened to every news bulletin on the radio. Nothing.

On Monday I returned to the Greek Department, did the necessary on the telephone, dictated to the PA who was temporarily attached, and two days later I did go to meet the quisling prelate, of whom my only clear recollection was the smell of his breath – mostly garlic, I supposed.

Taking a lift from the hospitality car back to the office, I glanced over the evening paper. There were the continuing reports from the war crimes trials in Nuremburg, but little else of interest. Then my attention was caught by a small heading at the bottom of the front page: "Police Clueless in Mystery of Missing Diplomat."

There were very few details. "Promising career . . . highly regarded in Washington," along with uncertain reports of his illness, with tactful hints of a mental breakdown having occasioned his recent return to London. Nothing to connect him with another unexplained disappearance earlier in the year, that of a nuclear scientist in America.

In the morning the office was full of chatter. It swirled round my head. For all the roar of the waves beating on that Sussex shore that I had not ceased to hear these past few days, I sat there in a pool of silence. Incredible silence. More must surely follow.

The next day I sought out Hacket and offered my resignation. I had not really thought it through. I had no money, or other job in mind, so I was a bit taken aback when he said, "Well, Tom, it might be the best thing. It's like this. Phil Kimball has had a word with me about you. He seems to have learned quite a lot about you for some reason. He says that while he, personally, would want to give you a first-class reference, he thinks you might prefer to go. Tom, I had the idea myself from our first meeting that diplomacy was probably not your line. Is that right? What do you think?"

I mumbled something that might be taken as assent.

"But, tell you what. Take it easy for a bit. I'll see what else we can find."

They found me a post in the Ministry of Works, as it then was. It looked after government buildings and property, and, at that time, lots of war damage cases and claims.

For the next thirty years I hardly missed a day away from my desk. In the evenings I used to make ship models and, an unusual departure, a very well-proportioned model of Big Ben and the Houses of Parliament – all out of matchsticks.

Now, long retired, I feel I must leave this record of events, which I could share with no one, and, even as I write, I have to wonder if they really ever happened.

THE END

ACKNOWLEDGEMENTS

First mention has to go to my late uncle Richard Miles, and to my cousin Elaine Moore, who discovered Richard's original drafts and gave them to me. I've really enjoyed reworking the story, and have learned quite a bit more about my uncle in the process. Without these two dear people there would be no *Requiem for a Spy*.

My sister Vicky Stevens has been brilliant, providing invaluable ideas for improvement and patiently combing the typescript for grammatical and punctuation errors (we are both somewhat OCD about this; I hope we have not overlooked too many).

I am deeply indebted to Professor David Dilks, not only for his favorable endorsement, but also for his insightful comments, his deep knowledge of the period and the subject, and his meticulous reading of the text – he pointed out some errors and anachronisms that slipped past even my sister's eagle eyes. My gratitude also to Andrew Roberts for his continuing support and for his laudatory blurb. I am indeed privileged to have two such distinguished historians in my corner.

Many thanks to my agent Tom Cull, who saw this book's potential, and to Reagan Rothe and his team at Black Rose Writing. Special thanks to Trevor Scobie for his inspired cover design.

Last but certainly not least, thanks as always to my husband Allen, for his technical expertise as we converted Richard's pages into machine-readable form, for his helpful suggestions and for patiently putting up with me during the many months that I was working on *Requiem*.

–Jill Rose, Florida 2021

ABOUT THE AUTHORS

Richard Miles RNVR (1917-1997) served his country all his life, in the Royal Navy, the diplomatic and the civil service. Many years after his death his niece Jill Rose revised and edited the drafts of his unpublished novel *Requiem for a Spy*, which was inspired by his own experiences. Jill, who is retired, lives in Florida, and is the author of *Nursing Churchill: Wartime Life from the Private Letters of Winston Churchill's Nurse*.

Note from the Author

Word-of-mouth is crucial for any author to succeed. If you enjoyed *Requiem for a Spy*, please leave a review online—anywhere you are able. Even if it's just a sentence or two. It would make all the difference and would be very much appreciated.

Thanks!
Jill Rose